D1528185

Secret
Correspondence

Secret Correspondence

MARCIA
GOLUB

TICKNOR & FIELDS

NEW YORK

1990

For information about permission to reproduce selections from
this book, write to Permissions, Ticknor & Fields,
215 Park Avenue, New York, New York 10003.

Library of Congress Cataloging-in-Publication Data

Golub, Marcia.
Secret correspondence / Marcia Golub.
p.   cm.
ISBN 0-89919-916-X
I. Title.
PS3557.0453S4   1990   89-48548
813′.54 — dc20   CIP

Printed in the United States of America

BP 10 9 8 7 6 5 4 3 2 1

I would like to acknowledge the help of Cork Smith,
Caroline Sutton, and Liz Duvall, and I would especially like to
thank Madison Smartt Bell for uncommon generosity and support.

For Bob

In memory of Hymie Golub

Painting isn't an aesthetic operation, it's a form of magic designed as a mediator between this strange hostile world and us, a way of seizing power by giving form to our terrors as well as our desires.

PABLO PICASSO

If it isn't art, it's madness, do you understand?

GABBY SEGUL

I pretend to be mad on purpose, for my own aims.

VASLAV NIJINSKY

It didn't hurt me, not one bit.

MOISHA SEGUL

This city is full of people who are slowly sliding down. . . . Most of them resist at first; but then there are these faded, aging girls who constantly let themselves slip over without a struggle, strong girls, still unused in their innermost selves, who have never been loved.

RAINER MARIA RILKE

Debbie Doobie for President.

DEBBIE DOOBIE

Love is always poor; and far from being tender and beautiful . . . , he is hard and rough and unshod and homeless, lying always on the ground without bedding, sleeping by the doors and in the streets in the open air, having his mother's nature, always dwelling with want. But from his father again he has designs upon beautiful and good things, being brave and go-ahead and high-strung, and . . . a successful coveter of wisdom, a philosopher all his days, a great wizard and sorcerer and sophist.

PLATO

You respond like a magic dream.

ILYICH KOLOKOL

"He's dreaming now," said Tweedledee, "and what do you think he's dreaming about?"

Alice said, "Nobody can guess that."

"Why, about you!" Tweedledee exclaimed, clapping his hands triumphantly. "And if he left off dreaming about you, where do you suppose you'd be?"

"Where I am now, of course," said Alice.

"Not you!" Tweedledee retorted contemptuously. "You'd be nowhere. Why, you're only a sort of thing in his dream!"

"If that there King was to wake," added Tweedledum, "you'd go out — bang! — just like a candle!"

LEWIS CARROLL

Visit Uncle Moisha, it shouldn't kill you the whole day. I know in the home he is lonely for a family face.

PESHA SEGUL

A dream not interpreted is like a letter unread.

THE TALMUD

This is my letter to the world, that never wrote to me.

EMILY DICKINSON

When this you see, remember me.

IDA TWEETY

Author's Query

For a biography of the artist Gabriella Segul, who disappeared in 1993, I am interested in hearing from anyone with reminiscences and/or correspondence.

LARA JACOB
320 West 83rd Street
New York, New York 10024

Lara Jacob had met Tom Campo before. In fact, she had known him almost her whole life. That was the problem. She wanted to be taken seriously, and he had seen her, till now, as a child.

She took a deep breath before entering the gallery. The door opened automatically, an action accompanied by the sound of chimes. A feline woman looked up from her desk. "I have an appointment," Lara started to say, but a middle-aged man entered. "Hello, Tom," she said, although she'd been raised to call him Mr. Campo. "I really appreciate your meeting with me."

"Not at all." He shook her hand and led her into his office. "I was sorry to hear about your mother."

"Thank you. The flowers you sent were lovely. She always spoke highly of you, and I . . ." Her voice trailed off.

"How about a glass of wine?" Tom asked. "I have a nice Chablis on ice." She nodded, smiling in what she hoped was a sophisticated manner.

"So, tell me about your project. A biography, is it? You know, we're planning a Gabriella Segul retrospective. The timing could be" — he snapped his fingers — "perfect."

Lara sipped her drink. "It's funny," she said. "It's almost as if I were brought up to write this book. The way my mother spoke of her, after her disappearance, I don't know . . . it was as though she were giving me notes. Then there's the diary itself, Aunt Gabby's diary."

"I didn't know she kept a diary." Tom leaned forward.

"Oh, yes. There's her diary, plus part of another. Also files of letters, quotes. Other stuff. She was a real saver. When we learned of Aunt Gabby's disappearance, my — why do you smile?"

"Oh, I'm sorry. I didn't mean . . . it's just funny, hearing you refer to Gabriella Segul as Aunt Gabby. You know, I didn't really know her. I may have met her once, but I don't think—"

"Wait," Lara said. "Let me set up the recorder. There. I'm interested in any reminiscence you may have, so—"

"That's the point, dear. There can't be a reminiscence of someone I didn't know. Gabriella Segul, to me, is a collection of artwork — two boxes of slides, really. The astounding fluidity of style in her work makes it seem as though a group of anonymous artists created it. That's part of the appeal, I suppose. And, callous as this is to say, the tragedy of her end is, too." He turned the bottle in its ice bucket. "You know," he said, "I've seen some photos, but mostly I think of your mother when I try to imagine her. More wine?" He refilled her glass and his own.

"How did you happen to acquire the paintings?" Lara asked just as the intercom sounded. A woman's voice came on, saying, "Mr. Rein in the solarium."

"Oh dear," said Tom. "Excuse me. Someone I must see." He left the room in a distracted huff. While he was gone Lara finished her wine and put the glass on the desk. He returned ten minutes later and immediately put her glass on a coaster. Lara tried not to blush. He poured another refill, which she felt too shy to refuse.

"About Aunt Gabby's paintings," she said. "How did you—"

"Oh yes," said Tom, looking at the ceiling as he thought back. "Let's see. I received a box of slides and a letter from your aunt."

"Do you still have it?" Lara asked. "I'd love to read it."

He laughed, as if Lara were terribly cute. "I knew right away that the artist was talented, but I never expected her cover letters to have value."

"It's not that." She hid her annoyance. "It's for the biography. Any scrap of her writing—"

"Of course. Well, the answer is no. I didn't save the letter, but I did hold on to the slides. Found the work quirky. Told the receptionist to set up an appointment. Somehow or other, it never got done. Months later a second box came. Again I tried to get in touch with Segul. It was around the time I was taking over the gallery. I was preoccupied with that — and with my mentor's death, of course. It slipped my mind. Then one day I was looking through old boxes of slides, ran across her work. I was struck by her . . . I don't know, magic quality? But at that point she'd already disappeared." He held his glass to the light and looked through it.

"One afternoon," he continued, "your mother happened in with a tiny painting, a portrait of an old woman. It seemed pure serendipity, that she should come into my gallery. Of course, I realize now she was making the rounds." He put the glass down. "Still," he said, "when I think how I almost turned her away. . . . She was so — don't be offended, but she was so unprofessional, the way she approached me, pulling out the painting. I was thinking how to get away, then I looked at the picture, remembered it. Found the slide easily. There it was, that incredible painting of the old beauty. Wrinkled hands—"

"Curly hands. Aunt Gabby calls them curly hands in her diary."

"Curly hands. Exactly. And her face. Old age, yet the beauty . . . oh, I can't describe it, I just remember being struck. Particularly the eyes. Green jade, completely unseeing. How do we see blindness? The eyes are normal-looking, but somehow . . ."

Lara leaned back. "Yes. She makes you see things that aren't there. That is, they aren't in the picture, they're in the life."

"And those strange abstracts," Tom said. "I still don't know what to make of them. How they pull you in, pull you out. The whole thing is rather erotic, but why? Circles, spirals, colors melting. What's erotic about that?"

"Mmm." Lara smiled as if at a private joke.

"Twenty years," said Tom musingly into his glass. "I was just starting out then. Frank Harme, who started this gallery, died twenty years ago. That's a long time. Too bad this couldn't have been done sooner."

Lara surreptitiously wiped her hand, wet from the cold glass, on her skirt. "For one thing," she said, "I was a child." She started to put the wineglass on Tom's desk, then remembered to use the coaster. "The material had to wait for me to grow up. My mother wasn't up to writing a book. The diaries and files just sort of, uh, sat around till I was ready. Besides, there was the disappearance. I mean, we don't know for a fact even now that she's dead."

"Yes. That came up regarding the paintings, too." Tom looked mildly consternated, like someone caught stealing cookies.

"We spoke to lawyers," Lara said. "There's nothing to worry about. In effect, Mother was executrix of the will. I, in turn— that is, she didn't have a will, but—"

"Your mother was your aunt's sister, right?"

Lara looked into her glass as if reading tea leaves. "No," she said. "Actually Aunt Gabby was a friend of my mother's. There were no relatives — that we ever found. Now, of course, distant cousins would come flocking from all over, but back then, when Aunt Gabby disappeared, there were bills to pay, police to badger, and . . . you know. The landlord called Mother, told her to pick up Aunt Gabby's 'junk' or he'd throw it out. This was the first she heard about the disappearance. She paid him the back rent, other bills. In a sense she bought the work. That wasn't why she did it, of course. I don't think she ever forgave herself for not knowing what had happened. Even when she was in the hospital. They gave her painkillers. She was hallucinating — something about her and Gabby as children running, King's Highway, alleys, tunnels. I couldn't make out much of what she was saying. I'm not sure it meant anything. You know, proceeds from the sale of Aunt Gabby's work go into a Gabriella Segul fund, in case . . ."

Tom nodded and glanced at his watch. "My," he said. "I've completely lost track of time. I really must get back to work. I'm sorry I couldn't be more helpful in—"

"Not at all." Lara shut off the recorder and gulped the last of her wine. "What you've told me will be useful." She shook Tom Campo's hand and walked as gracefully as she could through the door. Once outside, she ran a few steps, excited and tipsy and eager to get home so she could resume her study of the diary.

✦ ✦ ✦

October 30th, Friday — Aunt Sadie died again today. Root rot, I think. There's still Aunt Rose and my mother, but I can't help overwatering. She told me before she died the first time to bring her wandering Jew to the hospital. The plant was so big it took up the whole window by her bed. I told her it would steal her oxygen, but she insisted, so I brought it.

"This will be yours when I die," she said with her last breath. "Remember, let it dry out first. Don't drown."

I already had Aunt Rose's purple passion, inherited after her stroke, so Aunt Sadie must have seen my tendency. Later my mother gave me her succulent — just to take care of while she and my father were in Florida. They weren't planning to be away forever. It's called a mother-in-law's tongue. You can cut your wrists on its serrated edges, which I generally do when I feed it. There's no other way to reach the soil.

Oct. 31 — Been leafing through Uncle's diaries, still looking for a way in. Ten books in the blood of a cut-off tongue — appropriate ink for letters from the dead, I suppose. Who was it called Yiddish the only murdered language — Singer? These past two months I've been riffling the pages, willing a magic facility with translation . . . unsuccessfully. So then I try imagining him

7

into existence. Why did he write? Why does anyone write? To trick death? What is diary reading after all but another way to raise the dead?

Cold and bright today. Took a long walk. Supposed to meditate on art. Instead thought of James. Same old thing: why, why not? What did it mean, what did what mean?

Hey, it's Halloween. Let's dig up all the corpses.

Sunday — If Uncle haunts me, is it because of love or guilt? Good intentions are never enough. "Doesn't a man have the right to die on the street?" I demanded of my parents once.

"Rights schmights," they replied. "For this we sent her to college?"

To most people, Uncle was a shopping-bag man — in his late eighties, wandering the streets all day, most of the night, falling down either from epilepsy or muggings. A time came when we had to protect him, from himself as much as from others. But whenever my parents tried to persuade him to go into a home, he would screw up his face like a baby refusing a spoon. "No," he'd repeat, as if about to throw a tantrum. Only I knew he was trying not to cry.

When he died two months ago, it was like he flew away. They put him in the nursing home in January, then went to Florida to drown. I still can't figure out what this old Jewish couple was doing on a boat in the first place. Neither could swim, both got seasick. All my years worrying about colon cancer and heart disease were washed away by that improbable wave of event. Now, like the survivor of a shipwreck, I find myself lonely upon an island; nothing was salvaged but an old bag of bones, then he was lost too. At least Crusoe discovered seeds in his pouch. In January I'd fought for Uncle's freedom. In February I was his jailer.

NOTE: Call *Jewish Daily Forward* Monday. Place ad for translator. Must learn what he wrote.

Monday — James was crossing 57th Street today when I saw him. Lunchtime insanity, but he glided through the crowd as if he were a boat and it water slicing open to let him pass. Back-wash sluiced behind, and I was drowning in his wake. Cars and cabbies, buses and bicycles, people, dogs, and birds. I couldn't catch up. He was sailing down the avenue while I was still trying to cross 57th. I felt myself sinking in a swamp, as if hands were dragging me under.

I pulled myself free. Ran along the curb till I caught up with him. Recognized his cowboy hat, his low-slung jeans, his pointy boots, his silly, touching attempt to look like a Westerner. I went right up to him and tapped his shoulder, smiling in his face. And a stranger stared back.

I was so certain. That's why I'm terrified. It was like stepping into an elevator before realizing the shaft's empty.

Tuesday — Union meeting after work. Didn't go. Should, to show support, but I was tired. Heard Liz talking. Union expects trouble. There's strong opposition from the missionaries in accounting.

Why is it all the bookkeepers and most of the secretaries at PP belong to the same cult? They talk about Jesus as if he were a personal friend, tell Bible stories with the same relish others reserve for gossip. "Did you hear what happened to Mary Magdalene, how them seven devils went out from her that time? Well, I'll tell you." When not discussing the latest exploits of their Savior, they talk about the boxes the union is going to put us in. I hear them when I use the copy machine. They have learned not to proselytize to me. I can't imagine they get converts to either of their causes.

I'm counting on a union-scale pay hike to offset my latest rent increase. Can't believe I've lived here for 17 years, as long as I've worked at Publications Press, in this elegant turn-of-the-century building with turn-of-the-century plumbing. Landlord Green keeps putting "capital improvements" into my apartment, which I don't want but end up paying for. It bugs him that my rent is so low compared to what he could get on today's market. His improvements are never anything whimsical like fixing the plumbing or the elevator. He believes in getting to the issues — my windowed kitchen cabinets, my mirror-inlaid closets.

In the end, I begged him to raise my rent, only please leave my apartment alone — especially the lovely old mirrors. The glass was so dark, it merely hinted at reflection, was never crass enough to show fine detail. At 39, I found that surprisingly good taste for an inanimate object. But now I have closet doors that slide on tracks, in theory if not in fact, and Formica kitchen cabinets already chipping, *and* a rent more than double. Which is why you can find me five days a week sweating grease pencil at *locus schlockus*.

Going down to check on Miss Tweety before it gets too late.

Wed. — A man came up to me, a skinny man with shaved head: "I'll gladly pay you Tuesday for a hamburger today."

Later I saw him going through the garbage. A man in a business suit was yelling at him: "Go away! What do you think you're doing, you filthy tramp?" Can you imagine such a thing, to deny someone access to your crap?

James seduced me in the way of men — drew me in and left me there. His long gazes shied whenever I turned, fingers trembling like blind tube worms. I took his nervousness like a bouquet of flowers, but he was married, had a daughter.

The smell of my own power at first drew me like a goddess to incense. I didn't mean it to come to anything, and it didn't; that was the trap. Did he plan this all along, his game to hunt women like deer?

11:50 P.M. — Can't sleep. Thinking about Uncle. That we never really spoke didn't stand in our way. He understood that I understood him, without words. He knew his diary would explain.

His furnished room in Brighton: the linoleum rolling like the waves a block away. He wasn't a homeless man, but seeing him dressed in rags, digging through garbage, who wouldn't think him one? Who wouldn't have judged his family harshly for letting the old lunatic wander? I still believe he had the right to philosophize through trash. Every culture has its stories of crazy beggars who turn out to be secret saints. As far as madness went, I always had a sense that he was faking it, acting crazy as a protection.

If he hid himself behind this act of insanity, he had good reason. I only know some of what happened to him, but it was enough to make a man hide. Even so, glimmers of another self, the bright man with filthy pants, would shine out.

He was at the table with us one Friday night. My parents were talking about a friend of theirs whom they always called Meshuggina Sophie Herring. Most of my parents' friends had epithets. Fat Sadie. Little Sadie. Aunt Sadie. Skinny Moe. Moe Shirley's, a.k.a. Shirley's Moe. And the infamous Sam the Plumber.

I knew Meshuggina Sophie, of course. She didn't seem crazy to me, just different from most of my parents' friends. She always wore a dress with a rip in it, and she'd go out with toilet paper wrapped around her head to protect her hairdo. One time she came to our house when my parents weren't home. I was in high school. She sold me an old pair of her gloves, saying she needed the money, then proceeded to tell me the story of her life.

I was crying so hard I had to gasp for breath as this elderly woman told me how she'd been raped, then forced to marry her rapist. In the end he took her savings, leaving her pregnant. Which was why, in old age, she had to sell her gloves to the daughters of friends.

"You have a pen? You have a piece paper?" she asked, telling me to copy down her story. That's what I was doing, squeezing tears from my face like water from a sponge, when my mother came in. As soon as she saw me, she grew furious.

"What do you want to go and upset the child, Shayntze?"

"I didn't mean to upset her. Look, I gave her mine gloves."

After she left, my mother asked, "Did she sell you those gloves?" I nodded. "Don't ever let her in again when I'm not home. She makes up stories. You don't need to know from such things."

That was Sophie Herring.

The night my uncle was at the table, my parents were talking about how Sophie's 17-year-old grandson had just been killed in a car accident. My parents were tsking. Uncle was slurping soup. He seemed to listen and dream at the same time.

I asked, "Why do you call her Meshuggina Sophie Herring? Is she really crazy?"

Before my mother could answer, my uncle did, mumbling under his breath so only I heard. "She just acts like a meshuggina. To fool people." He laughed. I looked at him. He met my glance. A curtain parted.

Usually I'd see him at the table, singing to himself while my mother demanded, "So, let's talk about the chicken. Is this some chicken? Did you ever taste such a chicken in your life?" She was belligerent in her joy. Admit it, admit it! As if we would deny it. Yes, I admit it. I ate the chicken and it was delicious. My father would be tsking because she'd cut the bread unevenly. He was a butcher. It irritated him that the slices started out thin and got thick. "Can't you cut a straight line?" he'd ask in counterpoint. "Did you ever see a woman who couldn't slice a piece bread?" And there was Uncle, singing a soldier's song in Russian or telling no one in particular about the distance of Mars from Jupiter or how cows take grass and make it into milk. And I thought, "Who's to say he's crazy?"

Thurs. — Going through my crazy-letter file at work today, I realized it's been a year since we've heard from Debbie Doobie. I was about to mention this when Liz sent me to the stalls to look for Happy. I was annoyed. Happy has a problem common among the obese. She falls asleep when she sits down. As a result, whenever anyone can't find her, someone (me) has to go to the ladies' room and look at the feet.

Happy insists she doesn't eat more than a fly. If Liz or Suzy calls out, "Hey, Hap, you want something from Schwartz's? We're ordering," she says no. She couldn't eat a thing. She's had no appetite for days. Whatever you're eating makes her wrinkle up her nose in disgust.

She is also under the delusion she's a sex kitten and is always telling us about the men who try to pick her up, the photographers who keep asking her to pose nude for various men's magazines. She won't do it. It would be disloyal to pose for a competitor, undignified to pose for *Slut* or any other PP mag.

I have a theory about Happy: it's my theory of protective disguises. Fat is power. Happy is formidable in her fat — less likely to attract genuine sexual attention, while always sensing her unwilling allure. Whenever Happy gets on my nerves, I find her easier to bear if I speculate that she was seduced as a child.

P.S. Miss Tweety told me about the Indian again. As I was leaving, I heard the knight of the laundry room. Should I do something?

> Dear *Soap Bubble* Editor,
> I love the shows I watch and have watched since I was only 6 years old. But I can't understand why heavyset people are not part of the soaps. Fat people make up a large part of the world. I have worked with talented, heavy people in show biz. But they never get a chance because of their weight. I am myself a 300-pounder but am talented. Please help the fat people of America get a break. Fat people make loyal fans and like elephants they don't forget.
> P. Patts
> President of OFA (Obese Fans of America)

Friday — DREAM: James was still at PP. I asked him to translate Uncle's diary. Must have been because James is from Russia and Uncle was also Russian. In the dream the diary was in Russian. James said, "Da. Nyot nyet."

James left PP five years ago. How did he work this spell, to keep me under for so many years? A stranger with a Russian accent. A tall, skinny man with thin hair, cheekbones high as death.

The time he discovered me in the park I was alone, sketching. A shadow fell across my drawing. I looked up, saw the silhouette of a man. The sun was directly behind him. I couldn't make out his face. "Gabby?" he asked. "Vy howdy, ma'am."

Of course I recognized his voice right away. Who else did I know drawled like a Russian cowboy? "I can't see," I said. "Who is it?" And waited for him to say James Kolokol. The layout man from the art department, dressed in leather fringes and Stetson, peppered his Slavic-accented speech with incongruous "pardners," "you alls," and "ma'ams," betraying that his school for English had been the Western. He sat beside me and asked, "You draw, pardner?"

"Sorry," I wisecracked. "Forgot my gun."

He didn't get it, just stared till I grew embarrassed. I closed my sketch pad, tried explaining the joke. I didn't want to be rude but wished he'd go away. I wanted to finish my drawing. My lunch hour had already stretched itself beyond decency. But I also sensed his attraction and was excited by it, especially since I didn't reciprocate. Sitting in the sunlight, watching the glint in his glass-blue eyes, I felt beautiful. Sunlight makes anyone beautiful. And there was something supremely satisfying about being found out. I didn't want anyone at work to know about my art. I wanted everyone to know.

Maybe it was then that I fell in love. Clearly it was never anything but vanity. I was trapped by the image I saw in his eye.

Saturday — Being a woman of routine without obligations, how do I now establish a new order? Drinking's a ritual to replace nursing-home visits and worry. I feed the cats — Van, Fellatio, and Harry (pregnant again). Friday nights I water the plants, talk to them as the books prescribe. "Aunt Sadie," I said two weeks ago, "you're looking peaked." It's a one-sided conversation; she kept mum about her roots. When I think I'd like to phone my mother and realize I can't, I take out plant food and dig in her soil.

Sometimes I think there is an Uncle Moisha gene in my family and I inherited it. He gave me his diary right before he died. Ten books of a man's life, and I can't read anything except the few bits in English: little poems like "Sure thing, honey, if you got the money" and English newspaper clippings — particularly Dear Abby columns (20th-century wisdom literature). The articles are slipped between pages and are apt to fall out like surprise greetings. But some are pasted in, some underlined, Uncle's pale blue scribbles a mysterious iconography below. Most are from Yiddish papers, which I can't read. The English ones have stuff about Russia, science, bizarre murders, family problems. There are headings Uncle scrawled: "Space," "Inventions," "Medicine." I'm moved by their lack of meaning to me. Like finding dried rose petals in a math book.

When Tanta Menya died — a long time ago, when I was a little girl — my cousin Sylvia got the job of cleaning out her apartment. Opening a drawer, she found baby clothes from half a century before. My seamstress aunt had never had children but she'd had a miscarriage. All the little white gowns and swaddling clothes, handmade garments, were carefully folded and put away in mothballs, preserved for 50 years in a dresser. A lost fetus who would have been just another middle-aged malcontent was instead the secret grief of a lifetime. Sylvia was so touched that she ran away. She told the super to go through my aunt's stuff, take whatever he wanted, give the rest to charity.

I called the *Forward* several days ago. Ad should appear this Thursday. I'll wait two weeks for responses. Probably can read through them all and interview people in a few days.

Sunday — The prospect of doing art eroticizes me. Why? I expose myself, then if someone stares with Medusa eyes, I become a crazy woman lifting my skirt. Mustn't think that way. Listen to the ocean roar of traffic on Broadway. Swells of sound, like waves approaching and falling on shore. Due to traffic lights? All afternoon I looked out the window, watched the sky pass in glass reflections across the street. Clouds sailed from pane to pane. Sun went down in a blaze of gold.

Still light out — dusky pink. There's a large white building facing west across from me that turns red. Late afternoons, there's an alpenglow to all buildings facing west.

Repetition of form, of perspective; shadows of clouds, of other buildings passing across one another's skin — New York Canyonland. The Grand Urban? Could paint that. Idea's been done. Georgia O'Keeffe. Cliché now. Still, I can bring out the beauty of an afternoon city. Nothing I do will look like anyone else's, even if Georgia and I sat here together, dipping into the same paints. Maybe a drink. Should have gone out. Was seduced by the light.

> Well, I'am writting and hopeing to persuade you to write the Stories peoples want to read and learn about. Like Stories about Crime, Murder, Rapists, Sex, Suicide. These are the kind of Stories peoples are interested in.
>
> Yours Truly,
Mary L.
>
> P.S. Is there money in this kind of thing?

Monday (transcribed from small book) — Claw Day, 11:30 A.M.: Office empty. Everyone's getting manicured. I'm alone so can write how they giggled off to Claw 15 minutes ago. Liz, Suzy, Happy, Tessa, a few editorial assistants thus designated as being on the fast track. I've never been invited — not that I would go. My nail technique is strictly bite and tear.

Is this ridiculous or what? No one but me sees the absurdity of climbing the corporate ladder by editing *Soap Bubble* or *Stars*. Instead, they dress for success. The color of one's lips and nails is a statement, like a Rorschach you wear.

PP is a canned fantasy factory. As associate editor of *Soap Bubble, Sin, Slut,* and *Stars,* I ought to know. The company also publishes a series of romances, Gothic as well as historic, edited by women dressed entirely in black. There are ten of them in one office. They all wear thick makeup, especially black liner around their eyes. We call them the Caged Women. They live at the end of the hall. When the door opens, a toxic cloud of hairspray wafts out. On my way to the art department I catch them staring out of their lair with black-ringed eyeballs, bloody fingernails clutching the doorjamb, and wish I had a cross.

We publish confessions as well as romances. You may wonder what the distinction is. Confessions, of which our own *Sin* is a prime example, revel in sordid revelations of incest and gang bangs, while romances are rape fantasies in costume (vampire or ancien régime). Both appeal to a female readership's wish for submission to charming men, dead or alive. A romance will end happily ever after, with a marriage between the heroine and the hero who saves her from a wicked count or prince (depending on whether it's a Gothic or historic romance). A confession will conclude optimistically too, but only after years of punishment inflicted on the narrator by the narrator, to atone for crimes committed against her. One needs a strong stomach to read this stuff in the A.M.

Julie puts out *Sin* singlehandedly, although in my position as jill of all schlock I help copy-edit and proofread. In fact, my eyes are at everyone's beck and call. My red pencil swoops from stars to smut. Julie is hated by everyone in the company for various reasons, the major one being that she has her own office — with door *and* window. Every other editor shares her space with at least one other person, usually her managing editor. I am in an office with two editors and two managing editors. It is called the TV department, so we have a TV in here too. The size of someone's head, it's positioned on a file cabinet so that it looks like a robot. It's on every day from 11:30 to 4:00. I work with plugs in my ears.

In addition to producing these magazines, PP has an entire department devoted just to Goddess Comics. These "books" are full of such scintillating dialogue as "Well, Venus, I see our young friends are falling in love. What do you say we cook up some complications with Billy's brother, so these mortals will recognize true love when they get old enough to appreciate it?" "Excellent, Athena. I'll call my son. Oh Eros, oh Cupid, honey!" (They can never decide whether they're doing Roman or Greek.)

The Goddesses take themselves veddy serrrriously. They look down on us lowly magazine hacks. They act like they're artists working on late-20th-century illuminated manuscripts. Any correlation between their goddesses in bikinis and *Slut*'s goddesses without bikinis, their immortals' antics and the oppression of *Sin*'s victims by cruel fate, their divines' cloud-headed concerns and the worries that afflict the *Soap Bubble* and *Stars* celebrities, are purely coincidental, according to our gray-eyed Athenas.

The Goddesses are zaftig. One Goddess I particularly detest has yellow braids to her waist and is a cross between a Valkyrie and a lady wrestler. When we are in the elevator together, before the doors open, she says "Shazam!" and makes a magician's gesture with her hands. As Suzy says of our many letter-writing fans who confuse television with reality, the girl has "crossed the line."

Almost all the editors here are women. What men there are work exclusively on men's mags such as *Slut* and have substantially higher salaries. This fact is causing the union trouble. There's griping in the bullpen — the cave in the center of the office where prose and pose are ground smooth as wet dreams. Since I work on both men's and women's magazines, I'm the office hermaphrodite. My salary, however, is strictly feminine.

I don't care, can't get too involved with work. It's not real. It's what I do for a living waiting to be discovered. People say hello. I say hello. Life goes on. I cultivate invisibility. A voyeur, I watch from outside, eavesdrop on one-sided telephone talk. Take notes in a small book to add to a big one later.

Tuesday — Leaving Miss Tweety's, I saw the knight of the laundry room again. Second time in two weeks. Went back and told her to lock the door. You never know. Overheard man in Chinese restaurant: "Why does every woman I meet think she's going to end up a bag lady?" Snow flurries, then sun. Little girl in a pink snowsuit. Two-year-old cheeks so red, a painter would be accused of sentimentality to picture the cherub.

Wed., 11:00 P.M. — Just got back from Miss Tweety. Where does she get her energy? Says she's 93. Blind, going deaf. Got her to tell me again how she canoed with an Indian along a wild river in the Adirondacks. The child she was caring for — she was a private pediatric nurse — needed medicines from a town downstream and there was no faster way of getting them. This is one of my favorite stories. I love the thought of Miss Tweety doing this. Persist in seeing her white-haired, frail-boned, sitting upright in a canoe with a Plains Indian in headdress.

Frieda comes during the day to fix her meals, but at night Miss Tweety's alone. She could go into a nursing home but doesn't want to, has no family to force her. Sometimes when I am sitting here, the thought of that woman alone in the dark nags me till I go check on her. It's more than the appeasing of conscience, though. I like her. Am also fascinated by the old Christian. It's inconceivable to me that aged people exist who don't speak with accents. In fact Miss Tweety has an accent, which to my tainted ear is American but is actually Nova Scotian.

Her "apartment" is a converted maid's room. In the basement are five such rooms, four of which are now used for storage by cluttered tenants. There used to be another old woman living in one of them — Mrs. MacDougal — but she has since gone into a home. Miss Tweety took this rather hard when it happened last year and still misses her. They were quite a pair, the two old birds in the basement. "Ho, Tweety!" Mrs. MacDougal would call out from her room. "MacDougal, dear, is that you?" Miss Tweety would reply.

Her hearing has worsened considerably this last year. I sit in her tiny room on the bed next to her and shout. It is exhausting, but after I've done it for a while, it is hard to make the transition to speaking normally again. Last week, for instance, I came out and said, "Hi, Aldo," to the super in such a loud voice that I startled the poor man into dropping the garbage.

Miss Tweety's room is so small that one has to crawl sideways and bent, like a crab, to get between her bed and dresser. She has a tiny refrigerator, the kind kids have in dorms, and a hot plate. High above her bed is a small barred window, which makes the whole effect prisonlike. She has lived in this room for 30 years.

"I'm from seafaring stock. Moved in here determined to think of it as living on a boat. Everything has its place. No room for excess. My forebears taught me forbearance."

And she's been clever about decorating. None of the knick-knacks you associate with old people. My apartment looks more like an old woman lives here, with all the things I inherited from my relatives. Her toilet is in a closet she calls her library. She has shelves in there full of books — so full that I can't imagine how she gets up from sitting without banging her head. Being blind, she no longer has any use for the books. I just mention them to illustrate her cleverness.

Miss Tweety collects recipes and quaint sayings. She has a shopping bag of each and likes me to read stuff from them aloud when I visit. Today I read the recipe for plum pudding. She made me repeat things and hung on every word. We sat opposite each other on the bed, me in my little pink sweater, her in hers. I tried not to feel foolish as I shouted, "A pound of currants!"

"Again, dear, I didn't hear you."

The peculiar symmetry bothered and excited me. I thought of the scene as an allegory. Youth and Age. Life and Death. While I was talking to her, my mind was elsewhere, thinking about ourselves as a painting. Is it wrong to reduce Miss Tweety to art? She probably wouldn't mind. Maybe it is myself I am worried about, twinned with an ancient crony in the basement, cackling about pudding and cake.

Miss Tweety sat with her head toward me, her mouth open and salivating, trying to catch each word, as if I were reading a murder mystery aloud. When I was done, she said, as she always says, "That tasted good, you can imagine." Or sometimes she says, "You can imagine how good that tasted." I always agree, but the recipes sound vile to me, heavy winter cooking. She took many of them from the cooks in the great mansions she worked in. Generally, the recipes are for a minimum of 30 people.

Usually after a few of her favorite recipes, she shyly asks me to read some quaint sayings or poems. This is her other shopping bag, full of a lifetime's clippings from newspapers and magazines.

Today I read "The Master's Hand," one of her favorites. "That gives me chills," she always says, and I always put a shawl around her shoulders. It's about a battered violin that an auctioneer can scarcely bother to sell for a dollar or two. Someone comes and tightens the strings and begins to play. The crowd goes wild. The auctioneer shouts: " 'Three thousand once and three thousand twice, and going and gone,' said he.

> "The people cheered but some of them cried,
> 'We do not understand —
> What changed its worth?' The man replied,
> 'The touch of the Master's hand.' "

There is no doubt some Christian allusion here I'm not getting and don't want to, just as I don't quite listen when Miss Tweety has me read propaganda from World War I about the Communist infiltration of the U.S. — something to do with sex as a Red plot to sabotage our government by warping the minds of young people, ruining their morals with sexual licentiousness.

The hardest thing about visiting Miss Tweety comes at the end. She takes goodbye very seriously.

"I have to go upstairs now, Miss Tweety."

She pretends not to hear me for a while, till I stand up. Then she stands up — she's incredibly spry, more flexible than I am. "I just want to tell you, Gabby dear," she says, taking my hand in hers, "how much I appreciate everything you've done for me, how much your visits have meant to me through the years. I just want you to know that. And if anything happens to me, I want you to know you have cheered this old woman tonight and many nights."

"I'll see you tomorrow, Miss Tweety. You'll have a good night. Don't worry. You'll be fine and I'll visit tomorrow."

"Well, we never know, not at 93, do we? But I so enjoyed

hearing 'The Master's Hand' and 'Hilda's Plum Pudding Recipe.' It means so much to me. I just wonder what will happen to the recipes when I'm gone. All the cooks are dead, so I am their only caretaker. Imagine how good those dishes tasted. I have no favorites. I love them all. I just hope they don't get thrown out."

"They won't, Miss Tweety. And nothing is going to happen to you, not for many years yet." When I try to pull my hand free, she tightens her grasp. Her skin is so soft, a silken trap. I am amazed each time at her lack of wrinkles. Such white skin, hints of baby pink. Her thick snow hair always pinned neatly in a bun. The sparkling green eyes, unseeing but bright. She is clearly an old woman, but she is also clearly a beauty. And this astounds me.

"Well, we never know. I just want to say how much—"

And so it goes, me trying to escape her gratitude without being rude, her trying to keep me a little longer. Eventually I extricate my hand and leave. But I'm disturbed each time and try to think of what I can do with her sayings and recipes, how I can get someone to publish them so she can see her life's work live on after her. I just don't see a publishing market for a cookbook full of thick, sweet, sickening pudding recipes for 30 people, interspersed with sentimental poems about broken-down violins.

My Darling Editor,

I watched the last show of *Somerset*, the very last scene. I had watched those 8 people regularly for years. I kept up with their story lines. I love all of them. Four in particular were my favorites. Two of that four I loved most of all. And the one who is my absolute favorite, well you can imagine who she is, can't you? I heard the voice say *Somerset* was leaving the air. It sounded very final. Had you walked into my living room then, you would have thought a tragedy occurred. I was broke into tears. I know I can never see those 8 people again no matter how much I want to. This is more than I can take. I had read about it but I kept thinking such a tragedy wouldn't happen. You seemed so sure last month this thing wouldn't happen. I would value to hear your opinion now.

Yours in Sadness,
Miss Louisa Marie Smith-Patrick

Thursday — Bought the *Forward*. Ad hides in a forest of Yiddish letters, like Uncle. Who was he? A garment worker with artistic aspirations and epilepsy. One night he came home from the shop to discover his wife and children had left him. They took everything but the cot on which he slept for the next 25 years. I don't know why they left. I was an infant. All I know is what I saw: he was always alone, an outsider at weddings; everyone else was surrounded by family while Uncle stood alone by the band.

What crime did he commit, this embodiment of the Wandering Jew, to make them leave? Why did he always have to be alone, the odd man, the luckless soul? Was it that he was a dreamer married to a woman who couldn't dream? Will the diary reveal some awful truth?

Friday the 13th — Knight of the laundry room is at it again. Mr. Parks, the middle-aged black man on the third floor, goes about midtown with an attaché case, in a business suit. But every so often he heads to the basement dressed in silver foil. Has a baseball bat wrapped in foil too — his sword. Instead of fencing with it, he marches around the washing machines, presenting arms. Was he in Vietnam? I don't know. Something's bothering him. I don't want to be the enemy the day he goes on a rampage. Today I saw him on the train. He saluted. That's when I noticed the silver-foil medal on his chest.

Sat. — Scotch and cheese for dinner. Hot bath waiting. Want to talk, but not to Carol. That relationship's gone beyond friendship to family. I keep secrets from her the way I used to hide things from my mother. She disregards what I say, pries apart what I don't — another homemaker spy. I love Carol. And she loves me. And also Ralph, her husband. And Lara, her daughter. And Barbara and Fanny and Ellen and and and. My last duchess. She dismisses my worries, has the right to — her dad has Alzheimer's. My voice goes around. Living is telling a story no one else hears.

I never planned to have kids, still it's a kick in the pants that now I won't. When Lara was born, I realized time was running out. Began wanting a baby so much that it was like I'd swallowed and was being nagged to death by my mother. I remember diapering Lara at the time — a little soup chicken on the table. I'd suck her toes and she'd giggle. James was at PP then. I knew about his kid; his fatherhood excited me.

The time we were alone in Lucy's Bar, he took out a fancy red comb and asked, "What you think?"

"Pretty," I said, not knowing what he wanted.

"What it make you think of?"

It reminded me of a newborn animal but I was embarrassed to say that. "Blood?" I said. "The stones are like clots."

He gave me a dreamy look. "I bring for your hair. Like so." He combed imaginary locks to one side.

I was flustered. "I can't," I said. "It's beautiful but —"

"You like, take. You don't . . ." He shrugged. "Had it long time. Red in black hair. I think perfect, like painting."

"Oh." I started to put it in my knapsack.

"Put it on," he demanded. I pushed back my hair. "Not like that," he said. "Here, I show you." He sat beside me, staring as if I were an object he was creating. Then he touched me for the first, the only time. He pushed my hair to one side, stuck the ornament into my scalp. I didn't flinch, but later when I removed it I saw he had drawn blood. I have worn my hair that way ever since, as pinned in this enchantment as Snow White pricked by a witch.

Have to sleep soon. One more drink. When I'm finished, bath, then bed. Scalding baths make me sleepy. I take the hokey-pokey kind — put right foot in, right foot out, lalala. The heat is like life. As if I were dead and didn't know it till the water brought me back. Scotch tastes good. Only a few more sips. That heat, liquid life running through me. The way a leaf on a tree draws sap. Heat spreads through veins to tiniest capillaries. I open like a leaf, spreading myself wide. Like that stuff, what's that stuff? With an *i*, ith something. Ich? The stuff that runs in the veins of gods instead of blood. Ith ich? I always imagine that stuff gold like Scotch, only thicker. Ichor, that's it. Sticky ichor. A slow hot sap. I'd like to be a god. I'd like to be friends with other gods, sit around drinking nectar, feeling ichor like lazy gold melting to my toes.

✦ ✦ ✦

Lara Jacob rubbed her eyes. She had been reading the diary and going through files for several hours without a break. She stood up, stretched, went to the bathroom, washed her face. When she returned, she tried to work some more before realizing she'd had enough. She pushed the papers to one side, pulled the phone toward her. It rang a long time before a man finally picked up.

"Hi, it's me," she said.

"Yes."

"Hope you don't mind. I just — I don't know, I needed to talk. I've been reading the diary all day."

"How's it going?"

"I don't know. It can be so irritating when she pities herself, but I have to include it in the book, don't you think? I mean, her sadness was real."

"Why don't you let me take a look at the diary sometime?"

Lara pulled a lock of hair. "I can't. Don't ask me. Listen, are you free for a little while? Can you meet me for a drink?"

"In an hour," he said. "At Lucy's. I have things to finish." Without another word he hung up.

Lara stared at the receiver for several minutes before going to freshen her makeup.

✦ ✦ ✦

Sun. A.M. — Dreamt I translated my uncle's diary. He was proclaimed a genius, and I was a genius for having recognized his greatness. I did it just by looking at the books. In the dream I noticed that if I stared at the Hebrew letters, they moved, particularly if I didn't blink for a long time. The letters swam and turned upside down, found other partners; finally they spoke to me in English. I jotted down what they said. I do not remember what they said, only it was astounding.

P.M. — It's 5:30. In the nursing home they're lining up their wheelchairs to face the elevators: "Will I get a visitor? Will she?" The home's in Coney Island. Out Uncle's window you can see the parachute jump, a mushroom cloud in metal. In summer you can hear people screaming on the Cyclone, but far away, they sound like gulls. If you go into the TV room at the end of the hall and open the curtain, the ocean stares you in the face. It is startling to open an orange curtain in a falsely gay room and be struck by a gray eternity. The old women yell, "Shut the curtain. It's bitter cold. You want to kill us?" Summer, winter, they are always cold.

Sometimes Uncle and I would go in the TV room when no one was there. We'd look at the sea. Together alone.

The last time I was there I saw they had taken the boardwalk down. Just sand and scaffolding. Probably they'll put it back up, improved. I remember walking the planks as a child. They bounced if you ran; if you had no shoes on, you got splinters.

Why must things change? I want to hold on to what was, even if what's new is better. I didn't want Uncle to die. I didn't want my parents to die. Perhaps the secret is envy — the ultimate refusal of change is death. The deep freeze. Your body metamorphoses but the real you is frozen somewhere like a package of Birds Eye peas.

I used to come to the home and find Uncle clipping headlines from newspapers, as if composing ransom notes to himself. Now I keep trying to piece together a sense of him from tattered memories and a bunch of old newspaper articles. He was a street philosopher. He liked to walk alone, but the home wouldn't let him out. I'd get off the elevator and see him down the hall, his arms behind his back, looking at everything with a deep gaze, the sweetest picture of an old man. Tiny, bones as frail as a bird's, shuffling along, contemplating, not talking to anyone, never talking to anyone. I'd want to sweep him up, protect him.

Other times I'd find him on a chair in his room. "What can I

26

say?" he'd answer my "Uncle, what's wrong?" For a while he'd only say, "Escape. Before it's too late. Escape."

When he lived in Brighton he spent most of his time walking the streets. He didn't have the same sense of reality as other people. That was his charm. He was a mystery, his vision askew like his glasses. (Perhaps the Uncle Moisha gene makes one ear higher than the other? My glasses always sit awry too.) I expected wisdom from him, thought he might know the meaning of life, how to be an artist without giving up. He was an artist. He drew, played the mandolin, wrote stories and poems.

In the hospital he stopped speaking completely. He refused to look at me. Would blink his eyes hard, scrunching his face. At first I thought he was trying to communicate: one blink yes, two blinks no. Then I realized he was blinking me out of existence.

The doctors in the hospital said there was no reason he couldn't speak. It scared me, his refusal to hear explanation. He didn't understand that the doctors had saved his life. When an aneurysm exploded in his belly, they sewed him back together. He thought they were vampires who came every day for blood. I knew what he thought; without words I knew. But I didn't have the power to make him understand.

They said he'd never survive, but he did. He regained his strength and fight. At first, when he started kicking, I cheered. His actions were like a kitten's, he was so weak, and no one minded the old man's scratch. The nurses merely laughed, holding his hands down to stick him with needles and pins.

But the fight grew wearying as it dragged on, and the nurses didn't laugh anymore. He was surprisingly strong for an old sick man. They forced him to walk the halls, his gown open in back, leaning on a metal trellis hung with tubes. He looked like a jester with his stick of bells, but I pretended to see Hermes with his caduceus.

In addition to not looking at me or speaking, he refused to eat or drink. When he refused for over a week after they removed the intravenous tubes, they opened a hole in his neck, pushed a pipe into his stomach, and fed him by forcing food down his gullet. They tied his arms and legs down, held his torso and head, and stuffed him like a Thanksgiving turkey.

Bearded bone bag tied to a bed. He didn't acknowledge me. He closed his eyes tight when I tried to explain.

I knew a woman whose baby had leukemia. She cried because the sick child in his hospital crib turned away from her when she visited. The impossibility of explanation made me wish Uncle would die. I couldn't bear his incomprehension, his refusal to hear.

Then, on the last day of his life, he let his mask drop. He looked me in the eye, pulled back his blanket, revealing an arm bent like a chicken wing. I tried to cover him. His trembling limb terrified me. As I reached over, he whispered, "Drink."

I was as pleased as a mother whose child has had a high fever and now asks for a toy. I ran to get him a glass and held it to his lips, fighting revulsion and pity to suckle this ancient infant. When I looked at him, his eyes were sharp with a magpie's plotting. "B-b-books c-c-c-closet," he stuttered.

I didn't understand right away, but it became clear he was saying there were books in his closet at the home. He wanted me to get them. I said I'd bring them the next day. He gave me a funny look, as though he read my mind. My thought was that the books were a delusion. I'd never seen any sign of them.

"T-t-tonight," he insisted. He made a motion with his mouth as if he had a sour taste. "T-t-take b-b-books t-t-tonight."

"Uncle, I don't want your books. You need them."

"C-c-closer. C-c-can't see."

I put his glasses on his nose. The thick lenses magnified his eyes. They were wetly blue, globes without land. "P-p-please," he said.

So in the end I went. To my surprise there were indeed books in his closet. Ten notebooks — his diary.

People brought back from death say the pull of grief grabs one at the threshold, will not let one pass. Perhaps it's this Uncle wished to avoid. Still, I can't bear that he died alone. The tube slipped out of his neck, I was told. Or did he pull it? He wanted escape. If I had been there, could I have let him go? There must be a point to existence, a reality beyond the mundane.

Old man, show me something in your diary to give meaning to life.

Dear Maggie "Pussy" Morgan,

A Very Important Question I Been Wanting to Know for the Last Few Years but Couldn't Find Anyone to Answer. The question, Dear Maggie, is this. I know that according to Natural Laws and Science the Reason a Man has to have an Orgasm upon Relation with a girl is so that in the process his Seed enters a Woman's Virginia to Produce her to have a Baby. On the other hand I want to know why people tell me a Girl has to have a Climax too and if she don't it will not be a Complete Sexual Relation and she will become Discouraged. What I want to know is this. What really, according to Medical Laws, is actually happening concerning her to have a child when she has an Orgasm or reaches her Sexual Climax? Does any Sexual Fluid from her Virginia in her Orgasm flow into the Man's Penis? Or What?

I want to know, Miss Maggie, I got to know. Please write and tell me. Just what is a woman's Orgasm got to do (in Medical Laws) with having a Baby? I always thought it was not really necessary for a woman but that it was Very Very Important for the man. Because by Natural Medical Law and Science his fluid passes into the woman's Virginia with his seed to make the Baby. I didn't know there had to be seed for the Woman to Give Off.

To be truthful, Miss Maggie, I think what everybody calls Woman's Orgasm is just Sexual Secretion. It's just natural fluid flowing from her inner Virginia to lubricate the Man's Very Large Penis that enters her Tight Virginia like grease in a car. Her Orgasm is just slippery wet fluid oiling his Large Swollen Penis to let it slide in and out very fast so it won't rupture when he bust forth. All in all, Maggie Dearest, I think People should appreciate Girls more. Thank you very much.

Very Truly Yours,
S. D. Clepper

(You can write to me in care of the Buffalo Home for the Aged and Infirm — I don't live there but they collect my Male)

Mon. — Still nothing from Debbie Doobie. Should I try to contact her? I don't really want to get involved. She's one of our sweet lunatics who crosses the line, writing to us via *Soap Bubble.* Many people who read this mag think soap operas are real, that they're watching life broadcast to their TV screen direct from Mount Olympus. They write about praying for Morgana's baby, Brad's operation, and they seem to think we're gods — that if they tell us what is happening, we will intercede on the behalf of good.

"You better tell Clarissa Gwen's eyeing her husband. I can't believe that woman's gonna destroy another man. What is this power she has over them? Why doesn't she go to church?" a reader asks.

They are seduced by fantasy. In the beginning I tried to answer letters, explain that the soaps were fiction. Lonely, sad people would write back. In their minds, I was a hotshot editor in New York looking for pen pals. Now I just save the letters.

Fantasy is perfect power. You don't like what you said to your boss? Play and replay the scene till you get it right. Most people's feelings are locked inside; their emotions are powerful yet mute. But artists are suckled till they can speak. Muses allow them to drink the milk of dreams long beyond the age of weaning. Art is the clay breast at which artists suck fantasy. The breast can't be controlled, except in dreams. I was weaned late so remember chewing a rubber nipple in the dreamy between state. My mother couldn't say no. Instead, one day my father came after me with a knife. He got hold of my bottle, pulled it away. Put it on the cutting board and hacked it in half.

In art, I reunite with the fake breast. I resume the trance of pleasure — of nourishment and dream. Maybe that's why it excites me to create? Molding my Venuses of Broadway, fertility goddesses of art, I have touched something primitive. Hands muddy, I wouldn't have been surprised to see bones reflected in my hair by mirrors now lost. Clay figurines strangely beautiful, eerie. Before I ever took Art History 101, I'd set my fingers to shaping their pendulous breasts. The atavistic impulse is the same that has drawn shamans for centuries to clothe dolls in skins.

How can it be, since the urge bubbles up from so deep a well, that my work is not valued? Without esteem, how can I say I am not as deluded as the readers whose fantasies bulge my files? Where is the magic mirror that tells mad genius from the merely mad?

Tues. — Max and Lee's affair has become a scandal. PP is a small town. Gossip runs through its halls like a babbling brook. And the babbling brook is named Happy, who seems to ring a bell and shout, "Hear ye. Time for the editorial director's afternoon screw" whenever Lee heads for Max's office.

Part of it is Lee's own fault. She's an Oriental Aphrodite on a spurt of foam, so sexy I'm ashamed to meet her eye. Her body is right out of *Slut.* You wouldn't believe that a secretary in midtown could dress so much like a hooker on Broadway. I have seen her literally stop traffic on Madison Avenue, and remember, I'm a copy editor — I don't take my literallys lightly. I doubt there's a man in PP who hasn't suckled her succubus.

When she wiggles out of her chair, a groan goes up in the bullpen that sounds like far-off thunder. I feel sort of sorry for the guys — reading dirty stories, looking at dirty pictures all day, then seeing Lee bop braless in her tight T-shirt.

At least once a day she goes in Max's office, shuts the door: no calls are taken. An hour or so later she comes out, clothes awry, and runs to the ladies' room. There she fixes her makeup, combs her long black hair. Max's clothes are rumpled to begin with, but I notice he smells strongly of after-shave.

I once overheard a bathroom conversation between Lee and Suzy. Lee said she had been raped in a basement when she was in high school. Later I heard Suzy repeat this to Liz. They decided Lee was making it up.

Gentlemen,
I have sent this letter to several adult magazines. Please consider my suggestion. I am with the Navy. Most of the guys I talk

to would like to see more lingerie in the magazine. Even the girls we date would like to see that. Specifically we would like to see women raising their skirts or allowing them to be raised by male companions, exposing their lacy lingerie. It is important that the women wear the following: lacy slip, matching panties, fancy garter belt, silk stockings, high heels. We think it best if the lingerie is shiny. The girl could be seated or laying back with her legs open, exposing her sexy lingerie. We here at the Navy would appreciate also poses taken from underneath, to see up the dresses. I was urged to write this letter by a lot of guys at the base. Would you do us a favor? These magazines are wrapped in plastic so we can't open them. Could you give us a positive indication on the cover of your magazine if you have used our suggestions? Perhaps the term "raised skirt" could be used. I personally know there's a lot of interest in this sort of thing.

Sincerely,
John Ralfon, S1c., U.S.N.

Wed. — Green's trying to get Miss Tweety out of her apt. Says she can't take care of herself. Aldo told Frieda. Green says Frieda's "using the old lady as a meal ticket." Frieda was crying. It's clear to anyone with half a brain that Green just wants Miss Tweety's apt. He can get more money from a tenant needing storage space. That blond couple, the unbaked family — I bet they're behind this. Mrs. Unbaked told me once how much she needs a place like Miss Tweety's "for the au pair, you know."

Thurs. — Miss Tweety was a ball of fire tonight, wouldn't let me go, shot one story after another. I felt terrible, knowing Green's plot, keeping it from her. Telling would only upset her.

She talked about her house in Nova Scotia. Right by the ocean but she would never go in the water. "I come from seafaring stock," she said. "To me the ocean's full of dead people."

"Didn't you like to sit and listen to the waves?"

"Some people go for that sort of thing, but not me. I couldn't get far enough away from it. Gives me the shivers. Used to visit my grandparents all the time 'cause they lived half a mile further from the ocean than us. Hope to never see it again."

"But you like rivers."

32

"Yes. It's not water I don't like but the sea."

Then we got on the topic of apples. "Oh yes, I love apples, always did, always will. Now Frieda comes and gives me her homemade applesauce. I'd rather have a tart apple but can't digest it. But oh yes, I love a good apple. My grandparents had an orchard. I used to eat apples till I was sick."

Friday — Letter from Debbie Doobie today. Finally! For five years she used to write to us regularly about her campaign for mayor. She would always scribble incoherently all over the page. There'd be teases of reality, but we never knew what was real. We knew that she was or thought she was a tavern owner in a small town in Iowa and that she'd lost her job or property there. We knew she was perpetually running for mayor. "Nominate!" her letters cried. "Win! Debbie Doobie is the Republican for Mayor!"

It's strange, really, how we'd study our Debbie Doobie letters. Not just me, Liz, and Suzy. Even Max found time to scrutinize her craziness. Our fascination went beyond anything we'd have invested in a sane person. We'd spend hours trying to make out a scribble. Her letters opened the door into strangeness: "So this is how a madwoman thinks." Was it just voyeurism, then? A good chuckle? She'd cut out Frederick's of Hollywood ads from our magazines — drawings of women in peignoirs and corsets, their nipples poking through the gauzy material — and she'd write, "Too small" or "Send me a dozen."

Over the years Debbie Doobie began to reveal, in Debbie Doobie fashion, the truth about herself. She started sending us a series of local newspaper articles about her mayoral campaign.

The first thing we looked at after taking the carefully cut-out clippings from the envelope was her photograph. For years we'd gotten strange letters. ("Scoop! *Days of Our Lives'* Debbie Doobie: 'I'm more like my dad than my mom.' How to live a new life: 'Don't be afraid to tell the truth always.' ") Now we had a chance to see what she looked like.

Her round head was bowled by bluntly chopped hair. One great black eyebrow instead of two grew straight across her forehead. Her left eye looked left while her right eye looked right. She was slack-mouthed in the photo, as if caught saying "Duh." A scar cracked her skull on the diagonal.

From the articles she enclosed, we learned that Miss Doobie was indeed a former tavern owner who had decided to enter politics. In order to get on the ballot, she needed a petition with 100 names. She submitted the required document and her campaign was begun. Later it was learned that only six names were real.

I imagine this strange, ugly woman sitting at her table, scrawling with her left hand, her right hand, making up names, using ones from our masthead no doubt (themselves mostly pseudonyms, but she didn't know). Tongue curling out her mouth, painstakingly forging name after name, 100 on the petition.

Peculiarity peeks out of what would otherwise be boring local news. A droll journalist discusses the feminist significance of a woman running for mayor against the incumbent. Doobie's platform is revealed: she plans to renovate the downtown area, putting all accountants in one building, all beauty parlors in another. The articles give Doobie's qualifications: two unsuccessful tries to get on the ballot for senator, one for governor, one for president.

To us she writes, "Scoop! Debbie Doobie: 'Next to career, politics is my opportunity.' *Search for Tomorrow*'s Debbie Doobie: 'I came through with a million signatures.' "

In another letter: "Debbie Doobie and Frank Sinatra. Debbie Doobie and Elvis Presley. Debbie Doobie and Ronald Reagan. Commerce, industry. She owns one half of building with tavern. She sings. She dances. Upper teeth are false. Passed steno course. Bookkeeper. Spent all her savings. Has beer and wine license. Passed Bible course. Debbie Doobie whispers, 'I like studying.' Debbie Doobie speaks, 'I traveled alone but found friends everywhere. People were kind to me in Oxford, England.' Debbie Doobie cries, 'I may be mayor but I am very much broke.' Debbie Doobie and John Travolta: 'Age can't keep us apart.' Debbie Doobie's philosophy: 'I walk the streets and study them.' Debbie Doobie's advice on how to win: 'The people must decide.' "

Months later she tells us, "News flash just in — Debbie Doobie: 'I fly across the country to Paris, to Oxford, to Las Vegas.' A younger man loves Debbie Doobie for Mayor. Candidate has turned sad these past years. Member: Busy Bee Club."

Included in one letter was a picture of the leprechaun. You know the ad for a mail-order art course? "If you can draw this elf, then you have talent that we can blah blah blah." Next to it she had laid out the design for a billboard — a rectangle drawn on the page, with "Debbie Doobie for Mayor" printed inside and a smaller box drawn for her picture. Under it she wrote a new campaign promise, disclosing her plans for an ice-skating rink where Lawrence Welk's orchestra would play 24 hours a day.

After the newspaper articles appeared, Doobie's political career was washed up. She began to send us copies of telegrams she was mailing to famous people. She sent one to the U.S. attorney general, asking if she could have all her Social Security in one lump sum so she could pay her bills. "Then I will live in my house till November, sell it to live in Europe the rest of my natural life. I have my headquarters in my own house. Anyone who wants to see me, come on over. I'll fix lunch." At the bottom she had written, "I gave everything I owned to the Salvation Army. All the furniture in the tavern. All the furniture in my house. I walked east, I walked west, talking to people. They are on my side."

The last thing we got was a copy of a telegram sent to CBS. "Dan Rather and Walter Cronkite, be here Sunday around noon with TV newsmen. Don't talk to the neighbors. They chase my guests away. I live alone. All I got left is to talk to you and the TV. Regards, Debbie Doobie for Mayor."

That was the last message, which arrived over a year ago. Today, when I got a letter from her, I was so thrilled I yelped, startling Liz out of her chair. She was also glad. We laughed, saying that it was like hearing from a lost relative after a war. In the envelope was a letter that had been sent to Ms. Doobie, who had in turn sent it to us. It was a ruling regarding her petition to get on the ballot for mayor again. It stated that the signatures on her ballot were deemed insufficient. The director of the board of elections, Bill Boo, had signed the official document. On the bottom Debbie Doobie had scrawled, "Mr. Bill Boo Sr. goes to State Burlesque shows. Spends evenings in the company of women from PasQuale's Bar not his wife. It is useless to vote!"

Saturday — Stopped in at Lucy's Bar for nostalgia and beer. Remembered how after work we'd go there, James and I, the art department crowd. It's a seedy place, dark, smoky. I used to go, dreaming of a community. I had this fantasy of us being artists, everyone a genius. We'd be like the Impressionists— serious artists spurring one another on. It was never like that, though. Felt myself judged all the time. I'm not witty. Everyone learned, after a few of my gaffes, to ignore me. Except James. He'd sit next to me, talking like a Russian Ranger. I never knew half of what he was saying. The bar was noisy, his accent difficult to make out. I'd stare at his lips, trying to read them. One night I became aware of his mouth, his tongue. In the same instant we both recognized hunger — my hunger.

What he felt, whether it was his own desire or just mine that frightened him, I don't know. Which is probably why I keep tickling the bite, trying to draw an ooze of infection or some other explanation for the itch.

I still tighten around the absence of him, a man more fiction than fact. The person I last saw five years ago supplies a name and face to fantasy. He is a strange balloon I inflate with the idea of a man. I can't recall a tongue never tasted, but knowing this doesn't stop me. I blink bits of memory like lights, trying to form a picture from flashing bulbs. The way he looked into me, like he was staring into a still pond. The way he understood me, as if he'd read my soul's book. He showed me slides of his paintings once. Magus. With a wave of his brush he created Rembrandt cherubs to torture Bosch souls.

We went to Lucy's Bar a lot, the whole crowd. I'd listen to

people's stories. One night the conversation turned to me. They'd been discussing hypnosis. I think James mentioned a magic uncle who was a hypnotist. Someone asked me something, I don't remember what — it had to do with wishes. I was taken aback and grew dumb. They were waiting. I had to say something, I had nothing to say. James smiled like an encouraging aunt till finally I stuttered, "I always f-f-feel responsi-b-ble for my p-parents' d-d-deaths," and watched the air of conviviality drop dead at my feet.

My parents were alive then. I only meant that I believed my love kept them alive. When I was annoyed with them, I feared that that alone could make them die — to teach me a lesson. But I couldn't explain, with everyone staring. The silence tightened around me like a scarf. They looked away, smiles stiff, while the corpses of my parents sat on the table, waiting like roast chickens to be carved.

Do you know those dreams where you're in a classroom and suddenly you realize you forgot to put on clothes?

Sometime round April, I guess. I've lost track of time.
Dear Elvis,

Dropping you a line to ask if maybe you can find some time, but I don't think you will and this is foolish. You'll never answer this. Why should a big star like you care about someone like me? But it would be wonderful if you did and we could become friends. I doubt it.

I need someone to talk to. I have no one. I lost my wife and son, all my friends, even my mother and my dog won't have nothing to do with me. I'm a loser, yeah. I'm 21 but have lived through what a 40-year-old ain't been through yet. I need my wife back. All I can do is drink. It won't be much longer. Doc said a year ago if I didn't stop — well, that's not your concern, a star like you.

I am a fan. The reason is because your songs are special to me. Every word. I had a kingdom once. I need someone to help. Your music helps. I almost died last year, had me a nervous breakdown. Maybe you can't understand a nobody like me. I don't blame you if you throw this out. Most likely you have by now. I don't know why I send it. You are lucky you never been threw this part of life. I used to act like a 5-year-old. I believed if more people acted like that there wouldn't be any more wars or divorce. I can't be that way no more. I am alone.

My marriage means the world to me. Here's a picture of me and Betty and Timmy-boy. I will murder to save my marriage, if only that's what it takes. Have you ever knowed anyone detearreated inside? That has died, given up. Where the world has taken everything from a person, even a man's pride? Sure, you say I feel sorry for myself but it's different when it happens to you. Is it a crime for a superstar like you to understand the emotions of the little people like me?

Well, I won't take up any more of your valuable time. A big superstar like you has better things to do than read a letter from a nobody like me. So I will close now. Please write, if you find a few minutes but I know you won't. I love you anyways.

Tim Hunter

P.S. Please excuse the spilling mistakes. Here's a shot of my son Timmy. He's 18 months old now and precious to me. So's my wife.

Sunday — Came upstairs after seeing Miss Tweety and discovered Fellatio was sick all over the apartment. She's 21. I got her as a kitten my freshman year in college. An English major on my floor said, "Fellatio — lovely name. Shakespearean character, is it not?"

Nov. 23 — Suzy told a funny story today about her father— how he'd sit in the backyard for hours whistling back and forth with a red cardinal. "You know the kind of song they have?" she asked just as Julie was coming out of her office. Julie did a startlingly accurate birdcall. She looked so funny — her long dancer's neck, her lips pursed — we all started laughing. Happy kept saying, "Stop, you're killing me," and Suzy said, "Julie, that's so you." She even called Frankenstein in the art department to hear Julie's whistle. He brought along Ju-an.

Suzy continued to tell how her family was at a barbeque where her dad and a neighbor were talking. Her father told of his bond with the red cardinal; only thing was, the neighbor also had such a bond. The two suburbanites were pondering what this meant when it hit them: they'd been whistling back and forth to each other.

We were all laughing. Happy cried, "I'm going to pee in my pants." I don't usually laugh but I couldn't stop. It was like releasing a pent-up fluid. Suzy is so funny, though she lacks a self-image. Maybe that's what makes her the perfect mirror. Not a sycophant — the images she throws are ones people don't know they want. "You kook," she says. "That's so you. I can just see you yelling at that loony on Lex." She will mention an episode several times during the day, "You nut, you kook," till the reflected one thinks, "Yelling at that homeless man was quirky. I'm special."

Today, for instance, it was raining. So Suzy asked Happy whether she had an umbrella or was going to put a shopping bag on her head like that time she saw her walking down 57th. Then they laughed. I envy Suzy's laugh. People perform for it like jesters for a queen. My laughter is forced but I've my own talent: I can read faces like headlines. Today I read Happy's: "I'm the sort of person who puts a bag on my head in the rain. I'm a nut, how marvelous."

Later Suzy looked at what Liz was reading (*The Origin of Consciousness in the Breakdown of the Bicameral Mind* — so what? I've read it). She oozed admiration: "You're my genius friend. I tell people all the time. My friend Liz is a fucking genius."

Liz is bright, mind you, but no genius. A tough ghetto bitch, short, dark, she gives the impression that she smokes cigars. She doesn't like me — not since the time I discovered her hiding under her desk. I don't know why. I pretended not to notice.

I used to think Suzy was vain. Always looking in her mirror. She's a beautiful girl — eyes as green as a golf course, black hair, tall, thin. Then I overheard her tell Liz that mostly she feels she doesn't exist. Afterward I noticed she takes out the mirror when Happy is talking. Pretends to preen but mostly just stares. Happy is so full of herself. Suzy must feel like a stick figure next to a Rubens. Maybe she collects people to supply herself with an identity: "I am the friend of that kook, this nut. Geniuses surround me. That's so me."

Tues. — I pick up responses to my ad tomorrow. Will have Thanksgiving weekend to read them all. I have been fantasizing wildly. Find myself planning an intellectual friendship formed through my uncle's books. The translator and I work together to discover Uncle's genius. We publish articles. Give speeches. If the translator is a woman, we become best friends. If a man, we fall in love.

We are at my desk, looking at the diaries. Our hands graze. He looks into my eyes. With the hint of a Russian accent he tells me I am the most special woman he has met in America. He is older than me but not absurdly so — just enough to make him feel unworthy. He can't fight the attraction. And — you know how these things go in fantasies — we kiss, caress, fall to the floor amidst my uncle's writings. Afterward he tells me my uncle was a great artist, he sees I am an artist too. He recognizes I have genius genes, inherited from my uncle.

Wednesday — PP emptied out early. I waited till no one was around. Wanted to put on makeup, unobserved, before going to pick up the responses. When I finished, I saw a clown. Washed my face, started again. To see myself as a stranger, I went into a stall, came out with closed eyes. Kept them shut till I was in front of the mirror, trying to catch myself by surprise. When I opened them, I saw a face behind me and gasped. Lee laughed. I hadn't known she was in one of the stalls.

She was wearing a thin T-shirt, despite the coolness of the day. She claims to wear skimpy clothes because she's hot all the time. A short dungaree skirt slit up the leg as well as extremely high heels completed her ensemble. "How you doin', Gabby?"

Her sexiness is like a disease, but of all the women in the office, she's the nicest. Always smiles. I think she identifies with me. I get the feeling she thinks, "I am nice to Gabby so that someday someone will be nice to me when I get old." Lee is 23.

We are both outsiders here — I in my deadness, she in her

vitality. We're both ridiculed by the others. But Lee never says a mean word about anyone, not even the rapist in the basement. She told Suzy, "I don't know. I feel sorry for him. I mean, he was sick. I couldn't report him to the police."

I trust Lee. Even if I did something awful, like touch her breast, she wouldn't tell. So I asked about my makeup. Her eyes assessed my face professionally. She took a piece of toilet paper, wet it with her tongue. Told me to close my eyes, then bent over so close I was moistened by her breath. I didn't exhale, afraid of my smell. Her breast pushed against me as she fixed my makeup with a tissue. I stiffened my arm, to protect myself against the grazing of her softness.

"There now," she said. "Now you look beautiful."

I blushed, looked at my watch, pretended to be late. "Have to go," I said, and ran away. On the train I kept thinking about her, wondering if we could be friends. Finally rejected the idea. Lee's not very smart. Beautiful but vacant, not even a good secretary. A nice person but that's all. If I showed Lee a painting, she'd say, "Like a print dress I saw in Bloomies. Want to go shopping?"

I have to admit I have a crush on her. If she does that to me, the men in the bullpen must have balls the color of plums. Lee's creativity is in her sex. What art is to me, fucking is to her. I think she lies in bed, feeling her naked skin on the silky sheets, smelling herself, devoting endless hours to dreaming up what to do next to Max and other men, women, maybe dogs. A nice kid. We just don't have a lot in common. She thinks about sex too much.

Finally I got to the building where the *Forward* is. I went in. The receptionist handed me a letter.

"Where's the rest?" I asked.

"That's it."

"How can it be?" She shrugged and resumed typing.

"Will there be more? Should I check back next week?"

"If you want," she said without pausing in her work. "Run the ad again, see what happens."

I was so disappointed I almost started to cry. Instead I thanked her and walked away. On the train I kept fingering the letter without opening it. Wanted to wait till I got home. Not sure why. I guess I wanted to be alone. Wanted a drink. Felt nervous.

But I had nothing else to read, so finally I took it out — just to examine the writing. When I saw the name, there was a thud in my chest, as if the train had run over a body. The writing was tiny. I thought at first it was a woman's hand. I kept saying, "It can't be. I must not be reading it right."

The envelope said "I. Kolokoy."

So close, so imperfectly close. If I kept staring, would it magically become J. Kolokol or vanish, becoming something entirely different — M. Pickleberry?

I got home, poured a Scotch, sat down. Tinkled ice, sipped my drink. Pretended it was no big deal. There'd be more letters, and of course this I. Kolokoy was not James. Such a silly idea, James translating Yiddish, reading the *Jewish Daily Forward*. My Slav prince a Yid kid? Absurd. So part of why I didn't tear the envelope open the minute I read the name was that I didn't want to be disappointed. But I was also building to a grand climax, suspending my pleasure in expectation, in ridiculous expectation of something so huge I would swoon.

I told myself that if James had written it, he'd have known my name. He'd have remembered me that much. But I am an invisible woman. People forget me before I leave the room. Why should he remember Gabby Segul from PP or connect me with the ad? Then I realized I hadn't put my name in the ad, just a box number.

Finally I opened the envelope, braced for disappointment— and miracle. "Dear Sir or Madam," I read. "In response to your advertisement, I am fully qualified to translate the aforementioned diaries, being fluent in Russian, Hebrew, Polish, Yiddish, and English. May we meet to discuss the details of our possible arrangement? Please call the above number at your convenience. I remain yours truly, I. Kolokoy."

So here I sit, diary in lap, drink in hand, thinking about a translator and afraid to call. Here is his telephone number. He expects me to call, but I am under a spell. I sit, listen to music, look at the letter, look at the Uncle books, sip my drink, write to you, I dream and don't call. I have brought the telephone over to my side. It is eyeing me like a dog waiting to be fed. I dialed once but then hung up. I'm shy, don't know how to do this sort of thing. It's not just that. I'd rather hold on to the fantasy a while, pretend that for some reason J. Kolokol would answer my ad in a Jewish newspaper under the pseudonym of I. Kolokoy.

The thing to do is think about this when my head is clear, not after having a drink. What if my words slur? Don't want James to think I've become a lush. But I need a drink before calling. So I will call tomorrow, after one drink. I

Oh God, an incredible thought! James and I in a bar — how could I have forgotten this till now, how he wrote his name in Russian on a frosted glass with his fingernail and passed it to me like he was giving me his soul? I couldn't read it, of course. He told me what it said. Ilyich Kolokol. I watched the letters drip down the side of the glass till they vanished. Ilyich Kolokol.

Do you see? I. Kolokol. So close, oh why can't I make him come all the way? Kolokol, Kolokoy. A typo? But he wrote it in his hand. Could I have misheard James's last name all those years? Could he have changed it for some reason?

So strange. I know he wasn't Jewish. I can't imagine him reading the *Forward* like my father or uncle, snoring in a chair. Despite his accent, I never thought of him as Ilyich. That must be why I'd forgotten this. And yet it is such a good memory, now that I think of it. The heat in his eye when he pushed the glass to me — as if that heat melted the letters scratched in frost.

Not even in fantasy have I ever called him Ilyich, and far less amazing things happen in my fantasies. I could no more imagine calling him Ilyich Kolokol than I could hear him moan Golda Leah in my ear — my Jewish name, a gravestone name. Oh, but the look in his eye, now that I recall it, is seared on my breast.

He handed me that glass. I blushed and looked away. But I felt so . . . honored, as if a prince had kissed my hand.

Oh James. Ilyich. I blush now, trying to moan that foreign name. James, then. Ilyich Kolokol. I. Kolokoy. I want to believe such things are possible. I've always been that way, believed what I wanted, then cursed the Fates for leading me astray.

And yet, don't you agree that this is too close for coincidence? I don't believe in coincidence. I believe in fate. I've always believed I was destined to meet James again when the time was right for both of us. Often when I walk I relinquish control and call it destiny. I don't choose a direction but let fate lead me, as if I were a somnambulist, into his arms.

Dear Slut,

I'm sure many other lonesome gals would be happy to learn of my experience in the truly enjoyable pleasure provided by a dog. You can have pleasure 2, 3x a day. Just feed him ground sirloin and he's always available. I am 23. I need help. I'm married but my husband is away 2 months at a time. I stay alone so I bought a police dog, a wonderful handsome dog. One evening while my husband was away I was in the mood. Wolfie whined at the door. Still a pup, I let him in and resumed my position on the bed.

Well, within seconds he got in touch with my vitals. He apparently smealth the scenth. I went out of my mind with his tongue. After a few minutes I went to the bathroom and inserted my diaphragm. Then I resumed my position. By this time he was going nuts and so was I. I got in the dog position. Within seconds we were in action. I put on a jacket and had to assist him in guiding him in. Since the first time I no longer wear a jacket. Believe me, he is so gentle though satisfying there is not one scratch.

I always wear a diaphragm. I'm afraid this may not be safe enough. Would you ask your medical adviser if it is possible to become pregnant with a dog? I'm sure Wolfie and I would enjoy the ordeal more with no protective devices.

Wolfie has learned new tricks to add to my pleasure. Within an hour I reach 3, 4 climaxes. I'm oversexed but no man can take the place of my dog. I'd like an answer to my medical question. I want to keep my puppy happy.

Yours Truly,
Anonymous

44

Dear Judy Clars, Managing Editor, *Stars* Magazine,

I am a doorman in a building chock full of famous celebrities and I know other doormen in other buildings with other celebrities. I've had very unique glimpses of the stars and I think your magazine would benefit from being exposed by me. I could tell you what causes the bad temperaments of the stars, what they eat, what they leave over, how much they tip (I have a friend who is a waiter in a certain exclusive restaurant), who they spend their off-hours with, whether they leave their clothes on the floor or pick up after themselves (I know several maids), their strange reactions to deliveries, including a screaming fit by one superstar you wouldn't believe, and another famous actress accepting her deliveries while naked in her bed, which I may add she insists be made up in only the finest silk sheets (her maid is a *very close* personal friend). I also have information on blood on the aforementioned actress's towels and a brawl between a famous actor who lives in my building and a bartender nearby (another good friend of mine). I could tell you if Jacqueline Kennedy Onassis orders take-out Chinese food (she does) or pizza (she doesn't). Wouldn't your readers like to know how much she and others like her tip at Christmas to the doorman of her expensive building? You'd be surprised, believe me.

The article would be very unique, told as it is by the eyes of a doorman who is invisible to the stars who don't realize he is doing much more than opening the door for them or helping them into a cab.

Anxiously Awaiting Your Reply,
J. P. Lund

Dear "Soap Bubble,"

I think "Ryan's Hope" is disgusting. An insult to the Catholic faith. Our girls don't "make love" and get pregnant before marriage. Imagine an Irish Mother to condone such behavior. Tell her that the Irish people think any girl in that situation is a disgrace to her family. They expect virtue from their girls. In my married sister's apartment, when they watch it they turn it off. I'm 29, engaged, and I have never "made love," as you call it, and don't intend to. Surprised, are you not?

Regards,
Kathy Ryan

Please send me a free catalog of sex aids. I don't see what I want. Do you have a male doll that a woman can use without a man? I am a widow. Call if you don't believe me.

L. Pane

Greetings to All Peoples of Editorial Board of STARS Magazine:
Two years ago I wasn't as advanced in English like I am now. My highest mark is in English, sometimes acting like show biz (theater) in campus.

Dearest Editor! I think it is time to acquaint myself. My name is Idi Armah Yehu and I am 18 years, 2 months, and 1 day old being in 11th grade.

Dearest Editor! I always believe that success and failure are the consequence of remaining idle. I have lost my family. If I got someone to help, I want to be a big bug person through education.

Please, dearest Editor! try to get someone to help. Especially the STARS. Or other people. Or send me their address and I'll ask myself. See the list of names enclosed. I will read STARS monthly. I'll pay payment and need further information. How can I get this illustrious magazine? How much will I pay?

Thank you, dearest Editor! to the kindness of all you are going to do for me. Please, kind Sir, be cautious at everything you are going to do. I mean I hope you will send reply.

Dearest Editor! thank you from the bottom of my heart! If you want to know about world affairs, I can help. Who falls today may rise tomorrow!!! Please reply as soon as possible! in order to know that all Americans are cautious.

This is my list — Elvis Presley, Elizabeth Tylor, Dean Martin, Doris Day, Richard Burden, Marlo Brando, Bert Reynolds, Sydeny Poiter, Flip Wilson.

Your Humble Servant,
Idi Armah Yehu

Dear Sir:
So many girls claim to have boyfriends. How do you get around this and into their panties?

Sincerely Yours,
I. P. Rolls

Dear Handsome Dan Dick,

I'm writing to say what a great actor you are. I'm 13. I had an operation on my back. I'm wearing a cast and am on my back every day so I watch all the soaps. You are the best actor on TV. I'm dying to know more about you. How old are you? Are you married? Do you like girls younger than you? And many many more questions. Now I hope you will write to me. About myself, I'm blond with blue eyes and very feminine. I know all about sex, love, boys' bodies and of course girls' bodies. I dig older boys because they're so much older than boys my age. My last two boyfriends were 18 and 24. Think about that if you're not married.

Love and Kisses,
Lulu XXXX

 o
orry
o
loppy

Nov. 26 — Just called Kolokoy. My heart's still thumping. Woman with accent answered. His wife? Mother? Not surprised to hear from me: "Darling, Mr. Kolokoy would love to meet you." So now I know for a fact that I. Kolokoy is a man. He is certainly not James, but I keep trying to find ways in which he could be. James married to an older woman? Find out Saturday.

Carol invited me to dinner. Not going. The only family to be with on Thanksgiving is your own. I was determined to paint while the country carves. Instead am thinking about James. I know Kolokoy will not be James, but how could I have forgotten that time when he handed me his glass? Ilyich Kolokol: the long, thin letters of his name so like his legs.

He once said my art had "pulse." Other things too, excitingly unclear. Kept saying "you know." I never said, "I don't. Explain." Partly it was his accent — that odd Russian twang, as if Dracula's coffin had been delivered to Austin; partly it was his assumption that I did understand that made me smile my "mmm-hmm." He'd mumble the ends of sentences, leave ideas hanging, but I couldn't bear to reveal an imperfect comprehension so now am left with half-remembered fragments and don't know whether his comments were said in admiration or jest.

Even if I. Kolokoy is not James, he might

Stop, this is ridiculous. If you can't write sense, then write nothing at all. Dreaming on paper like this is masturbation. Think about something else. The Uncle books. Took them out today, stared at the letters, thought of genius. Many men existed who seemed mad and turned out to be visionaries. He could have been a great artist. A hidden saint. I won't say I believe in such people, only that I believe in possibility.

His notebooks look strange — yellowing pages, faded ink. The first of the Uncle books is small and unlined. Seven of the journals are unlined. That touches me, the correspondence between Uncle and me in our preference for unlined paper. Your own face, book, is as unlined as an infant's skin.

Sat. — Writing to take my mind off Kolokoy, who's due at 8:00. Almost 7:15 now. Anxious. Can't wait for this night to be over. If only I could laugh like Suzy. People like laughers. Instead I snuffle air out my nose — hmph hmph. James had a wonderful laugh. He'd spiral and I'd stand off watching. Oh James again. Pooh.

Still only 7:20? Intestines are writhing. Used to do that at Kensington Pigeon Art Institute while I was waiting for James. Always coming out of the bathroom when he arrived. That first class, he came up to me. "You Gabby?" he said. "From sudsy mags?"

I didn't like him then. His tone, the way he looked to my left, as if seeking someone else. What did he want? He just stood there, nothing to say. Finally I asked, "How do you like working at PP?" He shrugged. "Ve better sit down now."

His offbeat accent infuriated me. I didn't understand, hadn't seen his work. So many men wear masks, loving the image of the artist more than the work. They affect dreamy-eyed gazes if they're writers, hard-eyed clarity if they draw.

I'm a peripheral Peeping Tom. I notice things without gazing directly. People don't know I'm watching, so don't disguise their natures. I see them pick their noses, scratch their balls, all from the corner of my eye. I see them turn dreamy, and I see them turn cold. I sum up from the edges, confirm observations at a glance.

Kolokoy will be here soon. I'm afraid — what if he's a rapist who answers classified ads to find his prey? In a Yiddish newspaper? Still, I shouldn't have invited him to my apartment. Could have met him in a bar. I know he's not James. I've decided to give him one book at a time. What if he loses it? Why didn't I make a copy? My stomach's in a knot. I'm angry, and he's not even late. Should I ask if he wants a drink? Why did I put on this red blouse? I know I won't open the door and find a tall blond man whose eyes will widen in surprise, who will say, "Gabriella, is it really you?" I know that even if it is him, he won't have the audacity to take me in his arms, to pull me to him, to drink my lips, to cry, holding me as if I'd returned from the dead — or he had. He won't be standing there, he won't burn me with his gaze, he won't

He won't, he didn't, and he just left. Thank God that's over. I feel like puking, but somehow this Scotch is chloroforming the butterflies. I knew he wouldn't be James. Part of me knew he'd be an old man. Israel Kolokoy. How the gods love making a fool of me. ("Well, Aphrodite, what do you say we have I. Kolokoy answer the ad, knowing how Gabby still yearns for J. Kolokol?" "Neat idea, Athena. I'll call my son. Oh Cupid, Eros, honey!")

Mr. Kolokoy was in his seventies. I didn't exactly trust him but knew I could knock him down if he got funny. He was a tiny man with something of the rake about him, a boyishness that undoubtedly delights his grandchildren but nauseated me. It was the mixing of decrepit age and sensuality. I could see him taking me in, that hot-eyed Izzy Kolokoy. Now that I think about it, I know what it is. He reminds me of a friend of my parents when I was a child. Sam Shoemaker. Sam the Plumber.

The whole time Mr. Kolokoy was here I felt something pulling inside — an unpleasant drawing-in. I don't know how to explain it except as eroticized anxiety. A sexual feeling but not of desire or pleasure. More as if a taut string attached navel to clit, and there was an upsetting tug of war. Orgasm seemed the only way to release the tension, but thinking this while negotiating an agreement with the old man made the tendon tighten with disgust.

Make no mistake. Mr. Kolokoy was a perfect gentleman, an elf of an old man: his pointy ears, his delightful smile. Elegant hands. A charmer. He said, "So, your uncle was a Yiddish writer? I too am a writer in Yiddish. I will be honored to translate your uncle's works. May I take a look at them?"

I showed him the books and felt ashamed. I. K.'s hands are so clean, his nails manicured; my uncle's writing goes all over the page. There are newspaper clippings pasted in upside down, with Band-Aids, or not at all. We discussed the fee, then I took back all the books but the first. "I'd prefer that you translate one at a time."

"As you wish, Miss Segul," he said. Putting the first diary into his briefcase, he asked, "So, what do you do for a living?" I told him I was an editor. His eyes opened so wide that I almost fell in.

"You wish to include your uncle's work in your magazine?"

"Not at all, Mr. Kolokoy. I work in schlock. Fan books — you know, movie stars, soap operas?" I didn't tell him about *Slut* or *Sin*. Just the thought of them tugged queasily at my meat.

Mr. Kolokoy, however, didn't know from schlock. He nodded but I watched the information go right past him. If I'd had a magazine in the house, I might have shown him, but instead I thought, "Why should I put myself down? If he wants to think I'm the editor of some intellectual journal, perhaps he'll do a better job." So I let the matter drop.

"I will treat your uncle's writing with the utmost care," he said, zipping his briefcase. "I am honored to be entrusted with this translation. You will be pleased with the quality of my work, which I shall embark on first thing tomorrow. So I will see you at this time a month from now, if that is convenient?"

Then he did it, the thing I can't get out of my mind. "Till then, madam," he said, giving a slight bow with his skull. And that bow is still disturbing me.

It was in recognition of my womanness — is that why it disturbs me? I consider myself a feminist, think there should be no legal differences between men and women. In fact, I'd like no differences at all. Don't want men opening the door. Hate being in an elevator with them, not knowing if they're going to make me go first. They're so gallant when it doesn't count, but just see how many let you ahead when you're trying to get on a crowded bus. I do like to have my cigarette lit. Sitting in the dark with a man who bends forward to offer a heart-shaped flame.

This bow of Kolokoy's stays with me. I hate it, how it makes me a queen. Uneasy pleasure fills out my breasts, tightens my waist. That stupid little bow is upsetting my hormones. Caterpillar changes come over me. I don't want to be a butterfly. Prefer being a hermaphrodite, neither sex and both, but now am wet with new wings. Pull becomes pleasure, constraint heightens heat. I stand before the mirror to see a goddess of fertility. I am not at all pleased. Prefer to worship than be one. Heavy breasts are difficult to balance on my newly tiny wasp waist. And inside, the string of meat is like a leash tugging a dog from its nature. I jerk abruptly in response. Spill my charms like a bowl of fruit toppled by a mad dog. All because of that bow.

After he left I curtsied behind his back. Don't know why. Having acknowledged that old man's masculinity, I felt sick.

I wish we were not men and women. Why can't we just be human beings, all the same, our voices in the middle range, the same height, the same physique? What is a man that is not a woman? We all started as babes with just a bit of difference. Then breasts popped out and voices became shrill. Some grew tall, triangular — these now think their mathematical thoughts, plotting logic behind their beards. Perhaps if I had a brother, I'd understand. But I don't and so believe that if men differ psychologically from women, they must be as foreign as aliens from space.

If only we had no bodies and were just minds. As it is, I distort the differences, am extremely sex-conscious. See men as giant penises in overcoats, carrying briefcases, inclining glans slightly to acknowledge women. See women as wet wounds on the street. Pocketbooks all-too-obvious symbols of what they're trying to hide: that they are nothing but dark openings and the rest is fantasy. That's why I'd like to do away with it all, the man/woman thing. It makes it so difficult to talk to people.

Mr. Kolokoy looked more like a penis than most men. It was his bald head and the slant of his eyes, the way his eyebrows arched. He was small, hairless. I first noticed how phallic he was when he bowed to me. And I thought, "So that's how it is, is it?"

Dear Pussy,

I will send you whatever money you want if you know any Close Girlfriends with Blond, Brown, or Red Hair and ask them to come to any Hotel they choose. I'll rush up as fast as I can. Bring them or Her a Bottle of whatever She likes best to drink. A bag full of the Best Sandwiches. We could have a Ball eating and drinking together and listening to Soft Music from my portable tape recorder. First I'll give her Nice Money. Gift for Friendship and Togetherness.

Please, Dear Pussy, could you Come yourself on the Greyhound Bus to any Nice Hotel in Buffalo some future weekend you be free from your Employment? If you could check out a nice room in a hotel of your Choice, I'd really be happy to rush up and welcome You with wonderful things for us to enjoy for a weekend of Sweet Love. Just You, Darling Pussy, and Myself. I love You very much. The Picture of you in the Nude Position excites me. I approve of girls working in the Working World and I wouldn't stop you from your job.

Please, Pussy, accept my offer. But if you can't come to Buffalo due to circumstances beyond your control, I'd be grateful if you could recommend a Blond or Brown-haired or Red Head girl friend. I'll give her Nice Cash Gift, I promise, I'll do much for you Pussy in the future. I really love you, Pussy, the most. It's not just physical. Thank you so much.

A Devoted Fan

P.S. Can you send me a wallet-sized photo of you in the Nude Position, maybe with a girlfriend?

With warmest regards,
Samuel D. Clepper
c/o the Buffalo Downtown Home for the Aged and Infirm (I don't Live there. I Work there.)

Sunday — Spoke to Frieda. Nothing new about Miss Tweety's apt. She asked why they don't take Mr. Parks away instead. Haven't seen the knight of the laundry room lately. Hope he's OK.

Did a painting of Miss Tweety from memory. Part of a series of old beauties. Last summer Miss Tweety was sitting in front of the building with Frieda. Bright P.M. Cloudy green eyes, freshly painted scarlet lips — I never saw her wear makeup before or since. Texture of her hat: green velvet, pearl-dotted lace. It felt like the discovery of a new planet, this revelation of aged beauty. Don't know if she was beautiful in her youth. Anyway, I am pleased with the portrait. Hope rest of series works out. Have done other old women in neighborhood, intricately wrinkled. One has curly hands. Painful but fascinating — long, wavy fingers knotted with veins. I've permed Miss Tweety's hands somewhat in the portrait.

Must send slides around. Making art and not showing it is like masturbation. Lack of response dulls creativity.

NOTE: If weather stays bright, shoot slides.

4:30 P.M. — Creative depression. Going to paint again as soon as mood settles. Light in apartment great. Shot slides. Want to paint all day. Orgy of art. Just waiting for idea to land. Besides, putting it off this way adds to pleasure, like postponing coming till urgency drives you beyond will.

Liar. It's fear and you know it. Because suddenly this afternoon you remembered you have never sold a painting and you are almost 40. So now you approach the white canvas like the rolled-up eye of a corpse. If you had talent, it would have been recognized by now. How long can you kid yourself? Your artwork's just a wall of dreams keeping you from life.

Must show stuff. Everyone goes through this. Not like I've had no encouragement. Gallery owner's assistant in June said to try back after summer. Mr. Mauret? Check records.

5:20 — Just looked at portrait of Miss Tweety. I'm as horror-stricken as if it were Dorian Gray's. What made me think it any good? Can already hear Mauretshisname: "Derivative, sentimental."

Now I've done it. I'm terrified to go near fresh canvas. Instead I stare at the dead white eye, listening to a chorus of crows: naw naw naw. People don't know how their comments stick. I remember them all, their lips round as anuses when they said no.

Monday — Suzy has taken to sighing all day. Deep long sighs when she sits down, when she gets up. Sometimes when she's just at her desk. Does it constantly when we're alone. Why?

Been worrying about Uncle's book like it's a daughter on her first date. What do I really know about Kolokoy?

Tues. — In the home Uncle used to say "they" were after his feet. His ankles were swollen; the staff wanted him to take a diuretic to reduce water retention, but he refused any medication except the Dilantin for epilepsy. The more they insisted, the more certain he became they were poisoning him. They'd point. "Your feet are swollen. The medicine will get rid of the water."

"The d-d-d-doctors from the Workermen's Circle said d-d-d-don't take any pills but the D-D-Dilantuh."

"Your feet, Mr. Moisha, look at your feet."

"The d-d-d-doctors from th—"

He was obstinate. One day, when no one else was in the room, he whispered to me, "Look around. No one around here can walk."

It was true. Old people stared as Uncle paced the halls. He walked nonstop till forced to stay in his room for the night.

I told the nurses to give up. It wasn't so important that he take vitamins or a diuretic. They tried to trick him, putting medicine in his food till he was certain they were poisoning him.

54

Once I watched him take his pills. The nurse stood over him, to make sure he put them in his mouth. After she left, he spit them into his napkin. I had to tell her so she would give him another Dilantin, otherwise he might have a seizure. She came in yelling, shaming him, calling him a baby, an imbecile. She wouldn't stop. Uncle was shaking and looked about to cry. I felt like a traitor. All along Uncle had told me stories of torture, beatings. I never knew whether to believe him. I chose not to believe. But now I thought, "If she acts like this in front of me, what does she do when I'm not here?"

Wed. — Sitting with Miss Tweety just now I almost told her Green's plot to steal her apartment. We were talking about Mrs. MacDougal, who's so unhappy in the nursing home. Miss Tweety said, "If I ever had to go into one of those places, I'd die." There was a moment when I could have said something but didn't.

Why can't I stop thinking of James? I hardly remember him. I can recall his features one by one — high cheekbones, thin hair, Cupid's mouth — but somehow it's a cipher when I try to put him together. Yet this is the man who, when I invoke a flash of him, makes my muscles stretch with yearning like a snake that hears a charmer.

I have a photo. It was in a PP newsletter. He is one of a crowd of people in the art department. I study his face. At first there is nothing, till I will a thrill of recognition. I say, "That's him, that's James, there he is, that's his face," like I'm prompting a child to love Daddy. Why keep tickling this infection?

I wonder if he kept the picture of me as Sexy Death Doll they used in *Slut* one time? It was a head shot. I was supposed to be one of a gang of female terrorists. They do that at PP. When they need head shots, they line up the women editors and shoot them.

The photo I have of James is tiny but I've studied it. A shadow falls across his face. One side of him is kindness, the other mockery. He looks at me beyond the paper. The hollows of his eyes smile like death — insolence, disdain, and a cold cold longing.

✦ ✦ ✦

Lara Jacob bit the end of her pen. Sometimes she felt she understood her aunt too well. There was a certain sort of man who rooted in your mind like an impossible weed.

She got up, poured herself a Scotch. Stared at the phone, willing it to ring. When it did, she jumped. Fearing the caller had read her mind, she shook her head briskly, flinging out silly notions. It was Tom Campo. She hid her disappointment.

"Sorry to call so late," he said. "How's the book going?"

Fine, fine. She wished he'd get to the point.

"You know the painting Segul called *Self-Portrait*?" he asked. "The one your mother referred to as *Vaginal Bouquet*?"

"Maybe," Lara said, wondering if someone else might be trying to call. Hoping someone else might be trying.

"Well, we're planning this retrospective . . . and it occurred to me that your mother may have said it was one of a series of 'vaginal bouquets.' Does that mean anything to you? Do you know of other genital portraits, self- or other?"

Lara stared at the four mauve-and-purple pictures on the far wall, painted so thickly they were almost in relief. She'd always seen them as suggestive flowers. "I'm not sure," she said. She didn't know why. Maybe she just didn't want to share everything about her aunt with the world. Maybe she wanted to feature them in her biography. What was it her mother had said about those paintings — that Gabby called them inside-out Georgia O'Keeffes? Wasn't that the sort of thing that made a book sell?

"Tom," she said. "I'll look through my mother's stuff. See what I find, okay? Let me get back to you."

Sure, he said. You never know what'll turn up.

As soon as she hung up, the phone rang. The familiar voice on the other end was the one she'd been hoping to hear.

"How about a drink?"

Lara put down her Scotch. "Sounds great. Where?"

"You know where," he said, and hung up.

She stared at the receiver, furious at his insolence. Did he really expect her to drop everything, to run to meet him "you know where," because he wanted a drink and didn't want to drink alone? She slammed the phone down, took a gulp of Scotch, pulled Gabby's diary to her, began reading. She refused to be his puppet. Let him wait in Lucy's Bar. Let him wait all night. She wouldn't show up. Or if she did, it would only be after a good long while, when he himself was about to leave, disappointed.

Ten minutes later Lara Jacob put on her coat and headed out the door.

◆   ◆   ◆

Thurs. — Saw Mrs. Unbaked in elevator with her youngest daughter. She said something about her pregnancy. Then: "How's that old lady downstairs?"

I snarled. "Miss Tweety's a fascinating woman. More interesting than those with nothing on their minds but babies."

"Oh," said Mrs. Unbaked. "I'm not good with old people. I prefer the young. Full of life. This will be my fourth."

I said, "Babies are helpless but no one puts them in nursing homes." The elevator opened; Mrs. Unbaked ran out.

Slides are OK. Put together 20, including Miss Tweety. I *have* to do this. Suzy still sighing. What's wrong? I don't want to pry.

Saw shopping-bag man wearing headphones, picking through cans. Earplugs stuck out like a stethoscope on a child. I was happy there was some pleasure in his life. Suddenly he stopped poking through trash and stood staring like a rabbit, listening intently to some message in his ears. A news report? That's when I noticed there were no wires on his headphones.

Friday — Old man at the bank told me he dreamt he was on "Let's Make a Deal." Had a pacemaker on his head and was calling, "Monty, Monty." Monty asked what he had to trade and he said his pacemaker. Monty said, "Keep it." Then he said he'd in fact kept his old pacemaker when they put in his new one. He drew a picture of it for me on a paper bag. It looked exactly like an apple with a stem. His 15-year-old dog had just died, he said. He had been washing it and had found a boil the size of a heart. Cancer.

Next he showed me how to protect myself on the street. "You see this? To you it looks like nothing but a newspaper. It's a weapon, you know, against muggers. Look." He rolled it into a bat. "Tight, as tight as you can make it, see?" He took it, hit it against his hand a few times. "I may be old, but with this I don't have to be afraid. Any crook or no-goodnik starts with me, bam. It's all in how you roll it."

Sat. — Raining. Spent the day inside. Mysticism is a drug, I've decided. Behind trances and drinks is the wish to merge. We want to lose ourselves in something big — art, God, death. Are all fantasies of union, oneness with the breast of life that magically appears when we're hungry or cold, tired or scared? We drink ourselves into madness, whirl like dervishes, stand at easels. We must have silence . . . in which to hear our fantasies churn out perfect butters of omniscience.

If the impulse of art is erotic, is it because of the merging? When I stand at my easel, my eyes glaze just as they glaze when I have sex. Mystics speak of passion. A coincidence that the word has religious and sexual meanings? If you think that, look at Bernini's "Ecstasy of St. Teresa." The desire for loss of self pulls us to make love, to make art or God.

PAINTING IDEA: My uncle as an angel standing over me— old-man angel in baggy clothes. I am at his feet, aswoon in mystic ecstasy. Takeoff of Bernini's "Ecstasy of St. Teresa." Uncle is smiling. Show disturbing sweetness as in Bernini's angel. Sadistic intensity of smile. B.'s angel is about to stab the mad saint with ecstasy. My uncle has no arrow. Instead, he passes me a rolled-up newspaper.

Sunday — Watered the plants, fed the cats. The Uncle books watch me. I go through their pages, trying to imagine him.

58

Moisha Segul — what was he thinking when he clipped an article about Jesus on a tortilla? A Mexican woman fried a tortilla some years ago. When she looked at it, she saw the figure of Christ, crown of thorns on his head, on the bread. What could this possibly have meant to the old Russian Jew?

Why did he clip a series of articles about a 19th-century corpse found in a small-town general store? I read these pieces interestedly, wondering (as Uncle no doubt did) how the body got there. It was fascinating to learn that after criminals in the Old West were hanged, their corpses were given to circuses. And I was thrilled when the last article told of a discovery in the town records: the store had been a saloon. A traveling circus must have passed through, leaving stuff in storage there. Why it never returned to retrieve its hanged criminal remains a mystery, as does the criminal's identity and the crime for which his decomposition was made a small-town amusement. So does the significance of this to Uncle. Because part of my fascination is in picturing him, a tiny man wielding a large scissors, saving this tale from a mass of smudged print.

His Dear Abbys are evocative. Abby recommends writing letters to the dead as a means of coming to terms with grief.

Attention Dr. Jim Curly c/o SLUT, regarding: Five Ways Medicine Can Kill You

I have experiences to know that your expose is correct. I seek a photo of such outrage. In that photo the victim must be tied and show both breasts removed, the teats not in the right places. One living subject I saw (who is dead now, thank God) also had the uterus stolen. She claimed her ovaries were still there, then contradicted the claim by saying she took Ovarian Extract. She was aware she'd been robbed. I invite any person to send me such pictures. I want this photo to show to my granddaughter who doesn't believe me and needs to be warned.

Mon. — Surprise from Harry! Five kittens tangled in my favorite sweater! Adorable balls of black fur. Harry watched suspiciously as I moved them from the drawer. I don't know how I will bring myself to get rid of them. Maybe Miss Tweety would like one? They're so cute. Must get book from library about kitten care. Don't know who father is. Fellatio has never been in heat but I'm sure she's female. Van Gogh's castrated. Harry's always crying, rubbing, wiggling about the apartment like a woman in a tight dress. Should have had her spayed. Named her Harry but that didn't work. Concerned about Fellatio. She seems depressed.

Dec. 8 — Everyone at work is thrilled. The palm reader they go to says the union's going to pass. Black Angel also told Happy six months ago she's destined to marry a foreigner. She protested, "I don't know any foreigners. Who can he mean?" Judy giggled, in case we missed the point that the foreigner was Ju-an.

Ju-an and Happy are involved in a battle with all the earmarks of adolescent flirtation. Ju-an, who's from England, looks like Clark Kent. He and Happy shout at each other in the halls, for the amusement of their respective cohorts. I hear them when they come back from the coffee wagon, cursing and teasing.

Ju-an is generally very quiet, but Happy brings out the beast in him. He shouts, "Oh, Happy, dearest, please be mine. I'm madly in love with you, all 300 pounds of woman."

"Bullshit, Tink," Happy's voice will sound. "I wouldn't go out with you if everyone in New York had AIDS."

"They do," Ju-an cries. "That's why you must be mine."

"Tough shit." Then Happy and Judy run into their office, slam the door, and giggle.

Liz revealed today that she'd been to see the palmist. Seemed out of character for Liz. Half Jewish, half black. Sensitive, intelligent, rude, crude. I can't figure her out. "Black Angel says Tom was my son in a past life."

"What else did he say?" Happy asked. "Come on, give."

Liz cleared her throat. "He said we'd either have two kids in the next five years or we'd break up. But Tom might leave me anyway, even if we had kids, so I shouldn't do it unless we get married. It depends on his palm. Black Angel wants to meet him. Can you imagine! Tom would throw me out just hearing *I* went."

Then they all discussed the pros and cons of telling Tom. I think this Black Angel has a lot of nerve. He's planted prophecy in Liz's mind. If it takes root, they'll cry "prophet" while he reaps its homonym. I didn't say anything. Suzy was already relating her experience. "It was weird. Did he . . . breathe with you?"

It turns out he does this strange breathing routine to "get in touch with your aura." He did it for an especially long time with Suzy — about half an hour. He put his arms around her back. They inhaled and exhaled together. She tried not to feel his pelvis on her buttocks but "after a while it was all that was on my mind. He was humping me, you know? When he stopped and faced me, he had tears in his eyes. 'You are a very good soul,' he said. 'You are an extraordinarily good soul. A natural healer.' In fact, he had such good feelings from me that he offered to do my fortune for nothing on a weekly basis, to help me find my destiny. I told him I couldn't go so often and he said, 'Think of it as going into psychoanalysis.' I don't know. The weird thing is that I think he does have powers. I mean, he knew stuff about me. He knew about my father, for instance. He said, 'Someone you love is dying. You are a natural healer. I can help you find your center and save him.' "

This palm reader's fucked up, using that to hook Suzy. Anyone can tell she's suffering. Poor Suzy. He's holding her hostage. If she doesn't go and her father dies, she'll feel guilty, as if she could have saved him. And if she does go, she'll have this guy humping her — who knows what else he might decide she has to do to bring out her "natural gift"? I don't not believe in fortunetelling. That's why I'd never go. Wouldn't want to give someone such power over me.

What if he told me I am a great artist?
What if he told me I'm not?

Wed. — Cut work early to bring slides to Mauret. Told me to come back after New Year's. Why doesn't he tell me the truth, if I'm no good? How is one supposed to tell dreck from genius? Art is the side effect of possession, what's left after a god has his fun, but so is madness. I must believe in myself. Van Gogh took his stuff around. It didn't help, but he didn't give up. He was lonely, he

This is ludicrous. Van Gogh was rejected, I am rejected, therefore I am Van Gogh. What's wrong with this picture?

LIBRARY: Get Van Gogh's diary or letters.

A tiny voice inside me keeps saying, "I've an idea. Why don't you kill yourself?" Like it's a joke. The tiny voice says, "If you were serious about your art, neglect wouldn't matter." It says, "If you were really depressed, you'd jump out the window." It says, "Wheee!" and tells me to imagine flying. "Think what it will do to the Gabby Segul stock." Suicide as insurance policy.

I wish no one else's opinion mattered. I wish the world would come crawling to me but I couldn't be bothered opening the door, I was too busy working on a masterpiece.

What I must do is not think about success. I read too many art mags, trying to figure out the scene. Parties, openings. This one said this about that. The art world seems like a real place, as if I could travel there if I had magic shoes. Still, who does it hurt if I pretend that in the art world I am funny, that I make friends in Oz? Someone knows the wizard. I am introduced. He likes me.

I was at an opening once. A show by a girl I knew slightly in college. I don't know why she invited me. Perhaps she'd heard I was in publishing (ha-ha). It was a long time ago. I thought I could study success. I went to observe people drink wine. Everyone seemed to know each other. I eavesdropped on conversations about mutual acquaintances with names like Franz, Gaiea, someone named Persephone Lipshitz. I wanted to leave but forced myself to stay, gritting my teeth in a corner. A man eyed me, conspicuously alone. I didn't know how to escape— tried to smile, perfectly at ease in my solitude. He saw through me and came over. An older European man, he asked my name. I told him. Then he said something I will never forget. He asked,

"Should I know you?" And I said, "No. I'm nobody." He left. I went home.

I fantasize that in a museum someone recognizes me as a true artist. He starts a conversation and invites me to a party where I meet other artists. Before you know it I am the toast of the town.

When I imagine this, I get caught up. In such a dream, when I jump I fly. I imagine James. He holds my hand; his eyes drink mine. He says, "Why did you hesitate to step from your shell?"

Then before you know it I am crying. The crowd of dancing artists and poets and musicians sweeps me up. They swirl me around like white wine, and I am carried away from him, from James in a corner, his Russian accent, his wife and child. The world is at my feet, proclaiming me the artist they have been waiting for.

When I snap out of that fantasy, I find my face is wet and I've finished my drink. I splash water on my eyes. I'm allergic to tears. Coldness comes over me like after sex, particularly when you are alone and empty and it feels like defeat. Lovers rest in one another like spoons, but when you are alone and have pulsed around a void, despite the momentary pleasure, it is like having hiccups.

> To everybody I love at *Soap Bubble*. Yip! That's yous guys. I am a poet. Here is a poem I wrote about my favorite serial. I call it "Betty and Bill."
>> Betty and Bill weren't getting along,
>> So Betty went out and done Bill wrong.
>> Some time later champagne left its bottle,
>> when Kevin the Lawyer married Rita the Model.

Thurs. — Max called me into his office. Asked how long I'd been at PP. He knows it's 17 years, since we started at the same time. "That's quite a while." He laughed, so I laughed. Then: "I think you're due for a promotion, don't you?" What could I say? I smiled. "It's the union," he went on. "It'll put everyone in boxes. Management won't have the right to decide who to pro-

mote. If the union comes in, this company will fold. But if someone on the inside were to help us . . . if someone showed loy-
alty, she'd save everyone's job. I think we'd owe her something,
don't you?" I nodded, smiled inanely, hoping he'd think I didn't
really understand. What else could I do? Finally he let me go.
Ugh. As if I'd spy on the union, even if I wanted to edit *Slut* or
Stars. Should I tell Liz?

Friday, 12:12 P.M. (transcribed from sm. notebook) — Took a
half day from work. Dentist. Appointment at 1:00. As usual I
am too early. I'm sitting in the park. Warm, drippy day — unusual for December. Patriarch in shmatas walking by. Carries
staff and suitcase, like he's journeyed from a different century.
Woman sitting across from me, bundled peasant, looks like a
Van Gogh potato eater. Art stalks New York.

12:29 P.M. — Just finished conversation with well-dressed older
woman. We talked about construction in the park. "Building
building building," she said. "Everywhere is building." Then
we talked about meat and health. I said I wanted to become a
vegetarian but couldn't because I hate vegetables. She said, "Rome
wasn't built in a day." I started to tell her how my father was a
butcher, so giving up meat seemed a rejection of him. All of a
sudden her eyes bulged behind her dark glasses. With a start, I
thought, "She's crazy." But it was only that she had widened
her stare, expressive of something she was saying.

The fear of insanity: potential lunatics hiding axes beneath their
minks; girls who don't obey parents end up as hamburgers. On
the other side of kid worry is magic. The power of imagination
is packaged for children like candy. Believe, believe. Wishes come
true. Dreams are real. Clap your hands, boys and girls, Tinker-
bell will live, your parents won't die in a ridiculous boating accident, your own true love will appear, you'll see fairies, hear
gongs, your toes will curl. And if none of that happens, that's
your fault too. You must not have prayed hard enough.

They teach you to believe when you are a child. But if you
persist in believing when you are an adult, they call you crazy.

2:40 P.M. — Dentist appt. over. Thank God. White coats, chair with attachments, needle in mouth. Cheek still numb. Novocain wearing off.

When I'd get a toothache as a kid, my folks would put whiskey on cotton, hold it to my gum, teaching me how alcohol deadens pain. I was terrified of the dentist. Wouldn't let him drill. He used a hand pick while I bit, kicked, cried. When my mother was being worked on, I told dirty jokes.

I told him about the woman who calls the doctor and asks if she left her panties in his office. He says no and she says, "Oh, I must have left them at the dentist's."

My mother was making funny noises but couldn't really do anything with her mouth full of dental tools. I didn't understand the joke. I told it because it was about a dentist. Dr. Henie asked, "Who tells you such jokes?" and I said, "My mother."

One morning she woke me up. "Hurry, Gabbalah, get dressed quick-quick. We don't have time for breakfast. We'll be late for the movies." I dressed quickly, pleased and surprised.

She took me downtown to a big building. We entered an office. I was still looking for the movie theater when several nurses grabbed me, tearing me away from my mother, who was pulled into another room. "Ma!" I screamed. She was gone. I didn't know what was happening and I struggled like an animal. In fact, I have great sympathy for those animals on TV shows that get injected and tied down to be tested. The shows emphasize the danger the scientists are in, but I find myself rooting for the polar bears.

Because they held me down. I kicked, but they overpowered me. Came from behind the chair to force a gas mask over my face. I remember seeing stars, exclamation marks, circles. It looked just the way cartoonists draw pain. The next thing I knew they were all standing over me, saying, "There, that wasn't so bad." All I could see was a pack of false smiles like trick playing cards. White coats and blood everywhere. "Ma!" I screamed.

"Stop crying or we won't let you see her."

I was no more than seven but I screamed like a woman. Thick

red drool hung from my face. The nurses smiled their lipstick smiles, false, tight, as they removed their gloves and masks. I smelled anger. Adults forget what children see. The dentist was pulling off his face. I kicked my feet. They held me down. I was being murdered. I saw knives.

I heard my mother outside the room. "Let me go. She wants me. Let me go to her." They refused but she broke through. She ran to me, held me, sobbing, to her breast. "I'm sorry, mommalah."

I wept against her. "You told me we were going to the movies." Again I am reminded of those animal shows, when the mother elephant is separated from the baby elephant and they can't hold her back. Maybe it's a cartoon, because it suddenly occurs to me that the mother elephant has long eyelashes and lipstick, and the baby elephant is wearing a cap with a propeller. Anyway, the mother elephant breaks free and runs to the baby elephant, wraps her trunk around him, and he rubs his trunk against her neck.

Elephants are very sentimental, and they do have long memories. I saw a documentary about them once. When wild elephants find elephant bones, they treat them differently from other animal bones. They hold the tusks, sniffing them, as if trying to remember which elephant it was. Then they bury the bones, doing an elephant ritual of some sort, a funeral. I saw this on public TV.

My mother took me home and put me to bed, made me cereal, trying to woo my forgiveness. Whenever she came into the room, I looked away. She wept. "Do you forgive me?"

I hid my face in the pillow. "You lied to me."

Did I forgive her? Of course, otherwise how could she have betrayed me again and again?

Saturday, December 12th — Incredible great news. You won't believe this. I'm so happy I could scream.

I looked through this year's records and discovered that the Painting Place never returned my slides. So I forced myself to call. I figured they'd lost them. I was determined to show anger.

Instead they said they were keeping my stuff on file. The assistant curator said — according to the woman on the phone— that my stuff showed talent and originality. They're putting together a show of new artists and may want to include some of my stuff.

I was so surprised I didn't know what to say. Just said thank you, over and over. The girl said, "Send us more. I know Tom will be interested. He thinks you're really talented."

Can you imagine! I don't know what to do with myself; I'm overjoyed. I could just jump out the window. Forgive my exuberance. I wish there were someone to tell. I'm going down to see Miss Tweety. Maybe I'll tell her, but she doesn't know about my art.

Hey, just hold on there, Gabby girl. Get yourself under control. Keeping stuff on file is not the same as a show. And a show is not the same as selling a painting. And selling a painting to an individual is not the same as selling to a museum. And even selling to a museum is not the same as a permanent exhibition or artistic recognition. So don't get overexcited about this. It doesn't mean anything. People get their stuff kept on file all the time. And they're younger than you too.

Oh, screw you! I'm happy. Let me be happy.

Sun. — Gorgeous day for destiny-walking: letting streetlights lead, not stopping at reds but moving toward greens, following fate. If I walk along West End and the light changes at 72nd, I cross. If the light across 72nd hasn't turned green, I walk to Broadway. In this way I allow myself to be taken by chance. With whom am I directed to an accidental encounter if not James?

Imagining this, my heart gallumphs. I am unprepared. What if he doesn't know who I am? What if he stares blankly, betraying that I am nothing, was always nothing, to him?

It is then that I realize that the man ahead of me can't be James. He is the same age as James five years ago, and surely James looks different now. No matter how many times I tell myself this, I still race ahead. When I see a lean man wearing a low-hung belt and cowboy boots I think of James, as if he wouldn't have changed his style in five years because I haven't. I am faithful to his memory of me, still dressing like a frump. Old clothes comfort me with their associations; sweaters that belonged to my mother, flannel shirts that belonged to my father, second-hand skirts and pants that belonged to someone who died or cleaned a closet. Van Gogh was also a tacky dresser.

James, silly James. His Tex-Russian drawl. His Stetson. He wanted so much to be a real American, my Russian cowboy. He told me once, when he was wearing in new boots, that it was like bronco-busting, a question of who broke first. "My tvin hosses," he called them. "Vhoa there, little doggies."

I go to museums, thinking he will find me. I sketch, remembering the time he caught me drawing on my lunch hour. My pink shirt, the sun. A man's stare. The harmless delusion that beauty was mine. "Gabby?" he asked. I couldn't make him out, black against the sunlight. I shielded my face.

He sat beside me. I grew aware of his desire. It glinted in his eyes. I closed my art pad, folded my hands. He put on dark glasses to hide his attraction. Talking to him, I admired my reflection in the glass. When he asked to look through my pad, I let him, though I dreaded saying something stupid that would spoil his image of me in the light.

He said I was accomplished. I had style. "That girl, that Natasha, polecat. Stupid. You know." He made a discarding motion with his hand. My heart swelled with sudden love, as if he were a knight and I a maiden.

Natasha was a girl in our art class. He must have heard what she'd said to me, when she'd asked to see the work she'd missed the previous week. I gave her my pad. Seeing my sketches, she smirked. "If I didn't know better, I'd think these were the doodles of a tormented adolescent."

I was stunned but didn't want to let on I was hurt. When I'm stabbed, I pretend to feel nothing, or else I tell myself that the person who has insulted me has made a faux pas. I protect my assailant, saying, "She didn't mean it. The slight was unintentional." I learned to do this at my mother's side.

That afternoon, sitting with James on the bench, knowing he'd heard what she'd said and took my side, I grew generous. "She's just a tormented adolescent," I told him.

"Vy you protect?" he asked. "Downright no-good rotten skunk. Is willain, yes? Like vitch? You know vitch?"

Oh James. I enjoy writing his name. Ilyich Kolokol. Mrs. James Kolokol. Control yourself — this *is* getting adolescent.

Not too long after this conversation in the park I started going to Lucy's Bar with the art department crowd. The editorial staff acted like I was a double agent. I didn't care.

One time it was just me and James waiting for the others. That's when he showed me photos of his paintings. I was dumbfounded. Michelangelo was with me, drinking a Scotch. Color prints of angels, muscular clouds, gods. I'm not a fan of the Renaissance, but James could have made a nice living as a forger. I hated him for being so talented. I hated him for hiding it from me, from the world, for pretending to be nothing but a schlock-magazine layout man when all along he was a genius.

"How did you learn to do this?" I asked, wanting to hear about privileges of money, a Russian aristocratic tradition full of culture and cash.

"Taught myself. You know." The glint in his eye invited me in, said we were geniuses together. "Museums. I copy stuff. Masters. You know what you do. Books, Leonardo's notebooks. The usual, you know. Like what you call . . . alchemy? Mixing. Like anybody else." His humility infuriated me. I looked for the lie.

"You didn't go to art school? You don't have an M.F.A.?"

He shook his head, then added, "Oh, Kensington, of course. But that is social thing. What you think?"

After this I became obsessed, sick with the disease of him. I wanted him, I wanted to be him, to have that talent. I could have eaten him alive if that would have given me what he had. I say I was in love, but there was a strong dose of poison in the brew. I knew he was married. I'd never have an affair with a married man. What did I want? Friendship, respect? A magic mirror to make my peculiarities lovable, to supply me with a sense of self?

Mirror, mirror, in my lap, in my heart, in my memory, oh mirror, show me an image that is beautiful and talented and exciting. Show me that I was loved once, but the gods interceded to save a marriage. ("Say, Juno, do you see what I see? James and Gabby are falling in love." "Jumping Jupiter, you're right, Venus. Quick, call your son. We haven't a moment to lose." "Oh Cupid!")

What is the secret of eternal desire, an illness that neither heals nor kills? Simple. Whenever I realize I've stopped thinking about him, I tickle my fancy. In this way I've kept the infection itchy and hot.

Mon. — Union passed by 3–2 majority. I'm glad, though I haven't participated beyond voting. Celebration after work. Didn't go. What if Max called me in tomorrow, asked me to report on who said what while drunk? Now that the union is in, contract negotiations are next.

Brought Miss Tweety ice cream. Her enjoyment is so cute. I don't think Green can evict her. Saw the Philosopher during lunch — bald white-haired man who carries shopping bags, horn, bells. Looks like Santa Claus in civvies. If you give him money, he blesses you with his horn and bells. If you don't, he curses you. He doesn't remember me, although we've talked on a number of occasions. I don't like to be blessed by him. He wishes me fertility. Doesn't realize a single woman may not consider that a blessing. Madmen and saints lack a sense of the contemporary.

The Philosopher lives in a senior-citizen hotel in Harlem. He pretends to be a homeless lunatic, but he's faking — as much as anyone can be said to be faking who goes around blessing people with bells and horns. All I mean is that he's not a lunatic and he's not homeless. It's an act. It's his living.

Tues. — Should I go to Uncle's apartment in East New York, see if I can find the paintings my parents threw out when they moved him to Brighton? Maybe in the basement. I was in his apartment once. I was very young. There were drawings all over. I recall them dimly, like atavistic recollections of prehistoric cave paintings. Pencil studies of animals, people. I was such a little girl it feels like a dream.

For many years I forgot about his stuff. I was already an artist when I recalled the drawings. So it's not that I identified with him and followed his path, but more like walking the same path I bumped into him. In each generation there is one outsider/artist/lunatic/genius/nobody. "Nebechel," my parents called him. "He sits there like a nebechel." Am I the Uncle Moisha of my generation?

"Look what happens to a man," they'd tsk. "How he used to write, draw, play the mandolin. Now look at him." They always referred to him in the third person, as if he were an idiot.

They talked about me in the third person too. Coming out of the dark ages of Europe when they were both 13, they didn't believe in childhood. A child doesn't remember. You can do anything to a child. When my mother talked directly to me, it was of her death. She liked to make me cry; it made her feel loved.

I was already a loner, like my uncle but I didn't know that then. One day I saw him — not crazy Uncle Moisha sitting by himself in a corner singing a soldier's song in Russian, but a person separate from the family. I saw a man alone in the world, different, an outcast.

He was lost in dreams, he thought about stars. He got so caught up in the meaning of things he forgot to eat. I began to listen to him. He hardly saw me, the girl smiling as he spoke. He smiled back, and talked and talked, but he could have been speaking to a ghost. I wanted to be invited into his dreams and thought to show my interest like a key. He never recognized me.

I bumped into him twice — the first time on the IRT, the second time on the boardwalk. On the train I came up to him with a big smile. He backed away. "Who are you? What do you want from me?" he cried, running off before I could explain.

A few years later I saw him standing outside a circle of dancers at Brighton Beach. He was tapping a coin against the rail. I knew this was "to make them dance livelier," for he had told me many times how, tapping his coin, he made people dance.

Seeing him there, I went up to him. He smiled and laughed, but I sensed he didn't know who I was. I explained. I told him my name, my parents' names, and after a while I saw the light go on in his eyes. "So," he said. "How's Momma? How's Poppa?"

Uncle was always a mystery and a disappointment, and that is what I am afraid of. What if his diary is all gibberish? We are the artists of the Segul tribe, Uncle and I, shamans to whom the family says shah. I don't want to end up like him: walking the streets, talking to invisible beings. I see myself growing warped from aloneness like a twisted tree in a barren field.

> *Stars*, please forward. Thanks. I always buy your mag.
> Dear Cher,
> I love you as one tragedian might love another — 20 years of my own life has directed me to the mathematics of philosophy like a buttercup masterbating a pond frog. I've seen you everywhere. I want you to be my bellybutton dancer. I mean it. I want you, the belly dancer, to consider living with me, the philosopher. I see what you suffer with a sense of trembling humor. I am developing a new language. I need backing. Oh, sure, I can't throw a ball, but I can find determinants to complex matrices. I'm serious, honey. I'm developing a new language based on math, and I want you to be part of it. I'll name it after you even if you don't want to communicate with me. I want you to know that what I'm working on is the fact that anything can represent anything else. But how do objects become symbols for each other?
>
> Love,
> Barry

Wed. — In the train station today there was an end-of-world loony with a bullhorn. "Jesus is fed up. Jesus is sick of the whole thing. He is at the end of his rope. New York is going to be destroyed. That's why you have to mind Jesus now. He's really sick and tired. Disgusted. Jesus has had it up to here."

Went to the library after work. Took out Van Gogh's letters. When I first got to the library, I went to the bathroom. There was a red puddle on the floor. I stepped over it to enter a stall. When I came out, a woman stood at the sink, writing a note on a paper towel. I didn't immediately notice anything wrong. Then I looked down and saw she had no socks. I realized she was homeless. I rinsed my hands, thinking she might be writing a suicide note. I wanted to intervene, but how? "Excuse me. I notice you have no socks and are writing a note on a paper towel. You're not planning to kill yourself by any chance, are you?" So I didn't do anything. Later, when I returned, I saw someone had ripped the tampon dispenser off the wall and thrown it into a toilet.

Thurs. — Fellatio died either today or yesterday. Couldn't find her last night. She'd been sulking because of the kittens. I knew she was depressed. When she didn't come to dinner, I should have known. I opened the hall closet tonight and realized she wasn't sleeping. Wrapped her in a towel. Put her in a shoebox. Buried her in a vacant lot on Amsterdam Ave. Someday there will be a building on the site, people living in it. Only I will know they are eating, sleeping, shitting over Fellatio's bones.

Friday — A shopping-bag lady in Liz's neighborhood has a shopping-bag dog dressed in rags. The women at work find this hysterical. They make a point of collecting "loony" tales to compare after lunch. Happy mimics the boy with cerebral palsy who solicits donations on the corner. Suzy jokingly asks in Irish brogue, "Have you a quarter for a cup of coffee?" imitating an often-seen beggar with shaved head.

"Touched," we still say, *by God* is implied. I see evil-eye practitioners every day on Broadway. Paranoid may be the medical term, but might not lunatics be the shamans of our society?

My mother always gave money to beggars. She'd hand me a coin, saying, "Go, mommalah, give it to that man, a pity on him." The one-legged man was selling pencils. The no-legged man shook his can. "There's always someone worse off than you." Her stage whisper shamed the beggars (or was it only me she embarrassed?). "You must thank God for every little thing." When I was older and complained I was too tall, she'd say, "What do you want, to look like your friend Sara with her fat little feet? Be grateful you have legs."

I feel guilty. I keep forgetting to take nothing for granted. I must learn to appreciate my life. I feel sorry for myself, angry at fate. I can't will gratitude. Depression is despicable when life is mundane miracle. I know this. But still . . .

I complain of loneliness, that I am a prisoner in my home. "Be grateful you have a home," my mother's voice says. When I was in college, "Crazy Cat" used to stand on Madison Avenue reciting poetry. He looked like a Viking — horned helmet, bare chest, thonged sandals, leather kilt. A few years ago Suzy found an article about him in the paper. It turned out he was a famous Danish poet. The poems he recited were translations of his work. Since the people of New York didn't recognize his genius, he returned to Denmark, a sadder but wiser wise man.

I felt it was wrong to lock up my uncle. So what if he poked through garbage, walked the streets? Other people didn't see it like that. The woman from the bank called me. "You know, your uncle really can't look after himself. Why don't you do something?" My parents were alive then, but in Florida. I went to find him. He didn't have a telephone, was never in his room. I finally located him on the boardwalk. He was so happy to see me. He was in a panic because he'd thrown out his money and his bankbook. He didn't have a nickel to get food to eat. He said he threw all his money out with the newspapers. Maybe he had a seizure. He used to empty his pockets during fits.

I once saw an old immigrant who was as sane as me. Bundles tied at her feet, she observed me from her sunny bench as I walked by. A glimmer of recognition passed between us. We both knew we were the same . . . except I was lucky.

A woman asked me once if there was someplace I could let her sleep. I said no, then she asked if I'd just let her into my lobby, so she could get warm. She was dressed in rags. She was sitting in the dirt by the tree outside my building, ripping through garbage. I couldn't do it. I couldn't let her in. I felt terrible, but I didn't trust her. What if she started a fire? What if she told other homeless people about the soft touch on the West Side?

What if I were on the street, begging for a place to get warm?

Suzy, Max, or Happy will come up with a letter for my file. They call them "Loony Tunes" and think of them as ours, but they're not; they're mine. I am a file keeper by nature, with folders of report cards, letters, juvenilia. I still have notes from my mother saying she's gone to the grocery store and will be back soon. Even have the first chapter of a spy novel I wrote when I was 11. Someone once sent a story to *Sin* about how the narrator could fly, be invisible, speak to the dead. The writer must have been crazy. Julie knew I'd be interested, so she gave it to me. I Xeroxed it, put a copy in my file, sent the original back. I'm a saver. I don't know what I'd do if I ever had to move.

I have files of notes found on the street, cards left in library books. There are letters from my mother that I can't bear to read, her voice is so loud in her phonetically spelled, Yiddishly inflected sentences. They stab me with a blade of longing as sharp as a knife. I made tapes of her, my father, and Uncle talking. Their voices are alive, singing, kibitzing. Yet there's something ghoulish about making the dead talk about the chicken.

Suzy and Liz laugh at those who have crossed the line. I don't imagine a border so much as a border town. I am glad not to live in a magic world . . . because I believe in its possibility. Not that ghosts exist, only that they might. Perhaps it's insecurity, a streak of mysticism or madness, but I don't understand how people can be so confident as to say, "This is what there is. There is nothing else."

Am I playing, like a child who explores a haunted house? One must be careful when romanticizing madness, for the tramp in the basement may not be a saint. First you cultivate eccentricity. Then eccentricity cultivates you.

Sat. — Van Gogh writes: "There may be a great fire in our soul, and no one ever comes to warm himself at it. . . . Must one tend that inward fire . . . for the hour when somebody will come and sit down near it — to stay there maybe?"

I am setting myself up for a disappointment. I think entirely too much of Uncle, his diary. Can't help it. What did he mean when he said Sophie Herring acts crazy to fool people? His eyes twinkled. With insight, or insanity's glow?

Sunday — There was once an old woman who lived across the street when I was growing up. Rosemary. I don't know why, but I thought of her today. She would sit by her gate and call, "Girlie, come. I vant talk with you." She bribed me with sticky sourballs, dirty butterscotch, to stand with her for hours. Her accent, her lack of teeth, her wild switches of time and character — I hardly understood a word she said.

The boys called her Ragpicker. She walked along the streets, poking through cans. Mostly she cried to any passing child: "Come. I give candy. I tell secret." I listened till my mother freed me: "Gabbalah, it's time to come in now."

As best as I could understand, her husband had been a revolutionary, forced to leave czarist Russia. They came here, he built the house, then went to fight in the Russian Revolution and died, leaving her pregnant. Her son married a wicked woman who was trying to force her from her land. Her son died too.

One time she was in my house when I came home from school. I don't know why. She was sitting at the kitchen table. My mother kept smelling her dishrag, saying, "What stinks? Is it this shmata that stinks?" I was so embarrassed. We both knew it was Rosemary.

Her thoughts were wild. Her garden was wild. Bushes heavy with blooms lay on the ground as if drunk among the weeds, flowers, garbage. In the summer she gave me roses. Her roses had ants. Her candy had lint. Her dog rolled in the dust at her feet.

Most of what she said I didn't understand, but when Rosemary cried, I cried. Tears ran down my cheeks as she told story after story. "Vy he leave? Vy not take me?" I stood at her gate, standing on one foot, then the other, a girl flamingo.

Who was she? How did she get there, to her shack in East Flatbush from czarist Russia? A survival from a different time. Before the blocks of identical boxes went up, her husband had built their hut. "His two hands," she told me. "Vat happen him?"

The hovel was set back, so hidden by weeds that you wouldn't know it was there except for the gate. A path snaked to her door. Rosemary hobbled on it in front of me, the one time she took me in. It was dark inside; dirt floors uneven, windows without panes. She opened a drawer. There was something she wanted to show me. On the table crawled bugs. "Eyes," she said. "Hurt. Read me." Perhaps she'd gotten a letter. Whatever it was she wanted me to read, she couldn't find it. Instead she gave me a sourball and I ran away.

There was only one other time that someone besides Rosemary walked that path. It was because of a smell. No one had seen her for a long time. A neighbor called the police. Two cops took Rosemary away in a bag.

There had been a lot of rain that summer. It must have been during a storm that she'd gone onto her roof to put cardboard over a hole, slipped, and broken a leg. There was thunder and lightning. She was old, scared; lying on the roof she had a heart attack. How long she was alive up there, unable to call for help, no one knew. By the time the police came, there had been rats.

Did the wicked daughter-in-law inherit the property? Was there a daughter-in-law? I don't know. Rosemary's bones have been turned three times in some potter's field. They plow them under every ten years, to make room for the next batch of abortions, limbs, poor. The shack stood for years. Then, when I was in college, someone tore it down, built a brick box like the rest on the block. A family moved in. Now no one in East Flatbush remembers her. Except me.

Does it mean something, that I've told of a terrible life, a terrible death? I can't change that. But to be remembered, even as a mad Russian, must be better than to pass as a smell. So I will remember her: her black-and-white hair, her wild dark eyes. She hobbled so bent over that she looked like a question mark. I patted her little white mutt once and my hand came away with ants. He used to roll in the dirt and she would laugh. I never stroked her hand. She never knew my name. I was one of a tribe of girlies.

In a different age she'd have been burned as a witch, but at least she'd have been seen. Rosemary stood day after day at her gate, in rain and snow, covered in rags, a shawl around her small shoulders in summer and winter. She stood calling. Sometimes I pretended not to hear. Sometimes I couldn't bear to turn from my childhood games and pick up her sorrows. Sometimes I was laughing with my friends, roller-skating around the block, playing Chinese handball on the wall outside the candy store. I just couldn't bear to cry at her gate till my mother saved me, giving me an excuse to run away. "I have to go now, Rosemary. My mother is calling me."

What would she think, to see me crying now, and she dead 30 years? There's poetry in oblivion, isn't there? Think how many have lived since the world began, every life important to its hero, its heroine, though each died without leaving a name and exists not even in a journal for a moist hour. Rosemary was calling at the gate all these years. It must mean something, that I hear her now.

Can memory bring the dead to life?

> Dear Editor,
> Please write and tell me where is Maybury as shown on "The Andy Griffith Show"? Where is the town located called Maybury? The answer is very important. Because I am moving to this town called Maybury when I find where it is. Thank you very much.
> Love always,
> Aunt B
> Detroit, Michigan

Dec. 21 — Anxious to have back Uncle's book. Mr. K. should call soon. The diaries are like a row of toy soldiers guarding his thoughts. Each book has its own personality. One was written in a tiny, predominantly blue hand. It has a hard cover. The first page has the date and Uncle's name in English. The next book is tall and thin. Another is red. The two after that are school notebooks, covers marbled in black and white, thin blue lines dissecting the pages. Several of the seven unlined journals have sketches as well. They show skill. In spidery style, Uncle depicts cot, dresser, window, view beyond window. Sketches of things in his room? Some obscene pictures too. I blush for my uncle. He doodles. Eyes stare out every few words like scared children hiding in a forest. Sometimes I gaze at his writing. Feel on the brink of understanding but never fall through.

Uncle books. U.N.C.L.E. book. Funny. When I was 11 I was madly in love with Illya Kuryakin. I used to carry an U.N.C.L.E. i.d. card in my wallet, a cap gun in my purse. Kept a notebook in which I jotted down the comings and goings of handsome men I followed on Flatbush Avenue. Wrote in code in this U.N.C.L.E. book, making up messages that meant nothing.

Carol and I would pick out guys to follow. We wore "genuine imitation" leopard-skin coats, black eyeliner, white lipstick— 11 going on 40. Stood on the corner of Flatbush and King's Highway, smoking stolen cigarettes, pretending to be spies.

One day we passed a gang strolling on the avenue. One of them, a blond in a leather jacket, whispered as I walked by. He must have called me a Lolita, but at the time I thought he said "Lola" or "Lulu." Surely this was a signal between secret agents, so we began to follow him everywhere, him and his greasy-haired friend.

We named them Blondie and Shorty, stood outside bars they entered, followed them again when they left. We took notes on whatever they did, whomever they talked to, what time it was when they left the bar and walked down a side street, us in tow. When they heard us giggling behind them, they'd turn and we'd cling to the shadow of a wall. My eyeliner, my fake leopard coat, my cap gun and notebook. I wore my mother's high heels and had trouble walking. Click-click went my shoes on King's Highway.

There were movies at the time. Young girls following older men, taking notes on their amorous escapades. These girls acted out fandom's fantasies. It was all in good fun. That's what we were doing. But the danger was real, though I protected myself with a cap gun like any girl-woman turned on by a man's black leather and insolence.

I wish I could shake some sense into my child self playing that dangerous game. Because one day Carol couldn't join me. I followed Blondie alone. He walked into an alley. "Pssst," he called as I snuck by. I turned, my heart thumping. "Come," he said. And I went, my fear still playful, like a child tagged by It.

I hid my notebook in my jacket, determined to keep that from him like a good spy. Karate, cap gun — I was not unprotected. In the end Illya would save me or Blondie would turn out to be a double agent, on the side of good all along. But in the end Illya never came, the blond was a mercenary, and I lost my notebook. "What do you want?" he asked, understanding my answer differently from the way I meant it when I winked my private eye.

In a dream from that time he was chasing me. I'd been writing about him in my U.N.C.L.E. book, and I ran to hide in my parents' bedroom. I entered a closet and took off my clothes. Like Bugs Bunny pursued by Elmer Fudd, I was going to pretend to be dressing when he opened the door. The embarrassed hunter would blush away. Only instead of Fudd or the blond, the door was opened by a priest. He averted his face. "Will you kindly get dressed?" he said. "You are in a church."

THE FLATBUSH AVENUE AFFAIR
Chapter One: A Stolen Notebook

A scream was heard in the halls of the Hotel Picaro on Flatbush Avenue where Illya Kuryakin and Napoleon Solo were staying. As they ran out, trying to locate the girl who was screaming, you'd hardly suspect them of being agents for U.N.C.L.E., an agency of great importance for the free world. On their usually intelligent faces were expressions of terror, for if the girl screaming was Lulu Lane, they both knew something had gone terribly wrong. When they arrived on the scene, they were in for a shock. There, whimpering in a corner, was Lulu, an expression of terror and horror on her usually beautiful face.

Realizing she was not alone, she turned frightenedly, half ex-
pecting to meet horror again. When she saw who it was, Lulu ran
into Illya's arms. "It was so horrible," she said.

He could feel her body shaking. Napoleon Solo was amused,
watching his partner handling a situation that he, Napoleon, was
more comfortable in handling. Illya looked like he didn't know
what to do with the girl in his arms and was looking at Solo for
help, but when Napoleon looked more carefully he saw Illya didn't
really want help.

The halls had filled with hotel guests gossiping. Napoleon closed
the door in their faces. "Lulu, are you okay? Did anyone hurt
you?" Illya asked the girl.

"I'm okay," she murmured, "now that you're here." She gave
Illya a meaningful look, then cried, "The notebook! They must
have—"

"What notebook, Lulu? You don't mean—"

"Yes, the U.N.C.L.E. notebook with all our secrets in it. They
must have found it when they—" She burst into tears again but
quickly gained control of herself. You could tell she was a top
secret agent.

"What should we do?" Illya asked.

"I saw their car when they made their getaway. It was black.
Let's follow them. Quick, we'll take my car. Just hand me my
leopard coat over there on the chair. And my purse." She winked
at Illya. "It's got my gun."

Quickly the three spies ran out of the hotel room past the still-
gossiping hotel guests in the hall. "Which car is yours, Lulu?"
Napoleon asked.

"That one, the convertible with black and yellow tiger stripes.
Let's go. I love a good adventure, don't you?"

The two men looked at each other and laughed, Illya taking
the front seat next to Lulu. He wasn't going to lose out to Napoleon this time, not with a girl who was such a top secret agent
and loved adventure and drove such a neat car.

They were off, the wind whipping through Lulu and Napoleon
and Illya's black and brown and blond hairs. They had to get back
the notebook to save the free world, but like any spies they loved
excitement and knew they would win against evil in the end.
Little did they know the dastardly trick that evil was planning at
their destination, in an alley off King's Highway, for then they
might not have been so eager to arrive.

*

"For anyone who is sick of life, the thrilling life of a spy should be the finest recuperation." — Robert Baden-Powell, founder of the Boy Scouts.

December 22, Tues. night (transcribed from small notebook) — *12:01 P.M.* — Crystal blows in like a breeze, kid in tow. (*7:07 P.M.* — C. is free-lancer who comes once a week to drop off soap plot summaries. "Hi, hi." If window were open, she'd end up down the hall.)

12:05 P.M. — C. gives us Xmas presents: little erasers made to look like Chinese dolls. (*7:10 P.M.* — C. lives a marginal existence. She's sweet but out of touch. Not drugs, just naturally unnatural; e.g., last summer she came in wearing her winter coat and scarf each week until Suzy finally said, "Crystal, it's 90 degrees out." The following week she came without scarf.)

12:09 P.M. — C. introduces daughter: Pearl, 11-year-old curmudgeon. Massive child. C. drifts at her side. Together they bring to mind a Chagall — woman floating horizontal to cow. Pearl plops in chair, covers face with mag. Crystal strokes P.'s head. P. brushes her away like horse swatting fly.

12:18 P.M. — C. and P. leave. Suzy and Liz tell Happy how Crystal invited them over for wine last Christmas.

L.: "Did you know she ran away to join the circus?"

H. laughs. "Oh no. Did she really?"

L.: "Yes, she did. Classic. Small town in Ohio. Circus passing through. She was 15. Became their tightrope walker. That's where she met Pearl's father. He was the strongman. She showed us a picture. He wore leopard underpants and had muscles out the yah-yah."

"Oh stop. I'm peeing in my pants. You're making this up."

S.: "No, she's not. He had a very interesting muscle, hm, if you know what I mean. Boing! He could lift weights with it."

L.: "Pearl definitely takes after her father. She could turn out to be a bearded lady."

S.: "In that neighborhood she needs to be. I mean, that was a tenement. How can she live there? She has no choice, but really."

"Happy, she told us Samson never actually married her."

"Oh, Liz, now I know you're making it all up. Samson."

"Suzy, did she say his name was Samson or what?"

"Happy, really, his name was Samson. Samson the Strongman. That's what it said at the bottom of the picture."

L.: "Samson turned out to be a brute. No kidding, right? I mean this man was a classic brute from Central Casting. His leopard-skin drawers were a dead giveaway. And the gold bands around his arms and neck. He used to beat Crystal, and let's face it, that girl can't take too much beating. I mean, if he snapped his fingers, he'd probably break her neck. So she ran away from the circus, to become a ballerina in the Big Apple."

"Oh, this is too much."

"I'm not making it up. This is her life. Ask her."

Dear Manager,

I'm on my way to Haiti. I will keep in touch. I am sending you my fingerprints in case someone tries to play me. Remember to register any important letters you send.

Love and kisses,
God

Wed. — I'm depressed. I called ABC Gallery to find out about my slides. Some little twit said that they didn't have any interest in them. Then, in her nasal voice, she added, "Perhaps you are not far enough along in your painting to think of showing professionally."

I was flabbergasted but managed to squeak, "I'm sure that's not the case." The problem is, I'm not sure. In fact I agree.

Art is a wall between me and the world. If it is a wall of dreams, I should wave it away like colored smoke. To be an artist who is never any good is to be crazy. Should I allow myself to be imprisoned behind this wall? If poets see visions in it, yes. But if it is never to mean anything to anyone except me, and my whole life is sacrificed in the building of such a wall . . .

Behind the wall, everything is flattened into planes. Art makes me an observer of, not a participant in, life. I don't need friends or lovers, status, money, career. What kind of work is it when, on a typical day, I may proofread galleys about incest, followed by a fan-club newsletter, then be handed a photo of a Swede in braids tonguing an Oriental and told to come up with 17 lines, 40 picas wide, to fit the title "United Nations Relations"?

I can't get involved. That's why I'm still an associate editor. If it weren't for my art, I'd have left PP by now. As it is, I am shipwrecked and sleepy in the land of opium-eaters.

Thurs. — Carol called to invite me to Lara's birthday party on Jan. 10th. She didn't ask what I was doing New Year's Eve. We had nothing to say to each other. We've been friends since we were 11, so when Carol married, it was as if she betrayed me. Now whenever I'm with her, Ralph and Lara are around. I feel I don't belong — like Death at a wedding. If I were

Mr. K. just called. Needs another week on Uncle's diary. Nothing's wrong. I don't believe him. Claims it's Uncle's penmanship. Promises to have it ready by Mon., Jan. 4th, since a "nice Jewish girl like you must be busy New Year's weekend."

Sat., Dec. 26 — Terrible news. Ida Tweety died. When I went to check on her a little while ago, there was no answer. I got Aldo to open the door. Miss Tweety was in bed. We knew she wasn't asleep. Her head was bent like a fallen canary's.

I sat with her a while. It was creepy sitting in the basement with a corpse, even though she was my friend. When I went to see her yesterday I gave her an Xmas present — a clay sculpture I'd made. I thought even if she can't see she might enjoy touching it. She told me about the house she grew up in, a big house built in the 18th century, how it was always cold, even in the summer. The apple cellar especially. She showed me a photograph. She couldn't see it, of course, but she remembered it.

"All that snow. That was the biggest snowstorm we ever had in March. Can you believe it? In March, four feet of snow." Then she asked me to read "Adelle's Strudel." We had such a nice visit, I'd no idea anything was wrong. I shrugged off her solemn goodbye.

I can't just sit here, knowing poor Miss Tweety is lying dead downstairs, all alone. Going down to be with her.

Evening — Took a long walk, hoped the cold would numb me. Went to Miss Tweety's before going out. Door was locked. Had to bother Aldo again. He'd already called Frieda, who knew Miss Tweety's funeral arrangements. By the time I got down, the undertaker had taken the body. Aldo gave me the chapel's address.

Dec. 27 — Went to chapel this evening. Room was cold, empty. Miss Tweety's box was open, but I didn't look in. I'm still shaken. What should I do about her recipes?

4:35 P.M. — Who are the people in Miss Tweety's room? A man and woman are going through her things — must be relatives, but they're so nasty. A matched set of rudeness. I asked, "Who are you?" and he said, "Who are *you?*" I explained I was a neighbor. Neither said who they were — hardly paused long enough in their scavenging to look up. I felt sick, like I was watching rats chew an old lady.

"Excuse me," I said, "but there are some things Miss Tweety wanted me to take care of for her. Have you come across them yet — two packages? One's her recipes, the other's full of old say—"

"Hmph. The body's hardly cold and already this one's looking for souvenirs," the woman said, tossing her head.

I was so shaken, all I could do was open and close my mouth several times, like a fish. Couldn't think of what to say. Finally caught my breath. "You don't understand. They're not of any value," I said. "Except to her. She always kept them in that drawer," and I pointed. The woman stood between me and Miss Tweety's dresser.

"Get out of here before I call the police. There's a law against snoopers looking through a dead woman's goods."

I was afraid, more of myself than of them — afraid I'd cry. So

I left. Now I am crying, from fury and frustration. Can't bear to be misunderstood. It's not as if I want Miss Tweety's stuff. Just, I promised her. And those two rodents downstairs, they have no use for those old recipes. They'll throw them out. I just

Miss Tweety's lock would be easy to open with a long tool . . .

9:05 P.M. — Ugly couple still in basement, filling garbage bags with things. I feel sick. Try later.

10:40 P.M. — Still trembly. It was creepy down there, then that horrible sight, like a bloody silver ghost. Went down at 10:15. It was dark, dusty. I figured even if someone came in, I wouldn't be seen in the gloom. Spooky shadows dancing because hall bulb hangs on long wire. I worked the lock. It's a fragile lock, like poor Miss Tweety. Should have been a snap to break, but the only thing breaking was my will. Basements fill me with foreboding.

I startled myself a few times, hearing funny sounds that I explained away. Footsteps — I told myself people were walking upstairs. Humming — undoubtedly from electrical equipment. I kept calming myself from what I believed were unfounded worries.

Then I looked up.

"Present arms!" he shouted. I held out a cuticle hook. "At ease." He saluted, then marched to the washing machines. His silver wrap was so eerily effective that he actually looked like a knight standing at the end of the long passage. I carefully, precisely stepped by him, forcing myself not to show fear or enrage him by seeming in any way Vietnamese. I willed a cloak of invisibility over me as I left the hall, then ran up the stairs.

I'm sorry, Miss Tweety, but I give up. Foiled again, if you will forgive the pun. I tried, you know I gave it my all. If I expected to be haunted tonight, it was by you, not Mr. Parks in 3C. His threat is far more real than your kindly ectoplasm.

> I saw him standing over me,
> and I began to swoon.
> In his silver-foil armor,

with a silver-foil sword,
aglitter in the gloom of the naked hall light
stood the dread knight of the laundry room.

Mon. — Left work early to go to the service. At first didn't see anyone I knew — scavengers weren't there. Everything was strangely familiar. Christian funeral service — stand up, sit down. Recalling Hebrew-school tales of Jewish martyrs tortured because they wouldn't kneel, I held my lips tight against hymns, as if they might be spooned into me. Yet the service hardly differed from a Jewish one. Same clichés.

Afterward I saw Frieda, Miss Tweety's day companion. "I'm glad you could come," she said. "Miss Tweety thought the world of you."

I asked who the people in the apartment were. "What people?" she asked. "There are no relatives, I told the undertaker that. She had some cousins in Nova Scotia, but that's a long ways off."

"A middle-aged couple," I said, "were ransacking the place."

Frieda was furious, sputtering steam. She came back with me to the building and opened Miss Tweety's room. We stood stunned.

Clothing and paper were strewn all over. If there had been anything of value, it had surely been taken. The rest had been thrown about with abandon. I immediately opened her drawer, looking for the two shopping bags of recipes and sayings. Gone. I even got down on my knees, searching for them in the back of the dresser, although I knew it was hopeless. The drawer itself was empty, except for some old-lady underwear pushed to one side. We went through the papers on the floor. Not a recipe or saying to be found. The ghouls who'd robbed a dead woman had taken those bags just for spite.

We examined piles of junk — torn clothes too cheesy for rags were all that were left of her. I recognized the shards of my sculpture on the floor, but I didn't cry — not until I found Miss Tweety's cane. Frieda put her arm around me. "Why don't you take that?" she asked. "Miss Tweety would have wanted you to. Then you'll have something to remember her by."

So I took it, the cane Miss Tweety used to help her "see" outside. Long and thin, with a white tip like a magician's wand. It stands with all my other dead-people things. Aunt Sadie's flowerpot on one side, Aunt Rose's on the other. My mother's mother-in-law's tongue lashes out at the long blind eye, while Uncle's diaries stare sightlessly. I went through the rubbish outside, looking for recipes. Nothing. I feel terrible, that I've failed a friend.

Oh, Miss Tweety, if only you had given the bags to me for safekeeping each night. If only your foresight had consisted of more than those prolonged, torturous goodbyes.

Tues., Dec. 29 — The kittens' antics annoy me. Have to think of homes for them. Used to fantasize giving one to Miss Tweety. Now . . .

Everyone at work is pissed because there were no Xmas bonuses. Blaming union instead of pointing finger at management. Max shrugs: "You wanted the union." Bookkeepers: "No bonuses in ticky-tacky boxes." Could one of the bookkeepers be a company spy? Too obvious.

When I come home from work and there's no Miss Tweety, I feel an emptiness like a glass I need to fill.

Wednesday — Today was Claw Day, so Suzy, Liz, Happy, et al. sauntered out around 11:15, leaving me holding the fort. Not too long after, Max came in and asked where everyone was. Without thinking I said, "Sharpening their claws." When they got back, Max called them into his office, chewed them out. I overheard things like "The union specifies one hour for lunch. Bringing in the union was your choice. I'm sorry but you have to abide blah blah."

The rest of the day everybody cast the evil eye at me. I bent over my galleys, pretending not to see. Their glances were like ice picks at my back.

I can't stand my job. Because I have a compulsive personality,

I'm the only one who does any work. Even though they're only schlock magazines, I proofread as if I were a scribe working on the Torah. Who else consults *The Chicago Manual of Style* in order to decide whether "that naked nurse Lois" needs a comma between "nurse" and "Lois"? (It doesn't, because "that nurse" is restrictive. Very. She ties up legless war veterans with their IV tubes and performs fellatio.) Also, for your information, a set of lesbian twins is singular, even if its orgasms are multiple.

It's not as if our readers care. I take commas out. Suzy puts them in. I show her the entry in *CMS*. She pulls rank on me.

Why don't I just take a nap in the afternoon like the others? When you walk by the bullpen after lunch, you can hear the gentle snores of 15 editors working. Even Max gets his P.M. blowjob. The stairwell is so smoky with pot I think all the fire alarms must be turned off. People booze and shop and go to the hairdresser, the manicurist. And there I am at my desk, wondering what exactly the distinction is between "cum" and "come."

I should get another job, but I'm lazy, scared — 17 years, and it's so comfortable wearing sloppy clothes and sneakers.

What I'm looking forward to these days is reading Uncle's diary. He must teach me how to survive. Art is all that matters. He was a genius. I am a genius's niece. The rest is unimportant.

✦ ✦ ✦

Lara Jacob riffled the unlined spiral art pad, wondering what to do. She took out a legal pad and wrote: "Ed.'s Note: In view of Gabriella Segul's own doubts regarding the disclosure of the following, I thought hard about my right to include the—"

She ripped the page out, started again. "Ed.'s Note: Although Gabriella Segul made it clear that she didn't want the following disclosed, I think it important to air the ugly case in which—"

This page too she tore out. "It's the tone," she told herself. "I sound pompous, and I don't mean to. Maybe it's just, I don't know, am I doing the right thing?" She went into the kitchen. The phone rang. She took her time answering it.

"Nightcap?" asked the man on the other end.

"I want to ask you something," Lara said. "In general terms. If someone wrote about a secret and indicated he or she didn't want that secret published, but it was an important secret, and not one that reflected badly on the writer either, it's just—"

He interrupted her. "I'd publish it. Whatever it is. Look, Gabby left her diary behind. Even if she meant to cut something, she didn't do it. She must have wanted it known. Why else write it down?"

"She didn't know someone would read it. And publish it in a biography."

"Then why write it?"

"Yeah. I guess you're right."

"I don't know why you won't let me read it. I knew her too. I could help you with it. I'd just keep it one night, and I—"

"I can't, James, I just can't. It's too valuable. It's the only copy, and if something happened to it. . . . Besides, she writes about you. I'm not quite sure how I feel about you reading it. You haven't even given me your reminiscence yet, so it might—"

"Tonight," he said. "It's ready. Listen, I'm going to read that diary sooner or later, whether in manuscript or in your book."

"Well, later it is. I'll meet you at Lucy's at eleven, okay?"

✦ ✦ ✦

Thurs., Dec 31 — Happy New Year. My diaphragm waits in its plastic shell like a rubber Botticelli's Venus. I feel strange—erotic and full of hate. The confessional mood is upon me. I've decided to tell about Sam the Plumber. He was a friend of my parents, but you know how kids have special friends among adults. He was more interested in my stories than in kibitzing at cards. And I loved him more than my own father. My father, with his rough ways and bristled cheeks, lifted me like a side of beef. He held my waist in his two hands so hard I couldn't breathe and cried to be let down. Sam was always clean-shaven. He smelled of cologne. He was never too tired to talk to me.

One day he took me to his basement. I don't remember how or why. But I do remember he thought of everything. He even had a clean pair of cotton panties for me to put on. He put the bloody ones in his pocket. That was a revelation to me, that men's pockets go so deep they can hold a bloody pair of panties and a pretty pink ribbon. Which he took out and gave me, to make me stop crying. He told me never to tell. He made me take an oath, swear on my life and the lives of my parents not to say a word.

Sam. I wish he were alive so I could kill the old man. He made me promise not to say anything or "may I eat waterbugs for breakfast and dinner the rest of my life." He invented these outrageous oaths that were supposed to be funny. He made me repeat them solemnly after him, crossing my heart and hoping to die — which I certainly did. He told me that if I said anything my parents would stop loving me. He threatened to adopt me.

My drink has turned sour. Maybe I should stop. Is it a mistake, to divulge such a secret on paper? I never told Carol what I'm telling you. Who are you anyway behind this one-way mirror? Do I want the world to know this dirty thing about me? Yes, I want everyone to know that Sam Shoemaker, Sam the Plumber, Sam Ethel's, Marvin's father Sam, Sam who gets along so well with children it's a shame they only had Marvin and Marvin's not all, you know, there, that this Sam is a dead rapist.

People cried at his funeral, as if he were a good man. It galls me that he got away, free from taint, and I go through life washing my hands, washing my feet, scrubbing myself so hard I have sores all over my body and still can't wash his mark off me. Why should I go to my grave keeping his filthy secret? I can always burn this book, discard these pages later. For now, telling you what happened makes me feel clean.

IMPORTANT NOTE: Discard these pages before dying?

I remember how Lara used to display herself when she was two, running around naked. I couldn't stop her. She'd sit in my lap with her legs up, showing her poultry. Babies do that. There's no mistaking the sexual thrill they get out of it, but that doesn't mean they want to fuck. It's baby sex. I'd gently try to put clothes on her or get her to sit nicely. It made me uncomfortable. I demanded she stop acting naughty, so she'll probably blame me for her sexual problems when she gets around to having them.

Sam said he used to diaper me. Maybe I did something. Pictures of me as a child show a waif in rumpled clothes — big eyes, swollen lips, disheveled hair. You wouldn't know it to look at me now, but I was quite a dish when I was seven. People kept saying, "I could eat you up" or "You look good enough to eat."

I looked, in fact, like a child prostitute, a gypsy succubus— you know the tintype. Everything about me was unkempt. Maybe Sam thought sex was what I wanted. Maybe that's how he saw my thrill when he would visit.

I'm not making excuses for him. He was a monster, not my friend after that. I was tormented by the oaths he made me swear. When I heard him come in on Saturday night to play cards, asking for me as he always did, I hid under the bed. He bent down to ask what was wrong. He didn't try to get me out, yanking and yelling the way my mother did when Dr. Lublum came over—pulling down my pajamas, holding back my arms and legs, so the doctor could stick me with a needle as long as my thigh. I always figured she had to do this — hold me down for the doctor, lie to me about the dentist, not believe me when I told her about Sam.

Because I did finally break my oath. I had nightmares. Sam chasing me, vampires drooling that I was delicious, magicians with strangely pulsing wands. So I told her. She told my father. He called Sam, hemming and hawing. Then, without actually confronting him, my parents decided I had made it all up. There would have been blood. There was no blood. I told them how he put my panties in his pocket. My mother said, "Where would Sam get a pair of your panties? Stop making up stories."

I was a little girl and I got confused. I told them he made me eat waterbugs. I told them he was going to adopt me. I begged them not to let him. All the stories ran together, the things that happened, the things he told me. My parents kept saying, "Do you know what happens to little girls who lie? Don't you know about the little girl who cried wolf?" And I was crying wolf, wolf! and there was a wolf but no one believed me or saw him prowling around the door. And in the end, I stopped believing it too.

Years later, after my first adult sexual experience, I had a dream. I'd forgotten about Sam, thought I was a virgin but there was no blood. Then I started having a weird pain, a terrible feeling of fullness, of a long hard poker stuck so far up me that it was coming out my mouth. I'd dream every night of being impaled. In dream after dream I was in a basement. When I turned to see who was chasing me with a sword or a wand or a broom handle, it was my father. And I would scream, wake up screaming, "This isn't right!"

Then one time I turned and it was my uncle chasing me. He was dressed in a red-white-and-blue tuxedo and a top hat. Again I screamed, "This isn't right!" I told Larry about the weird dream I'd had one night after making love, only I said the man chasing me was dressed like Uncle Sam.

It was as if a curtain rose on the scene. I hadn't thought of Sam for years. Whether my parents secretly believed me or not, they stopped seeing Sam and Ethel soon after I told them. A falling out, they said, about the toilets. Sam was a plumber and the toilet in our basement never flushed right. When I was in college they made up, but that was years later. Before the fight, while Sam was coming to the house and couldn't get me out from under the bed, he didn't like me much. If I walked into a room, he'd eye me and say, "How's the little storyteller? You have some fairy tales to tell?" The adults laughed. They never noticed the edge to his voice.

I graduated from college and was still living at home when my mother gave me a gift box. A friend's daughter had just had a baby. She had to go out. Someone would be by to pick up the present. A few hours later the bell rang. I opened the door. Recognition glinted in Sam's dirty eye. Fourteen years passed before me like I was a woman drowning. I pushed him with the gift and slammed the door. He rang the bell. Knocked, pounded. I'd locked it but I was still afraid. I leaned against the door, holding it back with all my weight. Even after I heard his steps go downstairs, I couldn't look through the window. I was afraid he'd be there, looking in.

All day I felt in danger. Felt him looking at me, trying to get in, coming at me from closets, from under beds. Heard him in the basement, fooling with the pipes. I was afraid to pee. I knew he couldn't get at me from inside the toilet, but I felt him there. When I absolutely couldn't hold back anymore, I crouched over the bowl, watching the piss stream out of me to make sure a hand didn't reach up.

When my mother came home, I said, "How could you do that to me? Didn't you know that was Sam the Plumber?"

My mother giggled. "Oh that. You still remember that story?"

Bubble Editor
Dear Suzy,
I read your magazine all the time. I like Jane Ann Hope. I wish to have you forward this letter confidentially. I think she is lovely. I would like to take her up in the office of a child. I am a simple 30-year-old Canadian game warden situated here in the Beautiful Skunk Mountains. I have a cabin secluded in the hills. No one could ever find this place. Here's a photo of me in my uniform. Please send it with my letter to Jane Ann.
Ranger John Smith

Dear Jane Ann,
I see you on television you are having such a hard time. Why don't you come and live with me? I will adopt you or we could marry. The mountains here are beautiful. You would be happy. It's just the place for a girl like you to get used to. I'd teach you to do all the things a mountain woman should know. You wouldn't ever have to wear shoes. I am lonely here too as you are in the big city on channel 10. Let me know. I will send you the money you need. Don't bring fancy clothes. You don't need any.
Ranger John Smith

Saturday — Been hearing crying behind my wall. Mewing like a child. I stroke Miss Tweety's cane. The Venus I'm working on — I was so pleased at first with the sketch and watercolors, but lately the idea strikes me as stupid — Botticelli's Venus stepping out of a tub. Here I go, dangling ever over a swamp of doubt. People think of the victim tied beneath the sword of Damocles. How do you suppose the sword feels, knowing it's about to drop?

Kolokoy is due Monday. Soon I will know Uncle. He was an epileptic, a failure — does that matter? Epiphanies, scientists will soon tell us, are no more than the backfiring of brain cells (just as they now say that déjà vu is merely a precondition for epilepsy). No matter what, I will know him. It feels like a messenger is coming with the portrait of a king.

Uncle and I were once alone in the living room. I was about to leave when he mumbled something. He spoke to his shoes so I can't be sure what he said. It sounded like "Demons fight demons draw sword — a pencil, some paint. Grapes for the gods." He went on: "About her, what do you think? Wings not for all." Suddenly he looked at me. A sourceless light shone out of his eyes. His eyes were neon against his pink smile. He seemed to be someone other than Uncle Moisha. You know how that happens sometimes — you look at someone familiar and see a stranger?

In this case he was not just a stranger but strange. As if he'd come from another planet. He said, "The m-m-m-m-meaning of l-l-l-l-life—" Just then my mother came in with a bowl of apples.

"Have a fruit," she said, and I watched my uncle resume his idiot act. He did it so well that I have never been sure of what I'd heard just prior. Or whether he was doing it for effect, to put me on. Was he about to tell me something? Monday, when I am alone with the diary, I'll find out.

Sunday — Ice storm last night. Warmth yesterday caused moisture on trees, then water froze, encasing world in glass shell. Saw squirrel holding icicle in tiny, manlike hands, licking it. Felt

I'd entered a Beatrix Potter illustration. Afternoon's warming. Things melt away like a wizard's illusion.

Jan. 4, Mon. — Kolokoy is due at 8:00. It's 7:05 now.

(transcription from sm. bk.) *11:15 A.M.* — Liz just told Suzy that she and Tom broke up. He's moving out. She's sick of non-commitment. Do I detect a touch of Black Angel's wand? Now they're discussing union negotiations, which start this week. "Tactics?" Happy asks. Liz says nothing. Then: "Vogel claims PP can't raise salaries or benefits without going under." Suzy snorts, Happy giggles. "He's just playing with the numbers," Liz continues. "Negotiating stance. Right now the women's mags are in a slump, but we all know schlock's cyclical. They're trying to scare us into concessions." Silence. I feel them looking at me— am I being paranoid?

"Me, I'm tired of coolie wages," L. says. "But I'd like to know how it is management guesses the union's stance on everything ahead of time. I think we have a spy." Long pause. This book seem suspicious? Should I say something? Keep writing?

7:15 P.M. — It's clear Liz thinks I'm the company spy. I am a spy, just not for the company. I'm a free agent. A student of human nature. I eavesdrop on gossip, note hypocrisy. I observe how people talk to your face and laugh behind your back. Bent over my desk, quietly proofreading, I was always good at making myself invisible. Till the union came in.

If only Miss Tweety were alive. I'd like to go down, hear again the story of her canoe trip with the Indian to get medicine for a sick child. I feel I've failed her. Her cane leans against Aunt Sadie's pot. I'm thinking of putting it in Aunt Rose's soil, get the purple passion to climb it. How would Miss Tweety and Aunt Rose get along? There's that whimpering again. Is it someone's TV set?

7:35 P.M. — Too early to be mad at Kolokoy. Suzy has a new tendency. I noticed it today. "That's the Scorpio in you," she told Liz. Later: "Happy's such a Sag. You can tell by the laugh."

What would she say if she knew I'm a Gemini? That I'm two-faced because I was born under the sign of the twins? Uncle was also a Gemini. Does that confirm a diagnosis of schizophrenia? It's not that I don't believe in astrology. I don't disbelieve in anything, that's my problem.

Suzy's a Pisces. Says that's what makes her an empath. There *is* something of the fish in her. Maybe just her green eyes. But something else. Watery. The mirror thing too, like frozen water— how she shows you her face disguised as yours. Maybe I just see things this way because today she talked about being a Pisces — the narrative sense changing reality into fiction.

She talked also about being a healer. How she laid hands on her father, took his pain into herself. I'm worried about Suzy. She's fallen under Black Angel's spell. Even Liz the pragmatist has, and Suzy is much more biddable. When Judy started telling us for the thousandth time about being a pickle heiress (her father owns a big pickle factory: dills, garlic, tomatoes, you name it), Suzy said, "Judy, you're a Cancer, so watch that stuff. Carcinogens. Believe me. My father lived on hot dogs and sauerkraut for years." What would Suzy have made of Uncle? Who cares? In 15 minutes, Mr. K. will be here. I won't need an astrologer to read him.

Uncle was a man totally caught up in art. He lived in dreams. I admired his commitment. Whenever I came into his room in the nursing home, he'd be staring out the window. The other old people were phantoms. What was he thinking — of himself, a boy running?

Van Gogh writes: "He who is absorbed . . . is sometimes . . . shocking to others, and unwillingly sins . . . against certain forms and customs and social conventions. . . . For instance, you know that I have often neglected my appearance; this I admit, and I admit that it is shocking. But look you, poverty and want have their share in the cause and a discouragement comes in too for a part, and then it is sometimes a good way to assure oneself the necessary solitude for concentration on some study that preoccupies me." What would Unc

8:07 P.M. — Guess who just called, at the very last minute. He *said* he tried to call earlier but my phone wasn't working. Ha! He needs another week to finish the translation. Won't tell me what's wrong, only that Uncle's writing is hard to follow. Also said he'd had the flu. Why didn't he tell me that last week? I am suspicious. And anxious. I should never have given him the diary. Could he have lost it? Is he planning to steal it? We agreed on Jan. 11th as the deadline. I will accept no more excuses.

BUBBLE Editor Suzy James

In case you git this, we, the Retired Housewives of the country, we buy the groceries and are the group they try to make buy things they advertise on TV. I do my shopping early so I can watch your show. I like Password and One Life to Live. I don't like blacks. They have taken over Los Angeles.

I think and a lot of us agree the shows should be changed. If a hospital was run like you run yours, well you have too much murder and sex and these are daytime shows when kids watch. A murder was committed, some woman sleeping with someone else is disgusting. I watch the shows all the time and can't believe my eyes. I talk to a lot of women in restaurants, the laundromat. They say quit watching like them or just watch once in a while like them. I used to like the Doctors but with Steve and Ann its rotten. No wonder Carol left. How come that dr sent the other dr the picture when his socalled sister disapeared? Why didn't he put it in the paper? Doesn't anybody know what's going on? I have to keep up with everybody and all the shows so that things don't get more out of hand. I have my own work to do. Dr. Alrech could have used the paper like I said. Was he too cheap, hard to believe, him a doctor with all that money and all. When he and Mat and Stacy were in Joan's room she was alive. So the killer had to be wearing gloves. The great Jason could have checked this out. I told him. Then Paul hides the letter with the picture. Its about time you had him picked up for murder. Bout time you raped up that mess already. Vicky and Mr. Clay killed by Clarissa and she's off scott free. Is that nice? Why do you have to kill off the ones leaving the show? Mr. Clay could of just died without being murdered, him an old man and the killer gets off scott free, I don't like that. There she is, Clarissa, planning her viscious plans. Larry should open his eyes. Karen's not for him. My niece would be better. She wants children and has no past. I pray Kathy leaves and Tony marries Pat. I pray every night for Brian to get well, such a shame when things like that happen. The hospitals all being run by murderers and sex, no wonder things go wrong. Not like Dr. Welby's hospital. He knew how to run things. I always drink his coffee. Keep up the good work.

Sincerely yours,
Me

Tues. — Surprise, surprise, who do you suppose is taking Miss Tweety's apartment? Mrs. Unbaked is already bringing boxes down. They've decided to keep the au pair in the spare bathroom (she sleeps in the tub, the girl told me) and use Miss Tweety's room for storage.

The bank was a zoo today. On line, an old man and an old woman were fighting over his smelly cigar. People offered to save the man's place while he smoked it off line, but he refused. She called him an altah cockah and a son of a bitch. He said, "Where'd you learn to talk like that? Talk like a lady."

She said, "I'm no lady. I'm a human being."

I sided with her of course, yet I felt this tremendous pity for the old bastard. Another old man behind him said, "I for one like the smell of a good cigar" — it was a Dutch Masters — "and I'm going to light a cigarette right now." A black militant behind him said, "Why you do that? Smoke disturbs the woman. Go smoke off the line." The woman who'd offered to save the man's place offered again and was curtly told to mind her own business: "There's no law against smoking." Then the black guy said, "Yes there is. It's against the law," and the old man said, "So what are you, a policeman, a Nazi, you're such a law-abiding citizen?" The black man held back his fury and said, "It disturbs the people who don't smoke. It bothers her health."

I spoke once, whispering that I hate smoke, although actually I'm a smoker. Mostly I just shot daggers and pretended to be engrossed in Van Gogh's letters. Concentrated on not crying. I kept thinking of terrible things to tell the man, how his mouth was going to rot off from cancer, how he deserved it. But I didn't say anything. I'm a coward. And when I fight, I cry. Finally the man put out his cigar: "See, I put it out. You happy now?"

She said, "You put it out? You finished smoking it, you bastard!" and he said, "That's not true. I smoked it halfway and put it out, you tramp!" I could no longer keep from crying. I had to get out of there. I felt shame for the man though I sided with the woman: cigar as phallus; last outpost of masculinity, smoking in line at the bank; camaraderie of two old tobacco-suckers.

Suzy would make this a funny story. I lack a sense of humor.

P.S. Have decided the only way to clear myself at work is to find the real spy. Could be anybody. I am suspicious of all.

Jan. 6 — Remembering the few occasions James and I were alone at Lucy's Bar. We drank till I felt myself falling — in love with the dark, with art. I remember his grin. He was getting loaded — I thought he might be drunk on love too. At least lust. One time he smiled. Light darted out his eye like an arrow. He said, "I am hypnotist. Great conjurer. I hypnotize, put you under, no problem."

"I bet," I said, looking down to hide my thrill.

"Shall I put you in trance? Shall I make you do things till you believe? I do easy." He snapped his fingers.

"I believe you," I said. "But doesn't a hypnotist lack power over someone who fights him?" He stared. I feared he would make me reveal myself; I wanted to be under his spell.

In the beginning, when I realized I was drawn to him as to death, I tried to fight it. It was wrong, meaningless, ridiculous. The more I told myself I was nothing to him, the more I thought that a lie. "A married man," I said, "a man with a child." I didn't care. I was aware of my body, tight as I crossed the room, his hot stare sizzling my back as he took in my hips. When I returned to the table, he watched my breasts and pelvis roll, then looked away. I wanted him to look, I just didn't want him to know. I affected a businesslike manner: hey ho, buddies here. A toast to art, to comradeship! How silly I was, as transparent as lace panties. But he was soft in his intoxication. He didn't judge me, not as harshly as I judge myself.

I couldn't understand him. My drunkenness, his Dracula drawl, the noisy bar. My stomach churned from desire. I swallowed back hunger, sucked pretzels in the dark, rolling my tongue over every grain of salt. I can still feel that emptiness gulping inside; it takes a few drinks to deaden it now. But that night, when my need was new, I stared at his lips, reading them in the noisy bar. I leaned forward, intent on his words, then I was falling into his mouth, falling into a kiss. Maybe that is when it happened, when he hypnotized me into love. My lips reddened, swelled. I caught myself, pulled back before it happened, ashamed.

James looked at his watch. "One more, then I go," he said. I nodded. He accused me. "You know what you do."

What did he mean? The old femme fatale bit: you're seducing me for your own power? "You know," he said. "The others, children with crayons. But you — skill, pulse. You know."

So he hadn't seen desire flapping like a butterfly on my nose? "Doodles," I said, dismissing art. Relieved, pleased. Disappointed.

Why always this confusion of art and sex? I wanted his recognition, it made me real, so why did his accusation of artistry get me hot? It wasn't enough that he appreciated my work. I wanted to consume him. I needed to make him burn like I burned. I hid my ambition as a giant hides his soul in an egg. No one would guess that behind the mild-mannered (that is to say, dippy) demeanor of a schlock copy editor dwelt Superartist, flying through watercolor skies, traveling beneath clay underworlds, molding art and eroticism, madness and genius with her bare hands.

People said, when I was little, that I was gifted. "She should have art lessons," my first-grade teacher told my mother. So art lessons I had, at the Brooklyn Museum on Saturdays. I thought this was because I was talented. Years later my mother told me of the conversation she'd had with Mrs. Parofsky. It had been open-school week. My drawing of a house, a child, a mother, a father, was hanging on the bulletin board. Across the picture I'd traced the outline of my hand, filling it in with black scribbles. "What do you think this means?" the teacher asked my mother.

"The teacher says Gabby needs art lessons," my mother told my father that night. Even at age six, art and madness were as entwined as drowned lovers.

James. I taste your name. Write the letters on a glass. That night at Lucy's we finished our drinks and left, and we never met in quite that way again. It was raining. I was drunk and cried. It was silly. I am a silly woman. The heroine in a silly movie. I think tears will move an invisible audience; this audience has the power to change my fate. If they wanted to, the goddesses could call to him. "Don't be a fool," they could say. "Gabby wants you. Go to her. You can catch her crossing 59th."

I was stumbling as I left the bar, embarrassed by my tipsy gait, afraid too — a woman alone, one who's been drinking. "Control yourself," I demanded. Then I was fine, except . . .

I have come to think of James as a sickness, not fatal but something I carry. Years ago his fingers brushed mine for a moment and infected me. I feel this lump of love growing, benign but palpable, deep inside. I think about him, and who was he? A stranger who touched me with his damn kindness.

Still, an illness can be one's most valuable possession. It gives a shape to longing. James, my pot of gold. The leprechauns left him, it must be a joke. Because after I dream him a while, he vanishes into nothing. A few memories of treasure I clink.

James, you are my coins of indulgence. I play with you, allow myself moments with my gold. I remember certain looks, meanings implied. I make up conversations we never had, never would have, no matter how long we knew each other. My tongue would never have loosened around you, except in your mouth; in fantasy I am witty. Then I think, "No more." And so, book, fantasy, sickness, treasure . . . James. It's time for you to lie back in my chest. Your face rests beneath my pillow like a reflection in a pool.

Thurs. — If I ever wondered about Happy's feelings for Ju-an, I don't anymore. Frankenstein came back from the art department today with layouts. You can smell Frankenstein coming before he turns the corner. The man has worn the same leather pants every day for five years. He also has a terrible lisp.

He dropped off the layouts. We held our breath, waiting for him to leave. But he felt like talking. "Hey, Happy," he said. "Did you hear? Ju-an'th getting married. Thith thummer."

Happy came out and stared. It was painful to watch her clown face turn upside down. Her despair was wide open. I looked away, to leave her the privacy of her grief. Suzy and Liz soaked up her sadness like eye sponges.

Friday (transcribed from sm. bk.) — Bathroom conversation: "They never should have voted the union in. Jobs—"

"I thought you were for—"

"At first, but then I shhhh . . . is someone . . . *mumble* . . . sneakers? . . . must be Ga—"

Company spy setting me up?

10:40 P.M. — Took out watercolor sketches of Venus after dinner. Started oils. Shower cap must complement the flowery curtains. Clam-shell tub has to work as porcelain and abalone. My Venus of lust, emerging from suds. Allegory of me leaving PP. "We were waiting for you to step from your shell," James whispers. Mauret told me to check back after Jan. 1. I'm going to do it. The Painting Place still has my slides. Perhaps this will be my year after all.

Saturday — A sexualized imagination is not the same as an erotic one. The first has more to do with anxiety than with pleasure. I am about to reveal a secret.

James was still at PP. I decided to paint a nude self-portrait. Took off pants, shirt, folded everything neatly, ashamed and excited as I set up before the mirror. Artist and model painted and posed. A lust gathered. It seemed to come from outside. I was looking at my body as if it were someone else's. I desired and was desired by it. Perhaps it was a mystical experience, the lover and beloved are one; it didn't, however, feel religious. The brush became an extension of my hand, the canvas my skin. It stretched before me, receptive to every caress. I didn't touch my own skin. Compulsive circles, furious brushwork, merging colors, textures. My body responded like a plucked guitar.

When it happened I was so surprised that I fell to the floor as if possessed. Was it the demon of art — Narcissus, James? I never once touched myself, yet it was incredibly pleasurable, so powerful and maddening that I knew I would have to do it again . . .

I approach this sort of art with shame and desire. Can no more resist it than refuse James. It takes so much but doesn't leave me empty and alone. The climax only comes with the completion of the painting. And so, when I am back in myself (in ecstasy we leave our bodies), something is beside me like a lover. A new painting.

Most of these are abstract; only the first was figurative. I've never shown them to anyone. It would embarrass me. Is this crazy? Am I? I have confessed and am released, and am disgraced. I was only half kidding about the demon of art. Because, painting this way, an invisible intimacy takes hold. Possession, like ecstasy, can be sexual, mystical . . . or insane.

Why must I always stand before you naked? It's not that I feel no shame. I am wet with shame. Maybe that's why. You are a towel to soak up my secrets. Or am I trying to seduce you? Do I think I can make you love me on paper, through paper, that I can go beyond distance and death and stand voluptuous, my arms open? Will these confessions bring the dead back to life or make a man who has forgotten me awaken to his desire as one slipping from under a spell? If not magic wish, why keep writing this way?

Art, sex, power. I catch myself indulging in omnipotence. Communicating with the dead — reading their letters and diaries, writing back to them. I stare into the sunlight and trance a perfect world. I am astir with longings fulfilled.

The bottle stage of fantasy: staring at the light, twirling a curl, I once saw rainbows through lashes and thought how to control the spurt of milk from a rubber tit. Don't all fantasies shoot out a hole we manipulate with our tongues? Sex of course, but art too. We force experience to squirt completion. Oneness of art, oneness of sex, oneness of God too and madness probably and death surely. The paint and the brush and the canvas and the eyes and air are one, complete, full, just right. Mmm: the sound of breast. Perhaps it's all a matter of having one's holes plugged. Booze, cigarettes, art, sex, God. And when you're dead, clay covers your holes, at last you're at one. Now you're having a good time.

Dear Slut,
I enjoyed your article on spontaneous orgasm. I was lucky enough to actually witness one. It happened about seven years ago. I was an aide in a hospital. One morning a nice-looking fellow, around 22, came in for a physical. I did his preliminaries and told him to undress. All was routine. Then I told him to lie on his back on the table. I was holding his wrist to count his pulse and casually rested my other hand on his thigh. Well, suddenly this man's penis began to grow very erect. I stood there stunned for a few seconds, watching it, having lost all count of his pulse. All of a sudden, the man's entire body stiffened and he ejaculated right before my eyes. His semen got all over his chest and belly and even on the table. Neither of us said anything. He left before the dr. could examine him. It was a sight I for one will never forget. (Please don't use my name or I'll lose my job.)

Sunday — Saw Mr. Parks in basement. He asked about Miss Tweety's death. "A courageous woman," he said. "Afflicted but never self-pitying. There should be medals for daily living, don't you think?"
Lara's birthday party was as I expected — cute as all hell but more tasteful. I gave her waterpaints, paper, brushes, instead of the jewelry Carol suggested. "Thanks, Aunt Gabby," she said, quickly turning to the fashion doll Fanny brought. I'm not her aunt, but Carol is an only child, Ralph is too, so there's a scarcity of relatives. Carol doesn't want Lara to feel deprived. When I was L's age, nothing would have made me as happy as art supplies. I didn't have relatives who gave me such stuff.
Looking at her today, I experienced an epiphany, remember-

ing how I'd held her. Carol would give her to me at every opportunity, trying to make me a foster mother. That was around the time that Carol's father was diagnosed as having Alzheimer's.

When we were in high school, Carol's father used to sit in the living room, playing the harmonica and tapping his foot. We would have our guitars out and be singing along. He liked tunes such as "You Are My Sunshine." Carol's folky soprano and my adequate alto would harmonize, but he would get lost in a dream. He wouldn't answer when she spoke. She'd hit his knee: "Daddy, Daddy." He'd just stare into space or play the harmonica. This was one of the things I liked about him, but Carol used to go crazy. "Daddy! Damn it, Daddy! Yo, asshole, fuck you!" and she'd run out of the room. I'd still be sitting at his feet and see his perplexed look as he gazed after her, wondering what had made her angry. Or maybe who she was.

Like all epiphanies, mine's not profound when put into words. It was just, looking at Lara during the party, I noticed how her body is becoming womanly — in a seven-year-old way. Then it hit me that when a baby is born you don't realize what that means. The little girl I was looking at was Lara who will someday be a young woman and after that an old woman. Miss Tweety was once such a girl. And when I am a crone and Lara middle-aged, I will still see the baby I fed and the little girl I bought paints for and the young woman she will become, like animals digested in a cartoon snake's belly.

Lara played pin-the-tail-on-the-donkey, and I recalled the little Lara in my arms, so tiny and whole. When I'd give her a bottle, I'd try to place my mind in hers, think with her. I watched her suck; she was unabashed. I thought of my breast drained by a hungry child. I thought, "I will never know this feeling," and I began to cry. I looked away. Infants mirror the faces around them, and I didn't want her to feel sad. She wouldn't have known why.

One time, holding her, I had a terrible thought — of a mother leering at her child, making gorgon faces as the infant nursed. She crossed her eyes, exposed her teeth, stuck out her tongue.

It horrified me, to think of a baby forced to suck a witch's tit. I was scared, as if I'd become aware of a ghoul staring out of a closet. I turned back to smile at Lara to reassure her. I hadn't wanted to frighten her. And I hadn't, because she was asleep, unaware in my arms.

◆ ◆ ◆

Lara wished she could conjure the scene, draining a bottle from her aunt. She wondered, not for the first time, whether she should include her own reminiscences in the biography. But what would a seven-year-old's memories mean? What, after all, did she remember? That each year Aunt Gabby had made her a birthday card. It had meant so much, that someone painted such things for her. She'd tacked them to her bulletin board, from which eventually they disappeared.

What else did she remember? Gabby didn't look like other people's aunts. Sometimes beautiful, often frazzled, always odd. Her clothes never matched. Even her socks were of different colors. Jacket dirty, ripped, as if she couldn't be bothered. Yet she might also wear something extraordinary. Those peacock-feather earrings. Made them herself. From fishing tackle, she said. Lara recalled them in her hair, like another set of eyes. Janie would have laughed. Did laugh, in fact. Remembering this, Lara now cringed, for there was that too in her memories. How she'd wanted to hide her when friends came over. How Janie once called her aunt weird. "She's not my aunt," Lara said. "She's just a family friend."

And she *was* weird. The way she wore her glasses. They hung on a chain of beads and shells, which she called a specklace. Lara, alone with her, admired the jewels dangling down her cheeks, hanging on her chest. But if anyone else came in the room, she quickly turned her back on weird Aunt Gabby.

There was her funny way of talking. Fast, as if she might be interrupted at any point. Jokes made so softly that no one heard . . . except Lara, who didn't understand. Puns offered quickly, quietly, like wildflowers that die the moment they're picked. No one laughed with Gabby. They laughed later. "Gabby was here,"

Carol would say, chuckling with Ralph. A fragile woman, but what did a child know? The thought that she'd slighted her, favoring fashion dolls over art supplies, filled Lara now with greater shame than her aunt had ever caused.

So that was what a seven-year-old's memories were made of. But it didn't stop there. After Gabby's disappearance, when the family had transformed her into a household god, her few photos had hung on the walls, icons to the missing woman. Gabby caught blinking. "She could never bear to be looked at," Carol said. The blurriness about her edges — a woman not quite there. She must have moved, caught in the act of vanishment. Like the child in daguerreotypes who hops into specterhood — yes, there was something of that too in Gabby.

Carol spoke often of her lost friend, as if words could keep a ghost alive. "Gabby loved this part of the turkey," and she'd give Lara the neck. "Gabby used to say that." "Gabby would make that face." "You remind me of her, the way you hold your fork, the way you blink your eyes." Could a child inherit a friend's traits? Did they want her to? "I wish you'd known her better. She loved you so."

Twenty years of searching, and Lara still dreamed of finding her aunt, a ragtag lady on a bench. Would she recognize her, after so many years? And Gabby, what could she make of the child, now a woman, named Lara? Perhaps when the biography was published . . . of course, they had thought that when Tom Campo first exhibited her work, and it had come to nothing.

Oh, but the day her mother wandered into his gallery: a miracle! He'd been looking for Gabby, Carol had been looking for him. The slide he had and the painting she carried were like twin pieces of a ring that, matching, join long-lost bride and groom in tales. Oh, and the celebration. Champagne — even little Lara was given a glass. Music. They danced, laughed, sang. It was almost as if Gabby had come home.

✦ ✦ ✦

Jan. 11 — Do you believe this? Do you know who just called to say he doesn't have the translation ready? If he is not here by

Friday I will call the police. I told him that — not that I'd call the cops, but I put my foot down. "Mr. Kolokoy," I said, "you have broken your promise three times. I expect you to bring back my uncle's book on Thursday, whether you have done the work or not, do you hear?"

He was apologetic. I don't trust him. I have a tendency to blame myself instead of listening to my gut reaction, but with hindsight I can see that I misinterpreted premonition as sexual anxiety.

Why would someone steal a diary? Perhaps he has recognized Uncle's hidden genius and will pretend it's his? If that's the case, how will I prove it, when I can't read Yiddish?

What a disappointment I am to the people who have trusted me. Aunt Sadie's wandering Jew is a shriveled, withered clump in a pot. Miss Tweety's cane, rigid with condemnation, sees that the priceless recipes have been lost. Uncle's other diaries judge me for a fool. I have failed them all. I am not someone to leave a precious inheritance to.

Van Gogh writes: "I should want to show by my work what there is in the heart of such an eccentric man, of such a no-body."

It is good that he wrote to his brother and not me, for I would have misplaced his letter.

Tuesday — When Uncle first died it was a relief not to see him, not to trek to Brooklyn to confront his deterioration. Now I wonder if I sought a criminal like Kolokoy to kill him a second time?

His sad face would wrinkle into such delight when I brought him his own roll of Scotch tape. One time he told me how he missed his mandolin. Without thinking, wanting only to make him happy, I said, "I'll buy you a mandolin, Uncle."

He began to jump around like a parakeet. "You know what to look for?" he asked. "How to tune? Like this: la-la." He started to sing. The more he thought about having a mandolin again, the more excited he became. And the more afraid I was. Overstimulation, the doctors had told me, brought on his seizures.

"Calm down, Uncle. Please," I said. Instead he stood up and danced. I couldn't control him. I thought, "What if he plays the mandolin in the middle of the night?"

He went on, singing, hopping from one foot to the other. I knew I wouldn't keep my promise. Like a traitor I smiled, hoping he'd forget. When I came the following week, he didn't ask about the mandolin. He never asked about it. Maybe he did forget. Or maybe he knew I wouldn't live up to my promise.

I went to the Garden Cafeteria today. Uncle used to hang out there, before we put him in the home. It's a Chinese restaurant now. That made me sad. It would have infuriated Uncle. They painted over the mural that was on the long wall, took out the counter where you'd push your tray past blintzes, potato pancakes, Jell-O. No more old Jews smoking cigars, sipping tea through sugar cubes. No more alarming yellow light that made me feel I'd wandered into Van Gogh's night café. Instead it's red-and-gold Chinese screens. But it smelled good and I was hungry, so I went in.

After ordering I looked around. At a table in the back sat my uncle — an old man in baggy clothes slurping soup. A Chinese version of Uncle Moisha. He was watching me. He sipped his tea loudly, belched, then spat into his napkin, hawking phlegm. In all these ways he was like my uncle. I thought, "If he hands me a fortune cookie, I will take it seriously."

Wednesday, Jan. 13 — Mrs. Unbaked was in the elevator with her daughter, who has a black eye. I asked what happened. She said, "Mind your own business!"

Drizzling again. Death on my mind: those horrible crows picking apart Miss Tweety's room. Vision of Christmas future? Some years ago, when Miss Tweety could still get around alone, she bought me a birthday card. It showed a man and a woman playing tennis: "On your birthday I hope you score." I didn't know how to react. "How sweet," I said, holding in surprised laughter. I'm sure she didn't know what it meant. "And I hope you do, too," she said.

When I first told Uncle my parents had died, he said, "That so? Fat people don't live long. Not healthy. The paper—"

I interrupted him. "Uncle, they were in their eighties. They died in an accident. It had nothing to do with weight."

He paused till I was done, then: "Fat people get taterribable p-p-problems and and and and they g-g-get taterribababble heart dadadadisease. B-b-better skinny like the Japanese. B-but—"

I tried a few times to explain, but he wouldn't understand. The next time I visited he said, "Your mother came to see me. She sat over there, by the window, all night she sat, eating candy and talking. She wouldn't let me sleep."

I explained that that wasn't possible. Again he told me how she kept making noise, unwrapping the candy. " 'Pesha,' I said, 'please let me sleep. Candy is no good. It makes you fat. You'll die of heart disease.' She wouldn't listen."

Long after her death, Uncle Moisha still insisted my mother came to see him. One time she fed him soup. Another time she took him bowling. A few times she and my father took him for walks in Brighton. People were dancing, singing in Russian and Yiddish. The sun was shining. The boardwalk was crowded. He was so happy. He clapped his hands. They all turned around and said, "Moisha, Moisha. It's been so long. Where were you? We always dance better when you're here." Then he clicked a coin against a rail, to make them dance. "It tells the musicians what notes to play. They kick up their heels, everything gets lively. Ah, it's a pleasure. But I get tired, the music ends. They all stop dancing and go home. Still, if I click my coin again, they come back." He laughed.

Social workers in the home would take him to parties in the basement. He ate their cookies, observed the customs of a strange tribe — the other inmates. "The women dance together," he told me. "They live here but are simple villagers. On Saturdays they pray." He did not consider himself one of them.

One time he told me he saw my parents swimming in the ocean. He called, "Come out or you'll drown," but they just swam away. When he said this, chills glided up my spine. I hurried to the room where they hid the ocean. "I'm cold," the old women cried, but I ignored them till I'd searched the gray infinity for my parents.

Another time I asked him about his work in the factory. He started to tell me, then in midsentence switched. "I used to work whenever I wanted and the shock of it to come in and there was nothing. I didn't know what happened. I don't know why she left. She never complained. All of a sudden she moved out. She got a job and moved to someplace called Greenwich Village and wouldn't come back. I couldn't move there. After so long in a big city, I couldn't go back to the village life like we had in Europe—" and he continued telling me how his wife had left him. He had never mentioned it to me before. I knew because my parents had told me, but as far back as I can remember he was alone.

How much longer must I wait to read his journal? It's as if months ago Uncle knocked on my door, and my life has been moving in slow motion ever since.

Carol called to see if I wanted to go to the Lower East Side for bras on Sunday. I said no. I haven't told her about Uncle's diary. It's not a secret, just something I don't want to share. They're going to institutionalize her father. He's been wandering— walking down the street, playing the harmonica, getting lost.

Dear Sir or Madam,
Could you be so kind as to tell me when the "Forest Rangers" was made in Canada? It is a good show. My Mother and my self watch it every day. Mother has had a hard life. She is a wonderful Mother. Because I was ill I haven't helped her as much as I should owing to my sister abusing her. This is the first time I have been able to see through no fault of my own. When she was a child she had to do washing, ironing, and cooking. Her Mother was hard on her. She never had a holiday. Just workworkwork day and night, night and day. They gave her crumbs to eat, then she had to wash out the cinders from the fire and sleep in the hearth.

Dad was hard on Mother. It is lovely to talk to you as I am writing now. Nobody cares about us. My brother doesn't do what he should. My sister doesn't worry. She abuses me and Mother who is old and sick and can't take it. What a life. I even learned the Piano so as to help Mother. I do what I can. Unfortunately, they don't teach me right.

Sincerely,
Miss May June
Montreal, Canada

Thursday — Mr. K. is coming by today . . . supposedly. It's 7:57. He's not even late yet but I doubt he'll show. I've had a drink, may have another. I know Mr. K. isn't going to come so why should

Guess who just left? I am furious. We had a terrible fight. I am so angry I can't even look at his translation. Keep seeing through a red haze. I want to burn it because it is in his hand, that tiny, constipated penmanship.

Here's what happened: he came punctually at 8:00, handed me the translation, explained he had left some words in translit-erated Yiddish so I'd get the flavor of the writing, common words that I probably knew but which he translated in parentheses. He's a pedant but OK, I thanked him.

"Don't thank me," he said. "You know your Uncle was . . . I don't know how else to say it, a meshugginer."

I felt something catch in my heart, like a gun clicking off safety. "I'm sure you're mistaken. You just don't understand him. He was a bit eccentric."

"Eccentric, shmendrik. He was a meshugginer. Bah, I'm ashamed to take money from you. Whole pages of repeated let-ters, numbers I didn't even bother to translate. I marked them in the original with a toothpick, you should see for yourself. Not only that, but he was a plagiarist. He writes a story about a Jew and a thorn bush, and what do you think? I happen to know for a fact he stole it from Grimm's fairy tales. Only he didn't even get it right. What do you want to throw your money away on such garbage? I write stories you could die from, weep like there was no tomorrow, I—"

"I'm sure my uncle's writing is not garbage. Perhaps you don't understand. He was sensitive. He lived a hard life. He was—"

113

"A meshugginer! A fool! I was sick, translating his mishegoss. Nauseous to the depths of my soul. That you, an intelligent editor, an educated woman, should choose to translate dreck, publish it for Americans everywhere to read, what they will think?"

"Who said anything about publishing? I never said—"

"OK, sure, keep your secrets. Fuel the anti-Semites in this country to point and say, 'Look at the Jews. A bunch of meshugginers.' You think I don't know? I am a real writer. Read my stuff sometime, my Yiddish stories, some of which were printed in the *Forward*, plus in Europe I was the crown of the intelligentsia before that pig came to power. You think I don't know what I'm talking? I don't know from anti-Semites? No one here even glances at my stuff. And that you should choose to publish dreck, I am—"

"Listen, Mr. Kolokoy, I'm an editor of soap opera and movie magazines. We are not publishing my uncle's diary. I'm sure your stories are very good, but we don't publish fiction."

"Fiction! You think I made it up? Soap operas. I'll give you soap operas. I tell you, your uncle wrote dreck."

"I won't have this. You didn't know him. He lived in hell. An old man, all alone, never understood. Can you imagine the hell—"

"I don't have to imagine hell." He tore off his coat. I was afraid. I didn't know what he was capable of. He undid his cuff and pulled up his sleeve, revealing his arm. "Demons. You think I don't know from demons? Your uncle sewed for a living, a pity, a shame, tsk tsk, how he sewed. I was not a tailor, Miss Segul. I was a piece of cloth. See how they sewed me? Your uncle could not have lasted a minute what I lived through."

I was appalled, all the more so because I was so angry I wished he had not survived, the bitter man. How many more died that were worthier than he? I was deeply ashamed of my bile. "Mr. Kolokoy," I said. "I'm sorry. I wish you had never been in a concentration camp. Your experience was hell, I know it. But my uncle's life, he wouldn't have lasted, it's true, but—"

"So that's it. If I had any worth as a writer, any true sensitivity like your uncle, I wouldn't have survived. You want to know how I survived. That's my business. We all did things we would not otherwise have done. Who are you, with your American ways, your apartment and food and job, to judge me? I don't write to exist, I exist to write. To tell about all of them. This is what you should publish. Americans must know. You can do it. You can save the Jews from such a thing ever happening again. You, Miss Segul, think of it. The Americans are a great people, a great heart. They will weep. They will remember. They will make sure such a thing never happens again. And it will all come from you, if you would just take a chance on me, an unknown writer from Poland. Please, give me a chance, let me show my stuff."

I couldn't stop him. He wept, he stamped his foot. Screaming, crying, whipping himself to a froth. Dr. Jekyll turning into Mr. Hyde. Rumpelstiltskin spinning his fury. I expected him to pop into nonexistence. I couldn't get across the impossibility of his request.

"The women from my town!" he yelled. "My mother, my wife!"

I was weary. I was moved. "Mr. Kolokoy, I'm sorry . . . I didn't know. I can't, I just can't publish your stories. It's not up to me. It's not appropriate. Here, I'll show you."

I went to get the latest copy of *Soap Bubble* from my bag but he screamed, "Don't bother. It's appropriate the Nazis should march in this country? Fine. Here's your uncle's dreck. Publish it. Have everyone here think this is a Jew—a crazy Communist, he should roast in hell."

"Mr. Kolokoy, I will not have you say that. I suppose you're not interested in translating the other books?" I figured he needed the money. Instead he pulled himself to his height of five foot one.

"I wouldn't soil my hands on such dreck. Good evening." He turned on his heels and marched out.

I'm still shaking. I'm all mixed up. Pity, fury. Absurdity. Plus I feel afraid. His rage. I am so frustrated. Why couldn't I make him understand? I am not a bad person, a bad Jew. I resent his insults against my poor dead uncle, but I feel for Kolokoy too. If I could publish his stories, I would, but he doesn't have exclusive rights to my pity.

To be honest, there's more to it than that. What am I supposed to do now? Where will I find another translator? His was the only response to my ad. If he's right and Uncle's book is crap, still it's his diary and I want to read it. Should I take a course in Yiddish, translate it myself? In 100 years I'll be ready.

Maybe it's voyeurism, to want to know the delusions of a little madman. But even if he was just an epileptic schizophrenic, I must know what went on in his brain.

P. S. 203
Mrs. Elk   10/18/59

REPORT CARD

Work: Good
Behavior: Good
Teacher's Comments: Gabby has a vivid imagination and draws well. But she daydreams out the window instead of paying attention in class. Please make sure that Gabby has a clean hanky every day.

---

2 August 1953

On this day I am beginning a record to set the truth down once and for all that Molly Segul is no longer my wife and if I should take her back into this apartment, she should live so. I am writing to set the record straight. I don't know what she says. She makes up stories. She stole my money. She stole my son and daughter.

I come home last month after sewing a whole day gray pants, blue pants, black thread, white thread, buttons, snip, snap. If I say a word to a neighbor, it's "Shah, Moisha, they'll dock us."

It's hot in the shop, stinking from bodies and wool. In summer, it's winter garments, in winter, summer. Machines whirr. Sometimes in the machine I hear a voice. Wasn't there a group of angels in heaven once, angels of the wheels? [Yes, the *ophanim*—I. K.] I think there is an angel in the factory. I don't pay attention. If the angel wants to *kibitz* [joke around—I. K.], he must wait till I go on my break. I'm not going to get docked because an angel wants to talk union.

Today the angel said, "Moisha, do not despair. Molly will be sorry. We hold you cupped in our hands. We spit on Molly, she thinks it's raining."

I laugh, my neighbors turn around. "What's so funny?" I just laugh, put my finger to my lips, point to the shop steward.

I come home, I want only a cold supper. I ring the bell. Sometimes Molly comes. "What's the matter with you? You can't use your key?" If I go to kiss her, she pushes me away. "Pheh, you smell from ladies' pants." I don't know how she knows ladies' pants from men's pants, but she knows.

It's maybe a month ago I opened the door. Every night since, I open the door and again am struck. On my mind is other things— the weight of the moon, the meaning of life. I have no time for nonsense. But that first time I came home, a terrible shock. Not a stick of furniture, not a mirror, a curtain. I walked as if into a grave. My footsteps, *vay* [woe—I. K.]. Ever since, I am surprised, then, "Oh yes, they left me." I'm used to it. It's calm. But at first it was like a spell. Everything gone. Darkness and a bitter bitter cold. The angel of the machine followed me, he held me down, singing in the voice of wheels a lullaby I could not fight.

When I awoke, I called for Molly, Estelle, Solomon. My voice mocked me. I walked around the apartment. She took everything, even swept up after herself, she wants I should think her a *balabusta* [a fine homemaker—I. K.]. My mother was so clean, you could eat off her floors. Naturally, Molly wouldn't want it said of her that she deserted her husband and left a dirty kitchen.

She took the food from the cabinets. You know what she left? A cot. Not even a little milk for coffee. She took my mother's dishes. My mother left those dishes for me. My mother, God bless her, always said Molly was a serpent. A poor woman, what did she leave

117

us? A few poor dishes, the kind you keep tea in, sugar, salt, flour. I remember her pudgy hands dipping in to take flour for gravy. I ask you, Molly needs those dishes? She could have left me that, the one thing of Mama's.

I want you should know. Every week I gave her my paycheck, she gave me a little cash, I should have a dime for coffee and a paper. The rest, in the bank. Turns out it's her bank. She left me without money to pay the rent. I had to beg by my brother. Joe gave me money. Pesha said, "Don't cry. She was never any good, that Molly."

Joe said, "Moisha, you shall prosper without her. But if she wants to come back, so come. Whatever was the trouble between you, between a man and wife there should be no trouble. We will see if there's something you can do."

They called Molly by her sister's. Violent, she says. Stubborn. Says I threatened my children with a steak knife. I, who can't cut a lamb chop if it's undercooked!

It burns my stomach. She wants me to die. I read in the papers worry is bad for the digestion. I have no worries now that she's gone. I can go to lectures, the library. Cooper Union, Times Square. I will soon find the Socialists again, go to meetings. Molly can't say no. She can't say, "Stop with the mandolin already," or "You're making a mess with your paints." Every day I improve myself. Someday kings will ask, "Tell us, Wise Man, how to rule the world." I shall say, "Stand up, Kings. It isn't fit you should kneel before me. I'm just a poor garment worker. Kings and tailors are the same in God's eyes, no? Divide up your wealth," I shall tell them. "Give each man a piece of land and a plow. Give each tailor his own machine, a few pairs pants, we shall work in peace [original in English—I. K.]." Piecework, see [original in English—I. K.]? Clever I am to talk to kings and remember the union.

That is what I should like to say. Molly stands in the back, weeping her eyes out, watching from behind the door, ashamed to admit the mistake she's made. Against my children I will not stand. But against that woman I set my heart all my days.

*

Friday, January 15—Uncle's diary is strange. I must glaze my eyes past Kolokoy's remarks to concentrate on Uncle's writing. If only I could have translated the books myself.

4 August 1953

A letter from Molly. Joe says they want to meet, her and her lawyer, I should make a settlement on her. I don't have time. If she wants to come back, come, otherwise I'm busy. She doesn't know now's the busy season by ladies' garments?

15 August 1953

Evil woman, I don't want you. I never loved you. I don't miss you. All these years I wanted to leave but didn't because of the children. I'm glad you're gone. You have freed me, the only good you ever did. If you knew how happy I am you'd come back. You were my heartburn.

9 September 1953

It didn't hurt me. Not one bit.

Saturday—I am like a woman with a limited supply of bread. I mustn't gobble. Go slow. I recognize oddness in what Uncle wrote. Also vision (albeit skewed).

16 September 1953

I, a fatherless child, am now a childless father. When I no longer needed a father, he came running. Who needs him, I thought. I was too nervous for his constant yelling. He didn't know. He wasn't really angry, he just had a loud voice.

I have tried to see my children. I told the lawyer, "About that Molly, if I shouldn't see her the rest of my life it would be too soon. Though if she wants to come back, I wouldn't let her stand crying her eyes out. We had no dispute, we never fought. She never said anything was wrong or that she was unhappy. I gave her whatever she wanted. All of a sudden I come home, she's gone.

Let her keep the *dreck* [you should excuse the expression, crap—
I. K.]. The children I must see."

The lawyer's eyes dripped from compassion. He said, "Mr. Segul, I'll do what I can. What more can I do?"

We met by the judge. Molly was there, her lawyer, my lawyer,
Joe, Pesha. The children refuse to see me. I want to say, the hell
with them, but should I chop off my arm because of a hangnail?

Children, God willing someday you read this. I didn't abandon
you. I put up a fight. Don't blame yourselves. I know who put you
up to this. I hold no grudge against you. I want only you should
know I love you. In my old age you will come. I'll be in the cafeteria. You will beg my forgiveness. I will bless you. You will take
me home to live with you.

Why else did my father pick on me but from too much love? He
had such hopes, naturally I was a disappointment. It wasn't his
fault. He expected me to know. In Uzlan I'd take a twig, measure
it the length of my pinky, set it between my fingers to make a
sundial. "Look how he tells time, the *greener* [greenhorn, a re-
cently arrived immigrant; said in a derogatory manner by immi-
grants who hadn't been in the U.S. much longer—I. K.]. Look at
him, Moisha Pupik, the dummy." He meant it affectionately. I was
too sensitive. "So, Moisha Pupik, what time is it?" he'd ask, and
I'd sulk.

After all, didn't he send money to Russia for a guide to bring
me, my mother, Yossel, and Menya to America? The whole town
left with the guide the Uzlan Society fathers paid for, but Zayda
[Grandfather—I. K.] was too old. His widowed sisters, the *tantas*
[aunts—I. K.], came to take care of him. I stared out the train at
Zayda waving till I couldn't see. My darling little grandfather, what
happened to you? There was war. Uzlan vanished, a dream.

Papa would tell strangers, "My son, he thinks he's an artist. He
thinks he's a writer. He can't make a living, my genius."

Why, Papa, didn't you talk to me? You're dead a long time but
look at the respect I give you. Even now, I address you, not "him,"
not "the imbecile." Why give a corpse such respect? You can't
answer. Should I say to people about you, no, not you—him. See

120

how it feels to be a him? I'll tell the world now how you, *he* would take off his belt, snap it before Menya, a little girl with big eyes. "I'm going to give you a good licking." She hadn't done anything. He was teasing her. He never hit her. Why did you do this? It disgusted me to see that small girl standing fascinated by a strap. You snapped your belt. You smiled. She was hypnotized.

Corpse, your mouth is sewn shut. You can't speak.

Papa, I'm sorry. I didn't mean to call you a corpse. I think of you and my legs tremble. I see you standing above me. Abraham, you had the right to sacrifice me. You stood over me, the knife in your hand. Tall, dignified, your flowing hair. I see you with your walking stick, leading the sheep. Father, forgive me. It's just I wanted your respect. I stammered in your presence. Oh, if only you had not expected so much of me.

No, you're right, Papa. I see your disgust, though your lips are sewn. It's my fault. I was too sensitive for a father like you.

Maybe I should go outside the school where my children are? I don't know where is this village they moved to. Why must she move to a *shtetl* [small Jewish town in East Europe—I. K.]? The ignorant woman, she only wants to live in the past. Remember this, remember that, weeping for the ones we left. It's gone, forget it. We have to move forward, to be modern. My children should be modern but she makes them peasants. Soon she'll teach Estelle to spin.

Tuesday, January 19—Uzlan. For years I heard my father and uncle say Illusion was the name of the town they came from. It seemed the perfect name for a place that no longer exists. Thatched roofs, dirt floors, paper windows made translucent with animal fat.

Old people come from the same vanished village. Miss Tweety's Nova Scotia is my father's Belorussia. I'm not yet 40 but already search my memory for words to explain the Brooklyn of childhood. I tell an invisible audience, "There was a candy store," and recall the horse-drawn carts of the knife sharpener, the junk collector. My mother as a girl would play above the hearth. It was cozy there, warm by the fire. She made it warm in her telling, turning hands into baby fists, hugging them to her with a shiver.

For my mother the time of hearths was the time of war. All wars blended into one. "We were children and the war was going on." "Which war?" Shrug. Russian, Polish, German soldiers marching one way, then the other. Soldiers everywhere. My mother danced for them. She was a little girl. They gave her chocolate. They must have been Germans. She told me once that the German soldiers liked Jews because they could communicate in Yiddish and German. It must have been World War I. In this way I piece together my parents' and uncle's stories with what little I know of history. A spy linking clues, I try to determine the course of events. I see my mother dance, too young to be afraid — nothing evil ever occurred in that magic land of war . . . that she told me. Older girls were hidden in cellars, but my mother danced for chocolate. Look what happens to little girls in Brooklyn cellars. No Germans misused a little Jew? So much for what I know.

After dinner my uncle and parents would seem to rest their heads together like pigeons, cooing about their Illusion. I miss them, so I invent them. They described Illusion in a few poorly translated words. I paint the scene with my artist's brush.

Parents, Uncle, Aunt Sadie, Aunt Rose, Meshuggina Sophie Herring — what do I know about any of them? Sophie married the man who raped her. Was she always meshugga [crazy— I. K.; ha-ha — G. S.]? Uncle roamed the streets talking to himself. Did he really hear angels? Aunt Sadie was a garment worker. Aunt Rose, a baker's helper. My parents bickered for more than 50 years, then went down to death still fighting. (Momma: "I told you this was a stupid idea, to take a boat, now we're dead." Daddy: "Shah, can't a man get some peace when he's drowning?")

Nostalgia is cheap. When they were alive I hated to visit. They picked on me, nagged. My aunts wrapped their love around me, strangling me in its vines. I hated seeing Uncle in the old-

122

age home. I never knew whether he recognized me — not some strange girl but me, Gabby Louise Segul, his niece who needed, who needs, to learn how an invisible artist can live.

Can't Kolokoy see this book is my passport into Illusion?

1 October 1953

I wish I were a bird.
I would fly away [original in English — I. K.].

Thurs. — How can I. K. not find the story of an abandoned man moving? Uncle writes of leaving his home forever. At the train station, moaning fills his ears with premonition. His grandfather shivers, waving a blue-and-white arm long past the time it can be seen. The boy pushes his head and chest out the train window, waving back. The boy who is no one's uncle knows he will never see his grandfather again. Nor the mud streets, nor the houses made of sticks. He will wander forever.

Writing in his diary, he sticks his head out the window and thinks he can still see his grandfather gazing after him. His grandfather has been dead the lifespan of a man. The boy who wept to leave him is dead now too. Yet the tears he shed mark the page, smearing the spider scrawl of his writing. They must have run down his cheeks as he remembered. I touch the traces of a dead old man weeping for another. I bear witness to my uncle's salt.

Did I. K. not notice where the water ran?

Fri. — Max came into the TV department while I was alone. He cleared his throat as if he wanted to talk. I ran past him. That's all I need, someone to discover us conspiring. They already think I'm a spy.

Jan. 23 — It's 5:30. The sun went down an hour ago. It reminded me of the sunsets I used to see from Uncle's window in the nursing home: parachute jump in the foreground of a Fauvist sky. When the sun went down Uncle's roommate would crow. He'd stand at the window, fill his chest with air, flap his arms, and caw till a nurse put him to bed. "All that noise," Uncle told me, "and he still can't lay an egg."

I dreamt last night that a narrator was telling how Uncle once received a letter. It described his grandmother ridding his grandfather of the habit of studying the Cabala. She was sick, but he was always off in the woods, studying. So one night she lifted herself from her deathbed, got on their skinny horse, and rode to where he muttered to himself the numerical equivalents of biblical words. Her plan was to terrify him into thinking he'd seen a ghost. She was successful, because "after that he didn't study the Cabala anymore."

The odd thing was that all along, as I heard the narrator speaking and saw my uncle reading the letter, I also saw my great-grandmother and great-grandfather acting out their drama. I saw her white skin and hollow eye sockets. Her face and the horse's face were like twin heads of death. And when the old man, Uncle's grandfather, screamed, I in my dream screamed too. I was both the narrator of the story and my own ancestor.

October 3, 1953

The woman was crazy. She'd make me a soup from shoelaces. Buttons and thread. Such a cook you shouldn't know. You couldn't drink her soup, a crazy soup. I asked, "Molly, what is this floating here?" and she said, "The bellybutton from a cat." If she admitted to that, what else did she put in?

Now I go to the cafeteria, take coffee, pudding, whatever I want. The Garden Cafeteria is full of intellectuals. Personally I don't much enjoy the company of people. They waste your time with "Pass the sugar, give me the salt." When they sit down I get up.

I like to be alone, to make notes to enter in this book later. But I can't keep track of the little pieces of paper. How many thoughts have I left on a napkin in the cafeteria! People wait till I leave, then run over — to clean up supposedly, but really to capture my thoughts, like birds, before they fly away.

When I am sitting in the cafeteria, sometimes an angel comes

124

in. Like today for instance. Angels love to make a surprise. He stands behind me, I shouldn't see him. I hear him, the angel of the wheel. I hear his motor running.

At work when I sew, the machine talks a mile a minute. "Shah," I say sometimes, putting my hands over my ears. "Can't you be quiet a minute so a man can think?"

When I'm in the cafeteria the angel pulls me to the ground and tickles me. He thinks it funny. Who can understand an angel's sense of humor? People can't see the angel going "Cootchy-cootchy-coo." Sometimes I play a game back. I make myself rigid, try to scare the angel into thinking he's killed me.

Today, when the angel tickled me, I refused to laugh. The angel figures this is no fun. He goes away. I open my eyes, I am on the floor. Everyone is standing over me, pointing, whispering, making a commotion. "You okay, mister?"

"Sure." I stand up, brush my clothes. "I slipped on the grease over there. You should wash the floor. A man could get killed." From grease they know. From lawsuits they know. Right away the man comes out with a mop and washes the floor. I left laughing.

Sun. — Though Uncle hallucinated, occasionally his delusions revealed a core of sense. For instance, in the nursing home he kept saying "they" were locking up his water. "G-g-go!" he said, insisting I was in danger. He forced me to put my ear to his mouth so he could whisper in it. When I didn't bend close enough, he pulled his emaciated body up, rising half out of his seat. There was something repulsive about the scrawny snakes of his neck, his wormlike struggle to put his mouth to my ear. I bent closer, an accomplice to his madness. There was no doubt he was mad. I was afraid. He was capable of anything, his mouth full of spit. He put his arms around my neck to pull me closer, keep me there. His breath stank. "The st-st-steam . . . lock up water . . . can't t-t-talk here. G-g-g-go, get help. Call . . . outside."

I looked at him. His eyes were clouded, an overcast sky through which I tried to detect a glimpse of blue reason. Again he forced me to give him my ear. "Steam locked. Can't breathe. Steal water. Body needs water to *breathe*. Shhh. Call police. Not here."

I tried to distract him. Asked about the sweatshop he'd worked in. "Talk later. Save yourself. Demons . . . kidnap you." I tried to interest him in the astronomy calendar I'd brought, the chocolate. He shook his head at my madness. Didn't I have ears? He was trying to save my life and all I could talk about was stars and candy?

I reasoned with him: "Uncle, I want to be with you. I came a long way. Don't send me off." Every Friday I had to leave work early to go there, it was such a long subway and bus ride. At night when I left, the neighborhood was scary. I used to fantasize being murdered — would he notice I was gone? So I was touched as well as distressed by his concern.

He stamped his foot. "The body needs water . . . to breathe." He pointed to his nose. "They lock up the water. Shhh, go outside."

"Uncle, later, after we talk."

Frustrated at not getting through to me, he shook his head and screwed up his lips, like someone who has stubbed a toe but refuses to cry out. Again he forced my ear to his mouth.

"Call p-p-police. G-g-go . . . before they lock you up. Too late for me. You must escape. Get help."

I tried not to cry. I didn't want to upset him more than he was. "Uncle." I knelt at his knees, as if we were posing for a scene in a religious calendar. "Please don't send me away. I came from far off to be with you. Uncle, stop acting this way."

I could see he was touched, but he wouldn't stop this silly game or fantasy or whatever it was. His eyes were misty, as if he were crying too, inside. That someone, at the end of his life, should weep over him was more than he had ever expected. He, a man who had not had the power to make his wife and children love him, had the power to make a woman cry. It was a revelation. Or it might have been cataracts I saw, the film of old eyes. I don't know what he thought as he looked down at me, weeping. He put his hand to my head as if to bless me, then placed his finger on his mouth. "Shhh," he said. His head shook. "Go!" He pointed at the door.

Strange, overplayed, these were movie gestures for an old man's rage. I even remember it in sepia, as if I'd entered his silent picture. But my tears were real. I remember the way his hand moved. He was holding himself back from hitting me, that I was so thickheaded when he was trying to save my life.

"Go into the hall," he finally said. "Better there."

I asked him to come with me. He said he wasn't allowed. So I went alone and got the nurse. "My uncle is acting so strange."

She laughed. "Mr. Segul acts that way. We changed his pills. The Dilantin was making him walk tilted." She went into his room. I followed her, worrying. "So, Mr. Moisha, what's the matter with you? Talk nice to your niece."

He looked at me as if I'd revealed I was a spy. The nurse was from India, a cheerful woman with a pleasant, laughing accent. What could he make of her? He didn't answer. He had a funny smile, as if he knew she was a demon playing with him and he was smarter than she. Finally he said, "Go away. I won't talk."

"Come on now, Mr. Moisha. You know me. We friends, right?"

He said nothing, then: "Everybody has to die, right?"

"That's right," she said in a gay voice. "Everybody die. Old people. Young people. You. Me. All die. It's OK."

He smiled. "Someday you too?"

"That's right," she began to sing again. "You, me, every—"

He interrupted her. "Tell me just one thing, then. What do you do with all the bodies?"

At the time I didn't realize what Uncle was talking about. It was the heat coming up, it must have been that — locked-up water, inability to breathe. He needed a humidifier. After the nurse left, he continued telling me to escape, insisting that he wasn't allowed into the hall. I had to prove that he was. I refused to go unless he walked me to the elevator. Finally he agreed but still wouldn't put on his shoes. Probably his feet were swollen from not taking his diuretic. He pushed me out as though he was so busy saving me he couldn't be bothered with them.

We were walking to the elevator, me trying to prove he could go out of his room whenever he wanted, him trying to save me from whatever was after him. A big scowling nurse with strong arms came up behind us. *"Mister Moisha!"* she yelled, making us both jump. *"Where* are your shoes?" I tried to explain, but she wouldn't listen to me. Or Uncle, of course. She made him go back to his room. As he turned, he looked at me as if to say, "I told you so."

October 4, 1953

I have been wondering why there are so many stars. Maybe God likes to impress us, but a few stars should be enough. I figured out today God made all the stars so we have a place to go when we die. Think how many people have died, animals too, and bugs *vay iz mir* [woe is me — I. K.], a whole planet for cockroaches.

"Why, I ask myself, should the shining dots of the sky not be as accessible as the black dots on the map of France? If we take the train to get to Tarascon or Rouen, we take death to reach a star. . . . While we are alive we cannot get to a star, any more than when we are dead we can take the train. So it seems to me possible that cholera, gravel, phthisis, and cancer are the celestial means of locomotion, just as steamboats, omnibuses, and railways are the terrestrial means." — Vincent Van Gogh, Arles, France

Mon. — Received a second notice from the library saying I've not returned some books that I returned. After work I went, found the missing books on the shelves. When I brought them to the librarian, I said I wanted something in writing proving the books had been returned. She refused, told me to resubmit my application for a new card. I've decided not to return the volume of Van Gogh letters till it comes.

7 October 1953

I was sitting in the cafeteria, two men were talking about glaciers. I've always thought of glaciers as floating ghosts. Cold, dead, yet why shouldn't they be put to use? So I turn to the fat man with the cigar and say, "I hope you don't mind, mister. I hear you talking about glaciers. Why is it you can't take the cold from a glacier and use it in my shop in the summer?"

They stare. Then the man with the red hair starts to smile. "You could take the heat out of an icebox, it should stay cold in there longer, and warm your house with it. You see? And meanwhile the icebox would stay cold, I say."

The red-haired demon guffaws in my face, wetting me from spit. "Da-da-da-da," says one. "Peh-peh-peh-peh," says the other.

I get so mad I start to choke. You see how they mock me? Because I stutter. In Russia I had no stutter. It happened when I came here, under the influence of learning so many languages. I would forget what language I was speaking. My father would yell. He didn't mean it. He was loud and to a child's ears he was forever angry. At Mama he'd yell, "What is the matter with the idiot?" It was only natural for a boy to defend his mother, so I'd say, "Papa, please. Yell at me, not her." Only the words wouldn't come out. I would stand before my father, going "Papapapapa" until I was sick from disgust and would faint.

I am named for Moses, who was himself a stutterer. When Moses was a little boy playing with his toys in the pharaoh's kitchen, the pharaoh decided to test him to make sure he wasn't after his crown. They put beside him a pile of burning coals that glowed like gold, next to it they put the pharaoh's crown. An executioner was standing by with a kitchen knife to murder the baby if he reached for the crown. The pharaoh's daughter had taken a shine to little Moses, he was cute as a button, so they knew they had to kill him fast before she got a chance to make a fuss.

Moses was no imbecile. Naturally he reached for the crown, but an angel forced him to pick up the burning coal. What does a child know? Moishalah popped the coal into his mouth. And so he was a stutterer all his life, though chosen by God.

Tues. — Van Gogh writes to his brother that he is shunned because of poor clothes but poverty frees him to sink down in a field. I see Uncle's muddy pants. V. G.: "The other with his dream air, somewhat absent-minded, almost somnambulist— that is the weaver." I remember Uncle's seizures, when he would sew invisible thread to invisible cloth. They had epilepsy in common, as well as art, the lack of recognition, even the relationship between brothers — the older brother becoming the artist/dreamer looked after by the younger and his wife. I long to tell Uncle not to mind those who mock him. I long to tell V. G. not to listen to critics who dismiss his art.

Easy to tell the dead how to live.

9 October 1953

I don't think it would be so bad to be electrocuted like the Rosenbergs. Once I went to plug in a lamp. I put my finger in the receptacle [he must mean "outlet," but he writes "receptacle" in English — I. K.]. The electricity flooded me in waves of jerking like a fish. That's when I noticed that pain and pleasure are the same. Sometimes, sitting on the bench in the park, I pass out from pleasure. People are jealous. They stare.

Wednesday — Suzy's sighs blow me around the office. I started to ask her today what's wrong when Liz walked in. I couldn't talk to Suzy about her father and my uncle's death with Liz there.

16 October 1953

I am in the cafeteria, writing in this book, I should remember what I write instead of leaving my thoughts on napkins. All around, men ball up napkins to wipe the sour taste off their lips. It comes from self-consciousness and the smell of fish. You could die from the smell of fish. Wherever I look I see fish. Mouths open to chew soles like leather. Leather soles [original in English — I. K.].

Everyone is looking at me. I look like a nobody but I write in a book. Everyone wants to know a writer, to ask questions. What do they ask? "Mister, I see you are a writer. Tell me, do you use a pencil or a pen?"

The most amazing thing just happened. I was sitting here in this cafeteria, minding my own business, thinking about the meaning of life and how a soul can become a fish. Sole fish [original in English — I. K.]. Because my name is Segul and I thought how close that is to *gilgul* [a superstitious folk belief among uneducated Jews that the soul can be reincarnated to make up for crimes in a past life — I. K.]. Today being Friday, I wondered if any of the fish eaten in the cafeteria are reincarnated souls. Soles. [English. He does beat this pun into the ground. Maybe you can edit it out of the final version of the manuscript — I. K.] Because if you come back as a fish and get eaten on Shabbes [Sabbath begins on Friday night — I. K.], you skip some steps on the ladder of souls. [Maybe you should delete this entry before publishing the manuscript, particularly when you see what follows. You wouldn't want people to think Jews believe this sort of thing — I. K.]

I am sitting at a table, thinking, when the angel of the wheels comes up behind me. I hear his whirr and hold myself rigid, I shouldn't laugh. I don't want to encourage him.

Instead, a big Negro sits at the table. "Moishalah," he says. "I have a message for you from *Tanta* [Aunt — I. K.]. Because you are a wise man, you will know what to make of it."

He tells me a tale. I write in the back of this book. After, I ask which *tanta* sent it. He smiles, doesn't answer. "All my aunts are dead," I say. "Murdered in Europe. Surely in heaven they know what's happened to us Jews." Maybe I offended him. Suddenly he gets up, walks into the men's room in the back of the cafeteria.

I watch. He doesn't come out. I worry maybe the angel doesn't know how to flush the toilet, maybe he got locked in (the doorknob is loose, I've gotten locked in there myself a few times). I go to find him. Besides, I want to ask what the story means, to discuss it with an intelligent angel. Also, I can't help it, I'm curious to see an angel at a urinal.

He's gone. In the sink is a piece of fish, a bite like a person might spit. I'm sure that has something to do with the angel's visit and all the reincarnated souls in the Garden Cafeteria, so I decide to do the *gilgul* a favor. I ate it.

I am not a religious man, the angel knows that, but I mean well.

Why should the fish suffer because the person who was to eat him got something stuck in his teeth? I am not without sin. Someday I too may come back a piece of fish and perhaps you will do a like favor for me. [Never — I. K.]

THE JEW IN THE THORN BUSH

There was once a peasant who did an old man a good deed. What kind of good deed? Who knows? He gave him a crust of bread, a sip of schnapps. Even a smile was worth more in those days. Anyway, in return the old man gave him a fiddle, and this was not just any fiddle but a magic fiddle. People hearing the fiddle would dance, and they would not be able to stop dancing till the fiddler ceased to play. The peasant thanked the old man and went on his way.

This peasant was the youngest of seven sons, and he was very poor. So he decided to use his fiddle to make his way in the world. He took leave of his family and went to seek his fortune.

Now, magic can be used for good or evil. This is a tale of how it came to be used for evil. What's wrong, you ask, with a young man seeking to make a living by getting people to dance? Should a fiddler not live off his music? Does a baker not live off his bread? But if you'd just listen a minute, you'd hear.

This was a greedy peasant, poor all his life. People who suffer from poverty in childhood never get enough to eat, no matter if all the bakers in the world baked white rolls only for them. He made a good living from his fiddle, after all. He played at weddings, in taverns, everywhere people danced. But he wanted more. He wanted to get all the money he could from the richest people.

And who did he think was rich? The priest, fat as a goose? The white-tunicked lord with his rings? No, it was the Jew who had all the money. He saw the Jew in his long coat and hat, huddled with his family by a poor fire, saying a blessing over a meal of potatoes and bread, and he said to himself, "Look, everyone knows the Jews are rich. They must have lots of gold, since they never spend any, even to give themselves a decent meal and warm fire." He decided to rob the Jew.

132

He waited by a thorn bush for the Jew to happen by. And, ill luck being what it is, a Jew came into the woods. *"Boychik* [young man — I. K.]," called the peasant, mimicking a Jew's voice. "Come give a hand. I'm stuck in this thorn bush and I can't get out."

"Let me help you, *tatela* [little father — I. K.]."

"Come a little deeper into the bush," said the peasant. And so he managed to convince the Jew to make his way into the middle of the sticky thorn bush, looking to give a hand. Then the peasant picked up his fiddle and began to play.

The Jew couldn't help but dance to the evil tune. As he danced, his clothes were ripped, his skin was torn, and he cried for the peasant to stop playing before he bled to death.

"You've been bleeding me my whole life," yelled the peasant. "Throw me all your money and I'll stop."

"Please, I don't have but a few coins," and the Jew threw them out of the bush. But the peasant, even to pick up the money, didn't rest. It wasn't enough. He knew the Jew had more, and he played and he played, till the Jew stopped begging for mercy. Even then he played some more and made the dead body dance. Finally he stopped, and he spread open the bush to see what had become of the Jew.

In the center of the bush was a young man, naked but for a rag hung in tatters around his loins. Blood poured out of his wounds. And as he lay there, the bush reached out a sticky arm and crowned him with a branch of thorns.

The peasant screamed and ran from the majesty of a dead king. He took his fiddle, and, smashing it to bits, he heard a voice that said, "Fiddler, fiddle thee to hell."

Well, this could be a story with, maybe not a happy ending, but a happier one, no? The fiddler, after all, was terrified, and he could be sorry for what he had done to the Jew. He could have repented and he would have been forgiven, and this would still be a sad story but at least the peasant would have learned a thing or two. But, I'm sorry, that's not how it happened.

The fiddler began to wander from town to town. As he wandered he began to think. And what did he think but that the Jews had tricked him into killing his own. So from town to town he went, and everywhere he told his tale of what the Jews had done to him. Everywhere he played this evil tune, though his magic fiddle was gone, and everywhere he made the people dance. They could not keep from dancing to his evil fiddling about the Jews.

For truly the man in the thorn bush was his brother, as are all men. As the Talmud says, "Whoever destroys a single life is as guilty as though he destroyed the entire world; and whoever rescues a single life earns as much merit as though he had rescued the entire world" [*Sanhedrin* 37a — I. K.]. But the peasant never realized that, so he fiddled his way to hell, and many dancers followed.

But what of the Jews murdered? you ask. What can I say? I like to think the thorn bush has become a throne and the innocent are dancing now before it, that the evil tune the fiddler played has miraculously turned to good.

[This is an answer? What is this, did your uncle go out of his way to offend? Not only is the story stolen from Grimm, but it is objectionable to Jews everywhere, the way he mixes Christian imagery with Jewish ideas, Talmudic quotes with allusions to the false messiah. If you publish this, you do all Jews a great wrong — I. K.]

✦ ✦ ✦

Thurs. — I can't stand I. K.'s snide notes," Lara Jacob started to read. She pushed Gabby's diary away. If only she had Moisha's original diary. What had happened to it? Why couldn't Gabby have found another Yiddish translator? Had she tried?

Lara took out her own diary and started to write of her frustrations. Then the humor of the situation hit her. Like a mirror reflecting a mirror, here she was, responding to entries in Gabby's diary that were in turn responses to entries in her uncle's. She smiled, wondering if there were a way to incorporate this absurdity into the biography. James would appreciate it, she thought, dialing his number.

"I'm working," he said, when he finally picked up.

Something inside Lara closed against him. "Sorry," she said. "Some other time." She started to hang up but he stopped her.

"You might at least tell me what you want, since you've interrupted me." He waited as she contemplated slamming the receiver down.

Instead she said, "I just wanted to know what you think of me adding notes regarding my own responses to Gabby's entries."

"Self-indulgent," he said. "You want participation, to be included, but this is Gabby's life. Let her have it. No one cares about you." He paused. "Look," he said. "I don't mean that the way it sounded. I'm sure you can work this out alone. Particularly since you won't even let me see Gabby's diary."

After hanging up, Lara swore she would never call James again. She'd no sooner thought this than the desire to be with him gripped her so hard it was like being squeezed by an incubus.

◆　◆　◆

Thurs. — I can't stand I. K.'s snide notes to me in between Uncle's sentences. He accuses Uncle of plagiarism. Hard to believe an educated man can be so stupid he can't tell the difference between a response to and an imitation of an anti-Semitic fairy tale. The Grimms' story is about a clever peasant who outwits a rich, greedy Jew. Uncle's story is about the subliminal eroticism inherent in Christian anti-Semitism and art, what it means to venerate an icon of torture. According to the fiddler, it is the Jews who have murdered another Jew, not the soldiers who drove the nails in or the artists who carved him from wood and hung him from rafters. I. K. doesn't see any of this. He is put off by the Christian allusions in the story. "It's all mixed up with Jewish ideas." A story, like any creative work, has to be true to itself.

Dear STARS,
Please be kind and send my letter to the manager of Archie Bunker. Why he call that is suppose to be Sally's husband meathead and polacks? If he hates the Polish people so much why is he on TV with that big cigar tell him there are plenty dog cigars on my lawn tell him to pick them up and dry them he can chew them instead of calling Polacks on the air. We are fed up on his

ugly bald head. Tell him to pick oats out of horseshit to pass time. Be sure his bosses get this letter.

Fed Up,
TV Listeners

26 October 1953

I have hung up my drawings all over the apartment. My pictures are worth a million dollars. I don't want Molly to get a nickel.

Jan. 29 — Van Gogh's "Night Café." Uncle's cafeterias. Uncle must have done paintings of the Garden, Dubrow's, Garfield's. My parents would have thrown them out, with everything else that mattered.

6 November 1953

I have decided to send my story about the Jew in the thorn bush to the *Forward,* they should publish it. [Ha! — I. K.] It would upset Molly no end, if I should become a famous writer.

7 November 1953

I wish, I wish, I wish I were a fish. [This masterpiece is in English — I. K.]

Sat. — I. K.'s handwriting is difficult to read. Small and European, hard on the eyes. It bothers me to think of him copying Uncle's strange nonsense rhymes in his elegant hand.

28 November 1953

I want you to know. It didn't hurt me, not one bit. I wrote to Molly, "Wife, it didn't hurt me. Not one bit. I want you to know."

Sunday — I. K. is jealous. Knowing this, perhaps I can cultivate a shoot of tenderness toward him? He's an old man. He needs the money. I pity him. Perhaps I can ask him to translate the

No, the ploy won't work. What he said to me, how mean his

136

face grew when he tightened his lips to call Uncle crazy! His eyes, gelatinous cold eyes reading Uncle's intimate revelations.

What am I going to do? Book after book stands guard over his thoughts. Their eyes stare, waiting to be emptied of meaning.

3 December 1953

I laugh at Molly. She took whatever gives me pleasure, but she didn't take the one thing I cherish above all. It's in a cigar box— a handkerchief folded neat. On it, my mother's smell from her soap, not fancy but plain. When I am sad I take it out, put it to my nose. I smell her.

By not using it for every little sadness, I have made it last 20 years. I hold it to my face, I close my eyes, I see her as clearly as if she were standing by the sink. At night I dream of her. She is about to turn around. Papa says, "Look at him, the idiot," but Mama doesn't mind. She is scrubbing a pot. I call. We haven't seen each other so long. Always I wake before she turns around. Someday I will meet her eyes. On that day I die.

Monday — Work is getting strange. Whispering in halls, sudden silences. Something's going on.

Happy told Liz today how her mother always referred to her father as "him." "Look at him. What does *he* want?" Liz thought this odd, but it reminded me of Uncle. What must it do to a man to be talked to in the third person his whole life? Uncle's father used to do it, my parents too. Even in death; I. K. talks to me between Uncle's sentences. Was there something about Uncle that made people treat him this way? (Was the question mark originally an ear?)

At the table with my parents and Uncle: Mother says, "He fell and cracked his head open. The trouble we have from him. Every day it's something. See the stitches?" She holds his skull to her stomach like a melon and points till Uncle pulls away.

Father says, "He doesn't pay attention where he walks. He's in a different world half the time."

Mother confronts Uncle. "Why don't you look where you're

going?" Uncle has not been listening so this sudden demand makes an alarming non sequitur. We're all staring at him. He decides to make the most of it, his opportunity to tell us about the buses. My mother sighs impatiently, as if she had expected an answer. She interrupts: "How's the chicken? Good? Then eat, eat. Here's ketchup." Sotto voce to me: "Disgusting, his manners. It makes a person sick, how he eats."

It's true. Pieces of skin hang from his hands and spray out of his mouth as he speaks. A bubble of fat sits on his cheek, bobbing up and down with his stutter. "The b-b-b-buses—"

"Shah, Moisha, eat now, talk later. Wipe your face."

Uncle would do as he was told but continue speaking. He'd get on a topic for the night — buses, stars, songs — and drive us away with his revolting habits and stuttering stories that just went on and on. He'd speak till we interrupted him, wait till we were through, then continue as if we'd never said a word.

My mother's table manners were hardly fine enough to warrant her disgust. In Europe she had been starving, so here she ate like a peasant. She gobbled potatoes, used her hands, reached across the table for the bread. She spoke with her mouth full, spitting food. Uncle's manners were bad, but he didn't eat greedily. Food was less important to him than words. He couldn't be bothered swallowing before speaking, so he sputtered his food till my mother pointedly handed him a napkin. My mother, on the other hand, couldn't wait to eat before talking. In the middle of an anecdote, she'd shove vegetables in her mouth, revealing mashed peas as she laughed.

Only my father had manners. How elegantly his long hands cut his meat. He swallowed his food before speaking. But when his dentures bothered him, he had the habit of spitting chewed-up meat onto his plate.

I read during meals.

I remember Uncle sitting at the table. He'd get caught in a dream and I'd watch him ascend. Sitting so quietly. That sad, cloudy look in his eye — far away, sorrowful. I'd want to gather him in, the skinny bag of bones, hug him, tell him I loved him even if his children didn't. Instead I'd look away. It seemed an invasion of his privacy to watch him then, his face so naked. Wondering, wandering, none of us knowing where he'd gone in his dreams . . .

My parents talked to me in the third person too. "She got her report card today." "How did she do?" "She did well." "She always does well." "She gives us no trouble." "Never any trouble from her." Then they'd look at me, nodding like birds.

One time my mother said to my father, "She got her period today." It was my menarche. My father was cutting his steak. The blood ran into his string beans. I saw his disgust, he couldn't bear the juice of his meat to flow and mix on his plate. I too hate it when the blood pinkens my potato.

He turned to me, raised his eyebrows. He was chewing, then he swallowed. I watched his Adam's apple bob, and my stomach turned around and around like a trick dolphin. I knew his look to be a compliment, a tip of the male hat. Nonetheless I fled the room.

"Why does she run away?" I heard him ask. "From a father she doesn't have to run."

And my mother said, "She's meshugga from shyness."

Tues. — Tessa refused to do Liz's proofreading today. She walked out, didn't come back for two hours. Liz is talking about firing her. People conspire in corners. What's going on?

3 January 1954

I am thinking all day of the root of a man planted in the soil of a woman. At night I go to Coney Island. My secret grows hard.

Men beside me sew, mumbling under their breath. I see them move their lips, telling lies to invisible lovers. I listen carefully to what men whisper to their liliths [female demons, named after Adam's first wife, before Eve. The lilith seduces men into spilling their seed, you should excuse me. She uses the seed to make more demons. Another of your uncle's fairy tales — I. K.].

I am interested in what people say when they don't know angels hear. I used to listen to Molly talk in her sleep. It was more interesting than when she was awake. She used to fight with a man named Shmuel. "Shmuel, why?" "Shmuel, when?" "Shmuel, don't do this to me." Shmuel, Shmuel, a whole night. Sometimes I kicked her to wake her up from her dream so she'd stop talking and let me get some sleep. I have to get up early in the morning.

I listen to conversations in the cafeteria. Mostly they talk nothing, but sometimes interesting things come out. "I know where the treasure is buried. Meet me and I will tell you where to find the jade box."

I heard this last week in Garfield's. I kept my head down, they shouldn't know I heard. I didn't look directly at them. They left quickly, so maybe they figured out I knew. As they were leaving I studied them to follow on the street. To tell you the truth, I'm not good at people's faces. These two men were of medium build. They had brown hair, brown eyes, like everyone. Both wore fedoras, one carried a cane on his arm like a lady's pocketbook.

Yesterday I went to Dubrow's. It was crowded. A woman sat, trying to start a conversation with me till I lost my appetite. I decide to go to Coney Island. I go to the boardwalk and have a knish. I look at people on rides. The boys ride with girls who hold them tight. I watched them hugging on the roller coaster. All around people were coupled like this was Noah's ark and I was a unicorn, which is why the unicorn isn't around anymore. [The female unicorn supposedly hid from the male, so the male could not reproduce after the world was dry again. Your uncle is a living anthology of old wives' tales. *Boubameisas* we call them, literally grandmother stories, connoting nonsense — I. K.]

Sailors and girls everywhere. The wind was laughing, pushing them here, there. I noticed laughter made the wind laugh. What with them laughing at the wind and the wind laughing at them, I was blown around like a piece of toilet paper. At one point I had to grab hold of a gate with both hands so I shouldn't be blown into the sea. I started to laugh. Sailors saw me. They laughed too.

Then it died. The rides stopped. Everyone froze. I heard a sound.

Click-click-click. A woman in a yellow dress with dots came to where I stood. Slit up to the *pupik* [navel — I. K.], her dress was as tight as skin. She looked like a cat with spots.

"What you holding there, a fence? I got something better for you to hold." I saw the devil had the face of a girl with gold curls. Her skin was made from butter. An indescribable hunger took me. I wanted to lick the butter from her, to melt it with my lips, make it run down her neck and onto her breasts. Oh, it was wrong. But I was like a piece of rye bread stale for a pat of butter.

She took my hand, put it around her waist. "There, isn't that better to hold?" What could I do? I was under a spell. The way she walked, me holding her waist, her hips rocking up and down like waves, my hand was a tiny boat. [I am seasick from disgust. I don't think you should read the rest — I. K.]

"You want to take me in the Love Tunnel?" she asked.

A voice that wasn't mine answered. "I want to take you in your love tunnel." How did I dare say such a thing? She laughed, the filthy whore. [I'm sorry, but this is what he wrote — I. K.]

"Sure thing, honey, if you got the money [original in English— I. K.]." She was surprised at the rhyme. Me, I wasn't surprised. People often fall into poetry around me. I'm used to it. I took out my wallet. She plucked a bill. How long it had been since I was with a woman. Molly was colder than pickled herring.

She guided me to a dark hotel. Her room was decorated with black lace like a web. I thought, *I am with a spider,* but I wasn't scared.

"You want me to take off my clothes or you want to do it?" [Miss Segul, take my advice, don't read any further. You can see where this is going. This is not for a young lady's eyes. I myself wouldn't read any further if I didn't have to — I. K.]

I went up to her, unzipped her dress. I couldn't help but notice how poorly the zipper was put in. I am ashamed of the desire I had. Remembering her long legs as she walked in her underwear, even now a pregnancy grows inside me. The best thing is not to think of her. I thought writing I would feel better. Instead I am filled with longing. She told me her name. Lola? Lulu? I forget.

Because I wasn't thinking of her name as I watched her buttery breasts roll toward me, my tongue dry like toast.

After, when we were smeared with love, she told me I should look for her any time. Not like Molly, that fish, with her dead staring eyes, waiting for me to do my business.

I begged her to come home with me. "I'll give you all my money." She pushed me away, twisting her arms behind to put on her brassiere. She would not let me hook it.

She stood there in her underwear, her maiden hair reaching out to me. I was filled with lust. I didn't know what to say. She slipped on her leopard skin, ordered me to zip her up. "Let's get out of here. I don't have all night." She pushed me out the door, down the steps. "Go away. I got business."

I begged her not to. She laughed. "Moish, come back when you have the lettuce and I'll nibble it." She clicked down the street like a seagull going after garbage.

Time stopped. The angel of the wheels found me. "Look," it said. All I could see was Lolly naked. She had the legs of a chicken. "What does it mean?" I asked, and the angel said, "Listen." I heard *click-click-click*. There was Lolly. She spread herself wide. Instead of maiden hair was a spider.

I screamed, tried to run, but the angel held me in place, tickling me. I could not move. The spider grew bigger, hairier, wiggling its legs, opening its mouth, pushing out its tongue. The spider was bigger than my head. It was coming closer, so that I could no longer see Lolly naked on the bed, only the spider between her legs. The horrible spider opened its lips, sucked me in. I screamed but my scream was silent for the spider ate all sound as it gulped me. I was in a hole and had no sense of myself, like when you sleep and don't dream. I was in the belly of a spider. Why? I ask myself. I am no Jonah to be swallowed. Not once have I refused my mission. When the angel said look, I looked. When the angel said listen, I listened. If the angel should tell me to take up a bullhorn and prophesy to the people of Coney Island or East New York, even Brownsville, I'd do it. You only have to ask. "Brothers!" I'd call. "Comrades! Workers of the World! God is fed up with this nonsense. Better you should unite."

142

When the angel released me, I was on the sidewalk. My head hurt from where I fell. My pockets were empty.

I am infected with her. I love her. How can I explain such love? I want to save her, the whore. [Miss Segul, what can I say? I hope you are not reading this. I am ashamed to translate it, ashamed you should think this is what is on the minds of Jewish men. Please remember: I have stories from good people murdered by Nazis. They are much more suitable for publication than this, excuse the expression, *dreck* — I. K.]

Dear Pussy,
Just some Brief Questions. What do you mean by Getting It On? What turns You on? How do You turn a Man on? Is it True that a man's Penis is a woman's Best Friend? What size Penis do you love? If there is ever a chance for me to meet you in any Private Place, would you like to offer a Good Man like me a nice Piece of your Ass? Forgive me, Pussy Dearest. When I wrote this My Penis was Hard. My Penis is 6 and ¼ inches long, 5 inches thick. Is that enough? Please, Dear Pussy, answer these Questions if you can. Please show yourself in the Nude position in the next issue. Thank you very much. Answer in care of S. D. Clepper, Buffalo Home for the Aged and Infirm. He will pass it on to me since he's a friend of mine, though he's much older. (Don't worry, I won't tell him what it says so as not to spoil your reputation.)
P.S. My Penis is curcumcized. Is that OK?

Feb. 3 — In a state of astonishment, I read through half-shut lids. How can I explain? It feels as though I read with held breath. Uncle is so honest, revealing. Sometimes I can't bear to look at the crazy tightrope walker dangling over my head. Other times I watch amazed as he crosses the void. If he falls, I am ready to turn away. I refuse to see Uncle Icarus plunge.

I can't stand Kolokoy's notes. What to do?

7 February 1954

I saw Lolly in a store. When I looked again it was a dummy in a window wearing a spotted dress. I went to the cafeteria. Two men were talking. One says to the other, "Everyone knows the Communists are plotting to take over the world." The other says, "Yes. If that got out, it would destroy the union." Then their voices got low, I couldn't hear.

"What's going on?" I turn to ask. By then the plotters snuck out. They must have realized I heard them.

Sounds like a plot to do evil and blame it on the union.

Thurs. — Tessa was talking to Max in the stationery closet. When I walked by they grew quiet. I thought I heard Max say something like "but it won't affect you."

Dear "Soap Bubble,"
You got to do something. Lois is trying to kidnap Mary's baby. I'm the only one who knows. I called my mother but she was watching channel six. My sister's TV broke. Everybody knows Lois is crazy. Don't let this happen to poor Mary again.
Ann R. Livi

Fri. — People are writing wherever I look. There are shopping-bag people in trees, behind bushes, on benches, on steps, in crowds, alone and in groups. They are jotting notes. I saw a man today sprawled across a step, writing in his journal.

An old woman once came at me with a knife. She was tiny, carried a big pocketbook, and shouted at invisible beings. I walked behind her, eavesdropping on madness. Suddenly she turned, plunged a butcher knife down, raised it high above her head, plunged it down again. Her eyes shot fire at some transparent monster between us. My life flashed: *So this is how it ends.* I was extremely interested but my legs had the good sense to take me away.

I see her every so often. Once on the train she sat next to me. I didn't recognize her till she opened her bag, gave me a sidelong glance, giggling till voyeurism prompted me to peek. There, in the darkness of her leather womb, smiled the insane butcher knife.

This man today with his legs jutting across the sidewalk wore the shreds of an army uniform. He was surrounded by bulging duffel bags. Since he was tidier than most, I wondered if he was new to the streets. I have watched people drift into madness. They start out clean, their bags neatly tied. They seem organized. Then the packages rip, the clothes tear. They start to mumble and wear mud. They disappear, come back with shaved heads.

I wondered what he was writing, so instead of going around, I stepped over his long legs. He had a clear, legible hand. His notebook was like this one — an unlined art pad of standard book size. I couldn't make out a word.

13 March 1954

On Pitkin Avenue, the women walk their vaginas [excuse me, but that's what he writes — I. K.], hairy little dogs pitterpattering at the end of leashes. I walk my thoughts. I saw Irving from my shop. He's talking to Sam the plumber. Arguing. I figure maybe I can learn something. I go over to listen.

Socialists, Communists, Russia, Palestine — that's what people used to fight about. What are Sam and Irving fighting about? Toilets. Times have changed. At first I thought they were fighting about the worker and the landlord. Then I realized that Irving is the landlord and Sam is the worker. Sam is yelling because Irving didn't pay him for fixing his toilet. Irving yells, "The toilet doesn't work," and Sam yells, "Go stick your head in the toilet. It's full of shit," and Irving says, "Exactly, that's why I won't pay you a cent." And so on. I am not interested in such trivial matters. I have no time for it. I went to look for Lolly.

I take the train to Coney Island, walk down a street. I smell butter. Heels click in the alley. I run. Someone giggles inside a door. When I look, there's no one. The frame is dark, shaped like a coffin. Inside, nothing. I pull my hair.

Molly runs away. Lolly runs away. Solly runs away, and Estelle. I am the man from whom everyone runs. Why? I must be special, that I make everyone run. They run as Jonah from the angel. They run because they know I demand more from the world than toilets and tablecloths. People must join hands and work for the union. Brothers should live in peace.

Sat., Feb. 6 — Thinking about Rip Van Winkle. Who was he but a ne'er-do-well? His wife never had a bit of good from him, except the time he lay on her belly and gave her a daughter. He goes bowling in the mountains and gets so drunk he falls in a stupor for 20 years. Wakes up, rubs his eyes, heads back to town: lo, wife dead, no one knows the old nut, but his daughter has a good heart. Maybe he's her father, you never know. She remembers her father fondly, though he was always a layabout, even before he deserted the family. She takes him in.

Now he sits on her porch, drinks her beer, talks to the other bums. Everyone loves the gentle man with his dreamy eyes, his quaint tales of trolls. But what would his wife say if she was alive? He spends his old age as if he's earned it, while she who worked herself to the bone lies forgotten, without even her own name, let alone legend. The case of a man who has slipped his skin.

Was Uncle another? This story about visiting a prostitute— was it something like this that made his wife leave? Did he hallucinate during sex? Vagina dentata. His wife, his children must have their stories. On the other hand, why care? He never did me any harm. I'd rather drink beer with Rip, learning the ways of trolls.

The phenomenon interests me, how people slip their skins. Take my parents, for instance. They were the sweetest old people, yet my childhood was bitter. They loved the idea of me, a child to liven up their old age, but had no patience with the reality and tortured me subtly. I wanted to hold that against them, but they got old, they needed me. They changed the stories, and I acquiesced in revision. Scenes of forced submission — to the doctor's needle, the dentist's gas, the plumber's tool — became tales instead of their martyrdom to my childhood. I began to think, "So that's how it was."

It left me confused. Perhaps I was born with an innate sense of the sour. My parents were sweet, yet the vampires who pursue me in dreams yell, "Goilie, vere you running like a meshuggina?"

29 March 1954

I saw a man window-shopping on Pitkin Avenue with a Torah on his shoulder. At first I thought he must be a scribe delivering to a temple, but what kind of scribe wears no *yarmulke* [skullcap — I. K.] and stops to window-shop on his way with the holy scrolls?

He stood ten minutes in front of some coats, comparing prices, then he left. No one stopped him. No one noticed him except me.

Is this supposed to mean something? [You tell me — I. K.]

Sun. — Unusually warm out. I'm in the park, writing to keep the man next to me from starting a conversation. He asked me the time just as I looked at my watch, then said, "Psychic." A lonely old man, smiling at everyone. I don't want to talk to him.

He's taking an article from his jacket pocket, unfolding it in the theatrical way of someone alone. Wants me to read it. I won't be trapped into sticky conversation about his wife's death and do I want to read her obituary. Now he's leaving. Good.

Glad I wore headphones today. Not just to drown out unpleasant noises — people whistling martial tunes, truck farts— but as protection against meaningless conversations. Protection too from the Rooster Man, cock of the walk. Bobbing his head back and forth, defiantly taking his seat too close to me.

He takes his seat, he possesses it. It's his seat and whaddaya gonna do about it? Whaddaya gonna do if I put my arm across the bench and touch you? Who gonna believe you if I take your hand, close it round my loose rooster neck, make you pull the skin up and down till my wattles throb and my comb turns red?

I don't trust him. Headphones seem a chinked armor as he sizes me up. Keep scribbling, doesn't matter what. Pretend not to notice. Look at watch. Sigh. Act like you have someone to meet. Look around, as if to see where friends are. Check direction from which help may be petitioned. No one near. Damn.

Smile weakly, show yourself oblivious to the cock's threat. Foolish to stay. Make no eye contact, don't smile or frown. Walk slowly, purposefully, away.

Better here. More people, though reception's not as good. Headphone wires act as antennae. Position tangles around neck, waist, dangle wires through specklace strings. Feel strangled by my own ropes. Spider in a web of absurdity? More like it, fly.

7 May 1954

In Europe hidden saints went around dressed as beggars — we called them *tzaddiks* [holy men, wonder-rabbis: in reality a bunch of quacks living off stupid Jews like your uncle — I. K.] and *lamed vovniks* [36 anonymous men upon whose good deeds, supposedly, the world maintains its existence. Who needs a world where my Gittel perishes and fools like your uncle publish their ravings? — I. K.]. If a person did good to a saint, he might be rewarded with riches [like a trip to the shower? No one was kinder than my Gittel. A beggar couldn't walk in our town without her giving him the food from her mouth — I. K.].

I understand now I was wrong to try to make a profit from what the angel gave me. Such tales as are given by angels are not for publication in the *Forward*. They sent back the story about the Jew in the thorn bush today. You don't take the words of an angel and scatter them before living corpses.

Why was this story told me, if not for publication, and by an angel no less? He said *Tanta* [Aunt — I. K.] sent it. A *tanta* who sends angels as messengers is not a *tanta* who sends a nut cake on Rosh Hashanah [the Jewish New Year — I. K.].

I read again the story. It was about how magic was used for evil when it could have been used for good. Instead of realizing I had been given magic power — for what purpose I don't know — right away I send it off to be published.

The power to make people dance, such power I always had. When I play the mandolin, people leap from their seats to embrace and sway. I never realized it was more than having an ear for music. Tonight I hurried to the boardwalk. An old woman was singing a Russian tune it was lovely to hear, but she had a thin, scratchy voice. No one paid attention.

I took up a penny and began to tap. Everyone's ears perked up like dogs. They formed a circle around the woman. Her voice became rich, lively, she herself grew beautiful. The people began to sing. They clapped their hands in rhythm to my clicking. They stamped their feet. Someone ran into the center of the ring and danced a *kazatske* [Cossacks' dance — I. K.]. Everyone else joined hands and ran in a circle. All because of me and my coin.

I laughed till tears ran down my face. Oh, how blessed I am to be chosen by angels to bring joy to the worker on a Friday night.

Tues. — I have a plan, how to have my cake and let I. K. eat his heart out. Rehire him! Whether he takes the job or not, he'll think I'm spending money on the diary, planning to publish it. That will gall him. Oh, I know he's just a poor old man who needs money. That's why it's perfect — he'll have to take my offer. Then I'll have a translator. If he doesn't, it will upset him anyway. Why shouldn't I do it? He tried to destroy Uncle. Uncle is an old man more vulnerable than I. K. The dead are naked and have only our memories to dress them.

22 June 1954

I was in the park today, in a meadow. The wind picked up bunches of leaves, dropped them in clumps. They swirled, strung themselves into an alphabet, spelled out my name. "Moisha," they wrote. Then the wind came and blew them all away.

Who writes to me in the language of dead leaves?

Wed. — Just called I. K. Mrs. K. answered. It was like calling my mother beyond the grave. When I asked to speak to Mr. Kolokoy, she said, "So? Whom may I ask is calling?"

I gave my name, started to explain who I was. Just like my mother, she punctured me with interruption. "I know I know. My husband talks of you all the time. He admires you tremendously. How he would laugh, working on your uncle's book.

149

He loved the work so. What happened? You can tell me. He came home the other night so upset I was troubled for his heart. He went, locked himself in his study. He's in there now. I tell you, he's been crying. He doesn't know I know, but I know."

"We had a disagreement. We lost our tempers. I didn't—"

"So, don't be that way. Tell him you're sorry. He'll accept your apology, then he'll be happy as a clown. Your good opinion, you don't know what it means to him. Tell him you didn't want to hurt his feelings. Go on. Tell him how you love the translation of your uncle's book."

"I didn't say—"

"You know, my husband is a writer himself. Here a nobody, not that I'm complaining, but in Europe he was an intellectual."

"I'm sure I—"

"Me — a nobody here, a nobody there. But him, I read his stories in Poland and never thought in all my life I should marry and live to hear him cry. Go, talk nice to him. He's a little lamb if you're gentle."

I felt sick inside, nauseous from shame. After all, I had called to wound this poor old man who had already been crying for days because of me. Now all I could think of was how I could get him to translate my uncle's diary without making him feel bad. Mrs. Kolokoy, dropping the phone with a clatter, went to get him. I heard her slippers shuffling along the floor. In my mind's eye I saw a lumpy bouba in a housedress. She knocked on a door.

"Izzy, open up already. It's the girl. She says she's sorry. She wants to make up and be friends. Come on, be a mensch for once. It's a pity to talk to her. She feels bad about the whole thing."

I heard him say something angrily in Yiddish. Then Mrs. K. spoke. "Israel, be a person. She's crying, she doesn't like you should be angry at her. Come on, Izzy darling, it would break your heart to hear her crying. She misses you. Listen, the man was her uncle. She didn't need to hear you curse her dead uncle, did she?"

I. K. said something, then Mrs. K. said, "No, she didn't say that. She only says she wants to talk." Slippers shuffled closer.

"Hello?" Mrs. K. asked. "Listen, boubala, he's so moved he can't speak. This means a lot to him, but he doesn't want you should know. Men are all big babies. We women are stronger. How else could we stand to give birth?"

She cooed like a pigeon till I was lulled. Then all of a sudden, "Izzy!" she shouted. "You coming or no?" A moment later she trilled, "So darling, tell me about yourself. What did you have for supper?"

This conversation, with its abrupt switches of tone and the intimacy of its assumptions, was so much like talking to my mother that I almost expected her to ask me if I'd been moving my bowels. She filled me with longing for that silly Yiddish world.

"So boubala, you're married?" she asked. When I admitted I wasn't, she screamed, "What? Never married? How old are you?" I told her I was 39. "Go on, and Mr. Kolokoy tells me you're such a pretty girl. He thought you were in your twenties."

I found it endearing the way she kept referring to her husband as Mr. Kolokoy. Aunt Sadie used to refer to my uncle Irving, who died when I was little, this way. He was her second husband, an old man when she married him. She always called him "Mr. Schneidermesser May He Rest In Peace." Her first husband, the lover of her youth and the father of her children, she called "my Davelah," and sighed.

"—maybe you'd like to meet my nephew Nathan, a lawyer. Tops in his field. Handsome isn't the word. But he's too young for you. I must know an older — oy vay, vay, my lukshen!"

Unceremoniously she dropped the receiver and went to shut off the water under her noodles. I heard her call out, "Come on already, Izzy, I don't have all day. The girl is waiting." I. K. said something that sounded conciliatory, then Mrs. K. returned.

"I'm sorry, boubala, I got to go. Mr. Kolokoy is too moved by your call to come to the phone. He's still locked in his study, weeping out his eyes that you should be so generous, he can't get over it. But he says you should bring him another book of your uncle's Saturday, after Shabbes, pay him half in advance. He'll translate it and call you when it's ready. So why don't you come for dinner? I must know a nice widower for you."

I managed to make arrangements to come after sundown but before dinner. I don't know how I will look Mr. Kolokoy in the face.

10 July 1954

Demons suck at you like mosquitos on a summer night. I am learning invisibility. I dreamt of Golda the Wise who taught me the power of the evil eye. She was lying on the cot in my apartment. She was sleeping so I shook her. "Tanta," I called. In Uzlan we called all old women *tanta* [aunt — I. K.].

She blinked her eyes open. I cried, "Oh, Tanta, I'm so glad to see you. I heard the Nazis murdered everyone. How did you escape?"

She put her finger to her lips. "No one can destroy us," she said. "What am I supposed to do?" I asked. She smiled. "Memories are messages from Tanta."

Thurs. — Macon sent back my slides today. I've a new tactic. I put the names of galleries into a hat. As soon as slides come back, I pull out a name and send them on their way again.

Uncle's diary is strange. I sense him standing on the edge of a well. I hold my breath and he jumps — again and again, no matter how many times I cry, "Look out!" He's already dead and can't be hurt. What does a "schizophrenic episode" (that must be what it is) 40 years ago matter? Still, I feel his pain raw. There are moments, reading the diary, when the present recedes and the past covers me like a quilt.

How does an artist cope with rejection? Uncle makes power of powerlessness. He covers his hurt with joy, insists he was lucky when his story was returned. I turn to his diary with fresh dread each time, but fascinated. Like watching someone dance on a ledge. The past is over, Uncle is gone. Still I find myself hoping he writes another story, paints another picture, does something, anything, to save himself. The seduction of madness: I can hear the sirens singing, but I'm tied to the mast, safe because this is Uncle's life, not mine. Uncle, that poor old man going the limit, takes the wax from his ears. I see him succumbing again and again. I can't warn him back. Can't prevent him from leaping into siren arms. Because he can't hear me past the artifice of paper, beyond death, because I am alive in the present, and his life is past.

Friday — A cloud of nausea fogs my reading of the diary. I understand I. K. and am trying to make him understand Uncle. Colloquy with Kolokoy: I argue endlessly with an imaginary man, trying to prove that Uncle's worth does not diminish his own. Like a hamster on a treadmill, around I go, understanding I. K., understanding Uncle, trying to get the two men to understand each other. Be friends and in heaven you can play pinochle.

There are two kinds of observers in the world. Gazers, like bellybuttons, come innie and outie. Even when Uncle stares out he stares in. The spectacles of self sit askew on his ears, his lenses reflect back so that his own image stands always between him and the world. As soon as his gaze lands, it causes a stirring; his eye is caught and he has to fly off.

Because I cry reading Uncle's book, must I dismiss I. K.'s writings? Like a fairy-tale cauldron, I am an insatiable vessel for story. If I. K. wants to show me his concentration camp tales, I am willing to read them. I'll weep and be moved, agree they should be published. Yet what he wants from me is something I don't have the power to grant. My eyes I give willingly, but I am nothing, a copy editor in a schlockhouse. Yet he persists in seeing me as the powerful denier of his experiences.

September 29, 1990

Gentlemen,

The Nazi's seem to get much play in your magazines. I want to know why you don't write about the Nazi's big sister, Communism. Unlike Nazism, Communism has enslaved 2/3 of the world already. The Nazi's are criticized because they don't hide their goals, wear uniforms, swastikas, and are open about what they want. Is that so bad? Communists infiltrate labor, youth, under the guise of lending a helpful hand but ultimately subverting them to their Communist ways. Reds kidnap, highjack, murder and are every bit as awful as the extermination practices of Nazi's. Why do you gloss over the Leftist monster who is at this very moment taking a bite of the free world? Why do you concentrate on the hate mongering of a small number of old Nazi's instead? Communists are being born every day. One wonders if it's a diversionary tactic on the part of the largely Jewish press to distract readers from the real threat of Communism. Print this, if you dare.

Anonymous
Skokie, Ill.

Sat. — Mr. Kolokoy was cold, waiting for an apology I couldn't give. What could I say? "I'm sorry, Mr. Kolokoy. You're right. My uncle was nuts"? I wanted to tell him about Carol's grandfather who in Russia was a poet and here a grocer, how at night he used to howl like a wolf.

24 July 1954

I was walking on Cropsey Avenue. A Negro woman in high heels asked for a light. She took a shining to me. We went to her place. She took off her clothes. I asked her name. "Lolly."

Her skin was like butter. "Why did you hide from me?" I cried.

She laughed. "I was lost, Sugardaddy. Got any bread?" [English transcribed in Hebrew letters — I. K.] She took all my money. I asked her to go home with me. "What about your neighbors?" she said.

"Shit on the neighbors." [The profanity is your uncle's, not mine. If you are a lady, read no further — I. K.] She laughed. We fell to dancing naked. I asked her again to come home with me.

"You crazy? Get along. Go away." She sat up. Her eyes glowed, her nipples burned. She extended her arm, pointed at the door. That's when I saw she was a secret angel!

"Forgive me," I cried. "Why didn't you say you are an angel?"

She laughed, her breasts shook, her belly pulled, and though she was an angel, I wanted her again. She saw my desire hardening. "Got any more dough [original in English — I. K.]?"

154

"Yes," I said. "Don't you see how it rises for you?" She laughed again. She had a good sense of humor.

"Show me your lettuce [original in English — I. K.]."

"What is this, a butter sandwich?" I asked. She took my wallet. It was empty. She kicked me out.

I went to the Garden. It's near the *Forward*. Intellectuals come for blintzes and sour cream. I take a glass of tea and sit in a corner, writing notes on the secret angel. Two men at the next table are talking. They are the same men I heard plotting once before, they are plotting again the same thing. One says, "If anyone took over the world, they would blame it on the Communists." The other says, "That would destroy the union."

They laugh. They are pleased with the idea. It suddenly hits me. These evil ones are part of a big plan to take over the world and blame it on the Communists in order to destroy the union. Here I am, a nobody, but I have all these magic powers given to me by angels. It all starts to make perfect sense. This is the mission Tanta had in mind all along for me to do — save the union. Instead I'm busy having fun with an angel.

I quickly copy down what the men say. One gets up to get himself a piece of strudel. I concentrate on invisibility. No one notices me, so I figure I've succeeded. When the man comes back with coffee and *lukshen kugel* [noodle pudding — I. K.] (they were out of strudel), I'm set.

A woman sits across from me, staring. I figure she can't see me, I should be grateful she didn't sit in my lap. I ignore her. She lights a cigarette, blows smoke on me. Finally she says, "So?" I don't look up. "You're writing?" That was when I realized the terrible truth. I was not invisible. I had lost my powers.

I don't answer the woman across from me. I pray only that she goes away or at least keeps quiet so I can hear the men's plot. She continues blowing smoke in my face. She sips her coffee loudly, making noises with her rubbery lips painted red like from a can.

She says, "So? What are you writing?" Her filthy smoke is in my eyes, plus she has broken my concentration. All I can think of is her stupidity, she should only drop dead. Bad enough I'm not invisible, but she's making a commotion. Why?

I can't take any more. A table opens up on the other side of the two men. I change seats. But this, I won't even call her a woman, she's a witch sent to keep me from my work. She gets up, sits across from me again, slurping with her rubbery lips, staring. By now the two men have noticed us. It's no good. I'll never hear what they are planning to do. So I say, "Nu [So? — I. K.], lady, what do you want from me?"

She says, "What you got to be so stuck up about, sitting with your little pencil scribbling on a napkin?"

I get angry like a kettle boiling over because when I get angry I stutter terrible. I scream, "Listen, you! I got important things on my mind. I just want to jot down some ideas before I lose them"— I know better at least than to tell her what I am really doing— "weighty things you wouldn't know from, a peasant like you. Go sit at an empty table. Why do you torture me? Leave me alone."

I hold up my hand, not to hit her but to scare her. Just a gesture, but she starts to scream bloody murder. "Police! Help! A madman, a lunatic! Help, police!"

The next thing I know the man behind the counter by the fish comes at me with a knife. He's yelling, "Get out of here! Don't you come back. We don't need you bothering the customers."

I cry out, my arms open to embrace him. "My brother! Comrade!" I cry. He waves the knife and tells me to go.

Now that I write this down, I realize that woman was part of the plot. There is going to be a war between good and evil, with good angels and bad taking sides. I am to save the world, the union, and she knew it. That was why she made a disturbance, to get me kicked out of the Garden. What I should do is wait outside the cafeteria, next time I will follow the men.

Sunday — I understand I. K.'s point of view. It enrages him that an educated American Jew is wasting time with a nut. I admit Uncle Moisha is an acquired taste. People knew him his whole life without acquiring the taste.

Paranoid schizophrenia, delusions of grandeur. I took Intro to Psych. Neurosis, psychosis. Still, might not such terms be symptoms of our illness, not Uncle's? The shamans of one society are the madmen of another. Who are our priests nowadays? TV idols. People send fan letters like prayers to the stars. I don't believe in spirits, but when the cats begin chasing invisible motes, lunging and pouncing at things I can't see, I am not so sure there is nothing beyond my perceptions. Who is confident of reality must tell me what it means. The assurance of a pragmatist, is that wisdom? Or hubris? If art, religion, and fantasy fork from the same river, why should one stream be less noble than the others?

There are times I catch myself reading Uncle as a fiction. I have to remind myself he was real. It is a niece's duty to remember. He was not a magic old man, he was Uncle Moisha. His attitude of a genius surrounded by morons is unbearable. He makes terrible puns. I get impatient with his gibberish. There are pages of repetitions I. K. was right not to bother with. Yet time and again he makes me cry. I love him, I miss him, my crazy uncle with his quirks. How typical is I. K.'s scorn? I want to protect Uncle from him, but it's me he has to fear. I hear someone whisper, "Meshuggina," and I cry, "Who is it?" to an empty room.

Dear Secret Confessions,

My father held a knife to my neck and made me do it and that I dont tell nobody course nobody believe me and he made me do it again and again and is it any wonder what happened and than he beet me till I lost the baby bled it dead and than he made me do it again when no one was looking and I finely got so disgusted what with his beetings and loving that I snuck out and runs away and comes to the city and the only work I could get but it was still better then doing it for nothing like Spike says its true and then I got arested and they want to send me back to him and hell surely kill me if I go back and I want to know dont you think it was wrong they sends runaway slaves back to their masters like we read in school and isnt nothing mine not to give away for nothing not even to the man that hatched me from nothing?

5 August 1954

I am standing outside the Garden. I figured it out. It was all part of Tanta's plan. That woman with the red lips was supposed to make me look ridiculous, the two men shouldn't suspect me.

My powers are back. When I tap my coin on the cafeteria wall, they run to get on line for something to eat. When it first happened, I laughed till I had to pee, then I made myself invisible and used the men's room. No one stopped me. They didn't see me. Now I am waiting invisibly for the two scabs to leave the Garden.

The editors from the *Forward* eat in this cafeteria. They always used to wonder who I was. One day they approached me, asked me to write for them. I said, "I'm just a poor garment worker. These notes are nothing. I'm making a shopping list." I knew it was important I should keep my identity secret. A king's power is in his crown, that everyone should bow, but mine is in facelessness, and I must save the union. Ambition is evil's weapon against me. It's not easy to have such power but everyone thinks me a nothing.

The crowd in the Garden is highbrow, that's how I figured out Tanta's plan. That they should let someone annoy a man writing is unusual. If they saw what she did, how she tortured me with her smoke and her questions, Mr. Garden himself would have ushered her out. Gentle but firm, he'd have whispered so even that shouldn't disturb me. "Madam," he'd have said, "can't you see the man is writing?" This didn't happen. I know she was part of the plan. Everyone thinks I'm a fool. I'm not crazy. I'm just pretending.

I can't wait to save the world and start going to the Garden again, the finest dairy cafeteria in New York. Meat is bad for your health. Maybe I should become a vegetarian? I have no stomach for killing. Do carrots cry when you pluck them from the earth like infants from nipples? Dairy is different. A cow likes it when you milk her. Dairy is the food of a cow's pleasure.

I'm standing outside the cafeteria. A whole army of secret angels is waiting to do my bidding. As soon as I find out the details of the plot, I will lead the forces of good against evil. Regiments of secret angels spread from my arms like wings. [Surely you can see your uncle was mad, Miss Segul. I pity him too, but you mustn't let that cloud your judgment — I. K.]

*

Fri., Feb. 19 — When I was a little girl my father used to tease me with his belt. "If you're naughty," he'd say, "I'll take a strap to you." He'd yank it and grin. It was never done in anger. Snapping it was a mock threat, like a trick he was showing me. He never hit me, but he would take off his belt, make the two ends meet in a loop, then pull the leather taut, hard. Years later I asked him why. He didn't know what I was talking about! In the face of his denial I am powerless to believe my own memory. If you do not believe yourself, what can you hope from others? I enter stores with my hands behind my back, that I may not be accused of shoplifting. I race ahead of other walkers lest they think I am a mugger on their shadow. Innocence is no excuse. Help! I'm being held hostage by my imagination.

FANTASY: I am on trial. The defense attorney speaks quietly, then builds to a roaring conclusion. "Wasn't your dress too short? Weren't you flirting all along? Didn't you want to be raped? Isn't that why you went to the basement with him, knowing full well what happens to little girls in basements?"

Too tired to get into it now but before I forget, I was fired today. Suffice it to say I'm annoyed.

15 August 1954

Last night I dreamt of Golda asleep on my cot. I hadn't seen her for a long time. I tried to awaken her. I shook her, called, "Wake up, Golda, you're dreaming," but I couldn't rouse her.

Finally I just sat, staring at my hands. When I looked up, her eyes were open, she was watching me. I was startled. "Golda," I said, "you were dreaming."

She said, "And you?"

Attention: Softball team

Hi guys — How sweet it is to hear that your jerkoff magazines are folding and that all you two-bit hacks are getting layed off. Well, lets face it . . . you're mags always was as bush as you're cunt team. Have fun looking for work, scumbags. **Vengents is Mine.**

159

Outside the Garden. Can't wait to see Molly's face when I save the union. That will teach her. Fascists are stupid. They don't even know I'm standing here, waiting for them to leave. They're getting up to use the toilet. I'll make my report in the new book.

Sun. — Uncle's superior airs covered feelings of inferiority. He didn't want to be bothered with people because people didn't want to be bothered with him.

Just read over my last entry. Writing distorts things. Minor incidents pretend to greater import than they had. My father was not a monster when he snapped his belt. People do things to children that were done to them as children. I see kind people every day titillating children with mock threats. Suzy, for example, brought her two-year-old nephew in a few months ago. She picked him up and said, "I'm going to throw you in the garbage bin, OK? Should I throw you away?" And he said no in a tiny voice that broke my heart. She held him over the bin, saying, "You sure? Shouldn't I just throw you away, get rid of you like that?" Again that little voice: "No." He didn't know she wouldn't throw him away. She was so big and he such a little guy. I wanted to say, "Suzy, I know you're kidding, but he's not sure."

When Lara was around three, I remember, we were playing a game where I was eating her up. I took her arm and said, "I'm going to eat you all up, OK? First I'll cover you with ketchup," and I pretended to put sauce all over her arm, then salt, mustard. The whole time Lara was laughing, willingly holding out her arm, then pulling it back, the way kids do. Carol said, "Stop it. You'll give her nightmares." It was just a game. She seemed to enjoy it. I didn't mean to hurt her. But I see now it was something of a rape.

I can't believe I forgot to write about work. Now my hand is too tired. It's just so boring. I can't be concerned with it. There's so much else to think about. Next time, I promise.

***NOTE: Don't forget to tell about being fired!

*

Monday — I always live up to my promises. PP's canning the mags but keeping Goddess Comics, effective Friday. Last Friday morning there was a memo that Publications Press is immediately ceasing production of all its magazines — monthly, bimonthly, and projects. Management offers its blah blah blah. The upshot is we have till next Friday to empty our desks.

You know the bubbles cartoonists draw over characters' heads? I've decided those are really pictures of the Goddesses' minds. This is why. Everyone's stunned, walking around like there's been an earthquake. Some guys have families, kids in college, they're close to retirement age. Me, I'm not upset, just annoyed — looking for a job will take time. I've got more important things to do.

After lunch there was another notice on the bulletin board. Anonymous — as if its stupidity, mean-heartedness, and misspellings weren't a clear signature. The handiwork of the Goddesses is as obvious as a crook's footprint in the flowerbed of one of their own comix (sic, and I do mean sick). Who would raise an arm with the legend (in Gothic boldface) Vengents is Mine but Shazam the Lady Wrestler? The best thing about being fired is not having to watch her pretend to open the elevator doors by magic.

I've spent 17 years at PP, so this ends a stage of my life. I'm not sorry. I've been lazy about looking for another job. I can stretch unemployment and severance checks, though I might not have paid for the next installment of Uncle's diary if I'd known. I don't want to cancel the project. The old man probably needs the money. Besides, I wouldn't want I. K. to think I'd lost faith in my uncle.

In the meantime I'm doing what I have to. Résumé looks weird: 17 years in a schlockhouse, despite two promotions, doesn't make me a hot property. Once I had the experience, I should have packed my blue pencils and split. I told you it wasn't very interesting.

Tues. — Confused feelings about Uncle. He was once an artist. He felt the brush lead the arm. I know I saw secret knowledge in his eyes. We shared a secret. The secret is we create from trance. And when you stop creating, all that's left is trance. And sterile trance is madness.

Perhaps I have misunderstood what I read. I hate doubting his sanity, hearing I. K.'s comments and nodding my head. "Maybe he really did have secret powers," I tell myself. You see, he was my uncle and his peculiarities were sweet to me, the way a father loves his daughter's nose, its hook identical to his own.

Feb. 24 — This is the best thing that could have happened to me. I am worried about some of the characters at work, though. PP is full of oddballs, like a small town with a streak of insanity running through it. I still don't know if madness bred madness or chose it to bed; i.e., did people go crazy at PP or were they hand-picked for it? Till now we've covered for one another. Idiosyncrasy is encouraged. Suzy laughs: "That's so you. You're a riot." It's as if a genetic faultline runs down the middle of our village. Insanity, idiocy, something has taken us over through the generations. Intermarriage of first cousins or the earth shifting its plates, whatever it is, a distinct line of strangeness cracks the corridor from art department to editorial, fracturing each in its path.

Frankenstein, for example, with his stink and lisp — who would hire him? And Heidi from paste-up. Liz will do fine, Suzy too. If only Suzy would be my magic mirror once before we go. I keep wondering how people see me — a nonpresence flattened like a moth? I sense my colors changing when others are around. I merge with the walls while they make their lunch plans.

Today they were talking about having a farewell lunch and spent the entire morning planning it. I lowered my head, camouflaging myself like a bug on a leaf. When, however, I am noticed, my skin sets to quivering, so I felt the vibration of stares at my back. I distinctly heard someone think (Suzy probably), "We should ask Gabby." I hurried to the ladies' room. Gave them ample time to make their plans before I returned. I don't want to be invited. If I were, I'd feel obligated to go.

I have known these women for years but still am uncomfortable. The secret, I've decided, is in knowing how to act. Literally. That's what I will do on job interviews. I'll even wear a costume. That's the main thing I'm concerned about — clothes. I've grown lazy at PP, wearing jeans every day. Can't see spending money now on an appropriate outfit. As Thoreau wrote, "Beware of all enterprises that require new clothes."

I happen to have beautiful clothes — the clothes of an artist. Color, texture, pattern. I create a Bonnard of my body. Show superiority in unconventionality. My knapsack is a masterpiece of embroidered fleurs-de-lis. It molds to my back like a sleeping lover. But is it appropriate for a job interview?

I have a "lady" costume somewhere. The brown skirt and beige blouse exaggerate a femininity not mine. I am like a transvestite. Have trouble balancing without sneakers. Tom Sawyer in drag, I don't know what to do with my hands. "Stop acting like a meshuggina," my mother would say. If I am acting, I may choose a different role. Uncle said Sophie Herring was acting crazy to fool people. Does that imply he was acting too?

My mother bought me the brown skirt when I graduated college. It's boringly brown, but it worked on interviews then. Silly to worry about clothes. The skill, not the skirt, makes the editor.

Friday — Last day at PP. Refused to deal with goodbyes. Separation, death — didn't want to get caught in it. People exchanged phone numbers. I avoided that. Around noon I hid in the ladies' room, waited till Happy, Liz, Suzy, et al. left for their lunch. It was quiet in the office. I shut the TV off, thinking, "At last I will never have to hear another Fab commercial." I took my stuff from my desk. I was tempted to steal correction fluid, pens. PP owes me something more than some months' severance. I'm like a spurned wife. They stole my youth. In the end I took nothing but my own junk and the memo pads with my name. What, after all, will anyone else do with notes From the Desk of Gabby Segul?

HAPPY WEINBERG: Gabby and I were very close. She often confided in me. We had long lunches in which she told me about her art. She offered to give me a small watercolor painting. I could kick myself now for not taking it. At the time I didn't want Gabby to feel I valued her friendship only because she was so talented.

When I first started working in magazine publishing, Gabby was already there. She seemed aloof. I don't think she ever really warmed up to the others, but she and I had a rapport. I guess she could tell I have the soul of an artist too, even though I can't draw. I think she also — well, I'm not sure how to say this, but I think she wanted to paint me. She never actually got around to asking me, but when you look the way I do, you get used to artists and photographers wanting you to pose nude. I never do it, but for Gabby I might have.

Monday — I've an interview lined up at Editing Ink, an employment agency, next week. Someone named Mrs. Felix just called. I've been trying to anticipate questions. The problem is *Slut*, though *Soap Bubble, Stars,* and *Sin* are no better. The function of all four mags was to supply dirty dreams for people without the imagination to concoct their own. *Slut* never pretended to be anything but a mechanic's manual on pleasure. Men make objects of women, women make objects of men. I'm an artist. I make objects of everybody.

Tuesday — I wonder when Kolokoy will call with the second translation. Been thinking about Uncle. I know he wasn't just crazy, there was more to him than that. I used to watch him dream in a chair. Blood squeezed from his arm like oil from a tube. He knew what I know, that art pumps deep. Each heartbeat spurts one's substance onto the canvas. Later, when a man slits open a box of slides, slips it unviewed into its return envelope while he sips wine from a plastic glass, ask the value of that sour Chablis and compare its vintage with the one squeezed from your body's grape.

Antony Hal's sent my slides back today, no note. I don't care. I stuck my hand in my hat; my slides are on their way. Art is all that matters. Uncle knew. He was uneducated. He perceived strangely, that was his power. If Dostoevsky (another epileptic, f.y.i.) spent his life sewing ladies' pants, might he not have heard angels too?

Mar. 3 — Answered several more ads. No other interviews set up so far. I'm in the park watching a little girl with her grandmother. What can they be talking about so merrily? I didn't know my grandparents. Family stories all centered on my grandmother's strictness, and that she was very clean. My mother would say, "You could eat off her floor." I used to imagine my father's family doing that, like dogs. My father would say, "You were not allowed to sit on a bed in Momma's house. You sat on a chair. You slept in a bed." In the nursing home I sat on the bed, Uncle slept in a chair.

The other thing about her is how she died. She was strangled by her intestines. It seems she often used a Yiddish expression. It sounded like *es drayt mir de kishkas,* and it literally meant her entrails were twisting around, strangling her.

Why did she say this? My parents thought it was probably a premonition. What she actually died of I didn't know till a few months ago, when I was looking up the adjectival form for "vulva" ("vulvar," f.y.i.) and came upon the following word: " 'volvulus' — a twisting of the intestine upon itself that causes obstruction."

Fri. — Why didn't I just apologize to I. K. when I dropped off the second diary? I wish he weren't angry at me. He and his wife are like the grandparents I never had. If only he hadn't bullied me about Uncle. Should I call? What would I say? I'm sorry, Mr. Kolokoy, that you don't like my uncle's writing, I'm sorry you were in a concentration camp, I'm sorry you can't get your stuff published in this country, I'm sorry I can't publish your stuff? I *am* sorry. For all these things.

Mon. — I noticed today how I grow deaf from self-consciousness, looking for my reflection in the other's eye. Reading between lines, I become engrossed in what my body is saying despite me — crossed legs, chewed fingernails, twitching lids. When I'm asked a question, I have nothing to say. I haven't been paying attention. I smile, broadly and too much. In the middle of my act, falsity strikes. Tight-lipped, dry, I become an image in a witch's mirror.

Who taught me to read between the lines, to concentrate on the pauses in which true meaning crouches? My mother was a spy who never listened to what I said, while what I didn't creaked as loudly as couch springs at midnight. "Where did you go last night?" "To a movie." "What did you see?" "I don't know. A love story." "How come you can't remember a movie you saw last night?" The accusation, implied but loud, would make me forget I had nothing to hide.

Suddenly during today's interview I knew I had to leave. I was ashamed of the sham, pretending to like Mrs. Felix, a woman I don't even know. I watched consciousness of my duplicity flit across her face.

She is very pregnant, so I was naturally afraid I'd say something inappropriate. You know how, when you are talking to someone missing a leg, you find yourself complaining how your legs hurt from standing or how you had to run all over town? You call that person Mr. Leg instead of Mr. Lane. Drool about how much you love leg of lamb. Anything stupid pertaining to legs, just because Mr. Lane is missing one.

The brain is a brat. It plots ways to embarrass me. Mrs. Felix doing fellatio, Mrs. Felix's calves in the air, Mr. Felix's pimpled dimpled ass, the moans and groans of the marriage bed. I couldn't get my mind to behave. What made it worse was that I never knew her unpregnant, so I kept imagining this very pregnant woman doing all manner of obscene things. I tried to cover these thoughts with a smile. The wider my smile, the falser it seemed.

166

As I was leaving, I wanted to say something friendly, so I said, "Good luck giving birth." She looked shocked. It was so stupid, tactless. She said, "I doubt I'll have problems."

Here was my chance. I could have said, "Of course not." Instead I said, "You never know," and proceeded to laugh. An imp must have possessed my tongue, because I went on: "I've always been terrified of childbirth. I've heard it's the worst pain imaginable. But" — I was trying to make amends, trying to get my foot out of my mouth; it was stuck, my tongue wrapped around it like twine. I kept talking, hoping to unravel the words, but they kept knotting into a noose — "there you are, with a lovely baby, and it's worth it. Not for me, of course. For you."

When I asked where the ladies' room was, to my horror Mrs. Felix decided to go too, saying, "The baby presses on my bladder."

"Yes," I replied. "I know all about it." What I meant, I have no idea, because all I could think was that we were going to use the bathroom together and I wouldn't be able to pee with her in the room. She went first. I washed my hands, running the water to cover the sound of her splashing. When it was my turn, she combed her hair. In the silence, I couldn't get my muscles to relax.

She walked me to the elevator. I was hopping from one foot to the other because my bladder was still full. We shook hands. She waited with me for the elevator. I got in. Then, as if I hadn't proven myself odd enough, just as the doors rolled shut I waved bye-bye. I opened and closed my fingers several times like a toddler on a carousel to her grannie. She'll never call me.

MRS. FELIX: I don't actually remember her. It was a long time ago. I did, however, go through my records. If she was the same Gabby Segul I sent on job interviews right before my daughter was born, she seems to have made a good impression. My chart says she had a nice appearance, seemed bright, soft-spoken, polite. I did note that her reserve might be taken by some as an air of superiority, but I also wrote down that she would easily find a place. I noted that she wanted to make the transition from magazines to books, but I didn't know how easy that would be after 17 years' concentration in one aspect of publishing.

Tues. — Could Uncle's oddness have stemmed from his hearing problem? He was partially deaf. The nursing home wanted to give him a hearing aid, but he refused to be examined. If a man can't hear clearly, what he hears he distorts. Deafness could account for the non sequiturs in his conversation as well as his increasing fanta

Mrs. Felix just called. She's set up an interview for me at Magazine Network, obviously a magazine publishing company. I must have forgotten to tell her about art *books*. I'll go, but I'd only accept a position on a magazine if it's art-related.

Wed. — Nervous about my interview tomorrow. When I'm with people I forget who I am, think only of the other person's desires — what is wanted from me, how to satisfy unstated wishes. I say things I think the other person believes, only to find myself defending opinions not my own. I must hold on to my sense of self.

The crying behind my walls has begun again.

Thurs. — Interview at Magazine Network: Mr. Bloom looked like an aging Huck Finn. A middle-aged man with chubby cheeks, reddening and shiny, like an apple.

Something happened between us, I'm not sure what. He seemed to like me at first, then I thought he only liked my legs. He stifled a yawn when I spoke; afterward I had trouble getting sentences to stick. I am like Alice — my self-image shrinks or expands, depending on which side of the mushroom I nibble. He told me about the magazines. I stopped listening, became caught in self-images. He spoke of the company's needs. I thought of the sparkle on my lips.

I smiled, to be friendly, knowing he was in love with me. And he looked away! Yes, that's it. He stabbed me with unspoken accusation. His face was disgusted and disgust undressed me.

He thought I was coming on to him when I was just being nice. The flirtation was his doing. I was at once both his victim and seducer.

He had been smiling in that way men have — deep looks, thirsty lips. I was being kind. I'm still young, only 39. But his disdain turned everything around, as if I'd been making lewd advances.

My lips, that was all, I was licking my lips. They're chapped and dry, but it made my smile vulgar, how I licked my lips. I stopped smiling. I tried to show interest in what he was saying, tried to remove myself from my legs and breasts, to become eyes. I am only eyes and ears. I have no sex. I am not a woman.

I wish we could leave our bodies, that our auras could meet and speak, and neither Bloom nor I would know if we were working with a man or a woman until Monday morning when I showed up. I hate being a woman. I hate having this load of flesh to carry with me always, to wonder what is given in homage, what in insult, to the woman or human of me.

We'd been talking about magazine illustrations, so I mentioned I'm an artist. He asked about my stuff. I started to tell him about the allegory I'm doing — 20th-century Primavera stepping from a tub, the allusion to Botticelli's Venus. That is what I meant to say, but in the middle I forgot what I was talking about. I watched the glaze spread over his eyes and was hypnotized by the horror of it. How bored he was. He thought me pitiable. Saw a spinster tottering on the edge of middle age, pathetic as those old women on Broadway, the ones with no bras.

This is what I thought he thought. Meanwhile the man was waiting and I couldn't remember my ideas. On Broadway the ladies, their breasts sagging to their waists, shifted their bags to give everyone a better view, muttering till I couldn't hear myself think. I watched an expectant look replace his bored one; this terrified me more. I sank into blankness, staring into the hole of his face, watching it stare back like Nietzsche's abyss. When it became apparent that I didn't know what I was about, he changed the topic, telling me about his daughter's Caldecott award. That's when I remembered what I wanted to say. It was too late. I felt as naked as a pig in a house of straw. The horrible inner wolf began: "I'll huff and I'll puff and don't you dare cry." Tears came to my eyes. I thought only of escape, how to leave before bawling. The more I tried not to, the thicker grew the clot of tears.

He must have seen my trouble. He jumped up, said, "Come, I'll show you the art department." His kindness almost pushed me over the edge but in the end did me good. I regained my composure as he showed me around. A man walked by. His long stride, his weedy carriage. For a moment I thought *James*, like a knight to my rescue.

Isn't it true that destiny could take my hand? It's not a fairy tale to think James could be working at the same place where I get a job. We could meet again after so many years. He'd notice me first. "James?" I'd say. "Now I remember you. You've aged some, but oh, James Kolokol, how have you been?" We'd slowly, over many lunches and nights in a bar, revelations, confessions, fall simmeringly into love like a magic stew.

Mar. 12 — If it's not art, it's madness. Do you understand?

Sat. — Could Kolokoy have sabotaged Uncle's book?

I don't believe that. I'm just looking for excuses. I can see in the original (marked by toothpicks) all the repetitions he couldn't be bothered with. I don't blame him. A person could go crazy from this diary.

Secret angels, magic powers. Look at it objectively: the crazy old bird's let me down. I. K. was right. I felt sorry for Uncle. That's why I expected . . . I don't know what. He had such a terrible life. I remember his furnished room in Brighton, the communal toilet. Each tenant was responsible for his own toilet paper, but Uncle used the *Forward*. The landlady complained to my parents, she wanted to kick him out. My parents slipped her money, appealing to her guilt as well as her greed. "You can't throw him on the street. You're also a Jew." They warned Uncle. "Use the paper we bought or you'll end up without a toilet."

His room stank like a telephone booth. He hid things. When he couldn't find them, he said they had been stolen. He wouldn't bathe or change his clothes. "Look at a dog. A dog doesn't wash. A dog doesn't wear clothes. He finds what to eat in the garbage. He walks all day. He's free."

"Yes," said my parents, "but you're not a dog."

They took him to the bank, they took him to the doctor, they took him for new glasses. He was always losing his eyeglasses. Before they moved him to Brighton, Uncle lived in East New York. The neighborhood changed around him, his building became a slum, but he stayed in the apartment where he'd been abandoned. Every night he slept on the cot his wife left him. He had no phone.

He became old, the only Jew in the neighborhood. Fridays he came to our house with horror stories — he was mugged, he was beaten, he refused to leave. Two boys began waiting for him. He'd come out of the station at 3:00 A.M. They'd be there.

"Why do you walk the streets all night? Where do you go?" my parents asked. "What's so important in Times Square, Coney Island, that you got to go see? Stay home or you'll get yourself killed."

He shrugged, wouldn't answer, wouldn't listen. My mother, in a dramatic monologue, addressed the audience. "Who can blame him? How can he sit in that house? What's he got there? Nothing but cockroaches to talk to." Uncle was slurping his soup, oblivious to her soliloquy. She suddenly turned back to the scene at hand.

"Move, I tell you! Move."

"Huh?" He slid from one skinny buttock to the other. His perplexed look made me want to gather his bones.

Where *did* he go? What *did* he do?

I see him standing on the outskirts of a crowd, watching whatever happens in its center. One time I ran into him on the train. "Uncle," I exclaimed, "hello!" He ran away. I couldn't catch him, he ran so fast on his chicken-bone feet.

The two boys waiting for him played like cats with a mouse. They knocked him down. The first night they stole his watch and wallet. The next night they took the bills hidden in his coat. On the third night they hung him upside down from a tree. They took turns whipping him with his belt, laughing to hear the old man scream. After that he was afraid to go home.

"Now's the time to make our move," my mother said like an actress in Yiddish theater. Quickly they found him the room in Brighton. Uncle was already starting to back out. He didn't want to leave the old neighborhood. "It's not so bad. They're only boys. They've had their fun, now they're tired of me."

My parents wouldn't listen. They went to his apartment, picked up his stuff. "Next time maybe they'll crack your head open like an egg for you. Then you'll be happy?" What did they find in his East New York apartment? "A forest of umbrellas," my mother told me. "Every time someone throws out a broken umbrella in this city, he finds it, brings it home. Buttons all over like mushrooms after a storm. Half-empty cigarette packs. Why? The man doesn't smoke. Pencils galore. You need a pencil? Here, take this one. It's got an eraser. An entire room devoted just to old newspapers!"

They threw out his pillow and blanket and cot. They threw out his sheets. They threw out his mandolin and drawings. "Such junk. No wonder Molly left him. Who could live with such a man?"

"How could you throw out his mandolin and drawings?"

"It was garbage like a child makes. Where he got so much paint God only knows. And the mandolin had no strings."

He forgave them. This I can't understand, that he could forgive them for throwing out his soul. He must have been crazy. Or else he was a saint.

Mar. 19 — Interviews too boring to write about. Old woman at Gorky Prints wore white gloves and a hat — I knew I was doomed. Bored girl at the museum was looking for someone to edit catalogues — ho-hum. Man with a limp, man with a pot-belly, lady with an attitude. Wonder how the others at PP are making out.

Mar. 22 — I had a run in my stocking and had to rush out for a new pair before today's appointment. Bought purple ones that caught me in their nylon web — sheer like a layer of cold skin.

I put them on and ran to the train. They began to droop. I should have turned back, but I was in a hurry and chose instead to ignore them. "How far can they drop?" I thought, as they fell in paroxysms of laughter, giggling like obnoxious twins at my feet.

On the train I bent to pull them up. A gleam in a male eye alerted me to the indecency of a woman fixing her hose on the IRT. What could I do but let them pool? I got off the train and rushed to my meeting. A doorman stood guard in an empty lobby. I got in the elevator, willing the doors to close before anyone else entered. Sealed in, finally alone, I hiked my skirt to my waist, pulled the hose up, tucked the extra material into my panties. Like scratching a mosquito bite, the relief was immediate — and temporary. My stockings stayed up till I sat down.

I grew angry — at the interviewer, my legs, my stockings, my fate. Who was this Mr. Shwein to make me feel absurd? The interview was short, my stockings were long. In heavy-footed despair I stomped out of the office, a purple elephant in hideous hide.

Back in the elevator, blessedly alone once more, I tore off the hose, put the traitors into my bag. When the door opened, I was straightening my skirt, looking respectable as all hell.

Two guards were hooting when I came out. "Nonsense," I told myself. "Why should anyone laugh because my stockings drooped?" Nonetheless they were looking at me and howling. "I'm just being paranoid," I decided. Then I saw the video screen. There was a surveillance camera in the elevator. I hadn't seen it, but it had seen me. Illya Kuryakin would have demanded that I turn in my U.N.C.L.E. card.

I can't bear to be laughed at. Suzy could make this a funny

story, but I don't think I can go on another interview. Every time I think of today, I shrink inside my nakedness like a clam. The odd thing is, I haven't thrown the stockings out. They are entrancing and I am an artist who can't rid herself of beauty. I must find a use for them — a collage? Exercising my power over them is the only way to exorcise their power over me. For the time being, they're in a drawer. I tied them around my neck a little while ago, to see if I could use them for a scarf. They began to tighten. They want to kill me. Or sense they're controlled by some magician who pulled them into existence from his hat.

Tues. — Called Mrs. Felix yesterday. She hasn't called back.

Wed. — Should I call Mrs. Felix again? Maybe she didn't get the message. Each hour that passes leaves me sick with dread. Could she have heard what happened in the elevator? Did someone complain?

Thurs. — When it rains, the streetlight outside my building gets stuck on red. Horns honk until it stops raining and the wires dry. Fury outside my window howls like a mad king's storm.

I can't live in this crazy city anymore. I'm going to leave. There's nothing keeping me here. Mrs. F. still hasn't returned my call. I can't call her. Silence speaks her rejection loud enough.

Red bloody sirens are tearing by. Now they're stuck beneath my window, bellowing bullhorns till only I and the fire scream exist. I am a scream screaming, like in Munch. A scream screaming . . .

In the distance, still circling like vultures of anxiety, they're tearing at my mind. My mother's psoriasis — the scales and bloody patches she tore from her elbows up her arms, ripping herself open with red-painted fingernails till all was blood and shredded skin. I screamed, "Stop it!" It made this horrible scratching sound, like a rodent behind a wall. I screamed, "Stop it!" over and over, to lock out the sound of her psoriastic frenzy.

*

174

Apr. 3 — Haven't had time to write in a while. Been busy. Cleaned kitchen yesterday, bathroom today. Reorganized my closets (including kitchen cabinets). Windows next, then I'm going to get down to the real work. Files have to be categorized. They're still in folders on sills. I've been putting this off because it's such a big job, but I can't see where I'm going till I see where I've been.

When I finish this project, I'll know what's next. My apartment clean, my files organized, I'll be ready to take stock of the situation, figure out what to do.

Important to accomplish something every day.

Mon. — Started working on my files. Didn't know how to begin so began at beginning — juvenilia. Schoolbooks, art pads, manila envelopes full of third-grade limericks, report cards, drawings (princesses with perfect oval faces, flip hairdos, curls like horns, bodices like breasts — Snow Whites crossed with Astartes).

Around 2:30 I opened a shoebox full of ticket stubs and romantic memorabilia. In it I found something I'd completely forgotten. As soon as I saw the cough-drop box, I knew what it was. My first rubber, filled with original cum (an orange sand now). Who was I, to save stuff like that? I remember being terrified that my mother would find it. I went to great lengths to hide it — in foil, in a cough-drop box, in my typewriter, in my typewriter case, in the back of my closet behind my boots.

Girlish romanticism? I recall showing it to Carol when it was still liquid. She was a virgin at the time and was impressed. I used to tell her everything. Now I haven't even told her about PP folding.

I recall a sense of life as biography then. Now I can't throw anything out because the past is irreplaceable. Having saved this condom so many years, what else could I do? I filed it with the fossilized french fry from a high-school beau. Tomorrow I will organize the file of my friends' letters. Always feel better when things are clean, thoughts organized. Have to catch up with my laundry too, put away winter stuff, wash sweaters, buy moth-balls. By the time I'm finished, Mrs. Felix may call. Something unforeseen may happen. My mother always said a clean house is a clean mind.

Thursday — Important to get out every day. Rest one's eyes from the morning's filing. After lunch today I walked to the library. The park smells sweet and in the library I had a brainstorm. I'd been thinking all morning that editing isn't the right field for me. I've never liked it, not the way I love organizing my files. This morning I began my family file. Am enjoying it immensely but can't do more than a few letters at a time. It's hard to read the letters without crying. When I cry, my eyes get red. This makes it impossible to read further.

Most of the letters in the family file are from my mother. Some are from my aunts. All three sisters wrote in the same phonetic way, just as they spoke. I can hear their voices, their inflections. The associations of words, ideas — so strange and perfect— makes me miss them till I can't bear it. That's when I stop. I splash cold water on my eyes. Scrub the sink or wash a sill. I have to be careful. Even with all these precautions, I often cry because of a little thing.

Today, for instance, I came across a letter from Aunt Rose, before she had her stroke. It sounded just like her, but what really got to me was the shopping list at the end. I'm sure she didn't know she'd mailed it. She probably spent the morning looking for it, and now she's dead. My eyes got so swollen they looked like bulbs I could plant in Aunt Sadie's soil.

I decided to go to the library, to look for the next volume of Van Gogh's letters. Once there, I couldn't keep from reshelving misplaced books. That's when it hit me — I should work in a library. Why wait for Mrs. Felix to call? I must take charge of my life.

I'm not the type to sit around wishing. I immediately went to a librarian, an attractive man with glasses. When I told him I was interested in working for the library, he exclaimed, "Oh goody!" He obviously loves his job and is pleased that someone like me wants to be a librarian. I am so happy. I think I've found my niche. I at once called to set up an appointment.

Seems a good sign, don't you think? He must have liked me. He certainly liked the thought that I wanted to work in the library. It is as if I have already made a friend. Perhaps this librarian and I might work in the same library. We could sit in the park on our lunch hour, reading side by side. We'd go to lectures, perhaps even fall in love.

Saturday — Ready to tackle my next big project, 17 years of crazy letters. A mess, but I've learned a lot by doing the other files. First I must devise a system. Chronological, geographical, thematic? By sex, magazine, subject? You can see the problem, and what about the ones that can't be categorized — fantasy letters, absurdly naive letters, crossing-the-line letters? I wonder if there's a way to mention this work to the library adviser?

Dear Madam,
I read with interest your article on Barbra Streisand. I imitate her singing. I have never had lessons. I have perfect pitch and sing soprano, alto, tenor, base, with or without music. I used to be a librarian. I was born October 19, 1909. They say I'm the prettiest girl in town. I sing in Church. My husband died last May. My son used to be the leading boy soprano but he got pimples. I'm busy as a beaver and happy as a clam. My other son was killed. It almost killed his father. Later he died anyway. He was so handsome when we married, and rich. I'm secure now. The neighbors say I'm having married men in my apartment. They call me. So what? Who's business is it? The neighbors want to put me in jail so they can steal my TV. Would you give me darling Barbra's address? I'm sure she wouldn't mind once she gets to know me. Stay well. Here's my recipe for gingersnap cookies. I made 1,119 cookies from this recipe for the Adam Smiths when they were here at a party. They have the recipe. I wish you everything you wish yourself.
Hattie P. Wilke

Dear "Secret Confessions,"
What I have to say is so ghastly and dark that I can't sign my name so you will to print it by Mrs. X. When I first married I was but 18, blonde, blushing, my chest white as Ivory Snow

flakes. It soon grew dark with his bites. My husband, I learned, had an appetite for dastardly acts to which I must submit lest he harm me with his masculine brutality. He thrust himself on me the first time though I was a virgin and he a man of experience. One day he bought a coffin and put it under our bed and made me to lie in it. I was not allowed to move. If I did he put the lid on the coffin, put it under the bed so I couldn't get out. He made me lie there, even if I had to pass water I had to do it in my coffin and I got depressed. I was going to kill myself. I got a knife and the next time he put me in my coffin I was going to plunge it in my breast. The devil whispered, "Why don't you kill *him*, Mrs. X?" I tried not to listen, but I began to think about it while lying in the coffin submitting to the evil practices my husband practiced evilly on me. I thought how I'd take the knife and teach him a lesson. But he got food poisoning instead and died and I buried him in my coffin and lived to tell my Terrible Tale.

Yours Truly,
Mrs. X

Dear *Slut*,

I would like to write an article for *Slut* magazine, a fine and useful publication, entitled: What this country needs is my $397875,343.02 in it. Lately I have been making $1.20 for the Salvation Army. I have written millions of articles for your magazine. I am founder and President of the Republic of Smithsonia. My money is in Russia. My real father is Nelson Rockefeller, as I proved in an article I wrote in 1965. After I get my money out of Communist hands, I will do a lot of good. I plan to run for President and bring about the second coming of Christ.

Cordially,
Jesus Smith

Dear Illya,

I am a spy in training. I keep notes in an U.N.C.L.E. book. I follow my neighbors, but I don't know how to get into headquarters. Where is the tailor shop? I am an American. I love freedom. I am glad not to live under Communism. But I am a Russian spy, like you. Can you help me understand this? You and Napoleon Solo are good guys working together but you, like me, are a Russian spy. So who are we fighting?

I know we are fighting the forces of evil. That's what I want to do. I'm not afraid to take chances. I am in love with you even though I am much younger. Do you think this stands in our way?

We have so much else in common, both being Russian spies working on the side of good and freedom. I am mature for my age, quiet and tall. People think I'm older. Please write back.

I can be a secret agent in Brooklyn. I'm sure there are forces of evil at work here. I already cover Flatbush Avenue around King's Highway and think I've discovered a gang of spies who hang out near the drugstore. One of them must have thought I was on his side and he used the secret password "Lola" or "Lulu" to me. Does that mean anything to you? I hope it helps. I'll tell you more in my next communication.

Sincerely,
Gabby Segul
(code name: Lulu)

Monday, April 12 — Terrible news. I lost my small notebook. It must have fallen out of my breast pocket. I didn't notice till a little while ago. I've searched the apartment. I've been up and down the streets, looking in garbage cans, in the gutter, under parked cars. I asked shopkeepers on Broadway — to no avail.

Everyone I spoke to understood my concern, except the pizza man. He smirked. If only I could remember what I wrote. There were several weeks' notes I hadn't transcribed. Now I'm afraid, sense myself being watched; feel exposed, as if someone came upon me masturbating. Notes, dreams — stuff I meant to cross out. There may have been something about James.

A peeper reads my secret confessions. I never wrote with his sticky hands in mind. I am not jumping to conclusions. It's a fact that if my book had not been stolen, it would be where I dropped it. Someone saw it lying there, open like a drunk woman's legs.

There was a shopping-bag man sleeping on the subway grating near where I bent to tie my shoe. It must have fallen then. Bag men sleep with their eyes open. If it fell, he'd have seen it. When I returned to the spot, he was gone. A homeless man could be anywhere in this city. What is he, after all? The shape of wrinkled rags snoring in dirt, a beard, a filthy face. I might someday give him money and never know my book's in his bag like a stolen child.

Be fair, Gabby. You only accuse him because he is a wandering Cain. It was the pizza man who acted oddly. Everyone else seemed to understand. But Bruno — I don't trust a man whose pubic hairs curl out of his face. That dirty look he gave me, as if staring through my clothes. I'm sick to think of him straining to make out my hand. Only children learn a protective pen early; I wish now my letters were more ill-formed, that he might throw my book away in disgust. If I could just remember what horrible revelation makes Bruno lick his lips. He wets the page with his fingers to turn it. His saliva moistens the dark passage into me. I can't bear his eyes, his tongue wet with interest.

Stop! You're driving yourself crazy. You don't know anything about the pizza man except he makes pizza. The homeless man asleep on the sidewalk, you know less of him.

But my name, address, phone number were in it, do you see? I am in danger. An unseen stalker. A rapist could have my book.

Why am I doing this, terrorizing myself like a child I hate? Yet I've reason to be scared. My secret desires are revealed in its pages, so now, peeled raw like an onion, I make my own eyes tear. If something happens, I'll be accused of provocation. If only I knew with what thoughts I've incriminated myself. From now on I must be careful. Yet the need for an imaginary witness overrides any caution I may be presumed to have learned. The fantasy of a secret empathy is surely a powerful illusion, to be worth the horrible exposure I open to again. For here I am, offering myself to the gleaming blade like a patient asleep on a surgeon's table.

Tuesday — The habit of diary writing is a drug. Nothing is real till I write it down. I must take you with me. Still no word from I. K. The second half of the payment would be a hardship now anyway.

Wed., Apr. 14, 42nd Street Library, Periodicals Reading Room, 1:58 P.M. — Waiting for my interview with the library adviser. I'm in a room of old men. Everyone's at work on a masterpiece. At the far end of the table, one man refers to points on a giant map.

Makes notes. Has ruler and magnifying glass. Across from me, a man with a yellow legal pad is writing on a page already covered with words. Crosses things out, inserts words in margins, between lines, sideways, upside down. Words on top of words in the scrawl of the insane. Mumbling to himself. Must be crazy — unless he's a poet.

The man next to me is TRYING TO READ OVER MY SHOULDER, THAT'S WHY I'M WRITING SO LARGE. I WANT HIM TO SEE I KNOW HE IS A NOSYBODY AND A PEEPING TOM. Good, that stopped him.

I look to see what he saw and confront your scribbled face. Half an hour till my appointment.

A tall hunchback — uncut white hair, magnifying glass with flashlight attachment — looks at items in the *New York Times*, writes notes on long slips of paper, places these between pages of a book. Puts his nose to the magnifying glass, turns on light, examines an advertisement of a woman in fur. Mutters. Belches. Farts. I shouldn't laugh. He's very old.

He wears a tie around his neck. Literally around his neck. His shirt is open and the tie is knotted around his stringy old man's neck. Has a jacket with kangaroo pockets attached by safety pins. Now he looks at the photograph of a bed. Ad for quilts? His nose is practically in the sheets. Staring, laughing. Stops. Goes back. Acts as if he sees someone in bed. Intensity of his stare, amused excitement . . . does he see a naked woman cavorting on the page?

I am observing all this peripherally. I don't want to stare, so it's hard to determine his actions. He seems to be bowing to a miniature seductress. He gets up, talks to two other old men. They know one another, talk about some free-lunch place. His voice surprises me. It is very deliberate, no accent. I would never match that voice to the old hunchback. He must be 90. The other two are younger, in their seventies. They tolerate him, entertained by his seriousness. He puts on a hat. The others laugh. He searches through his pockets, takes out reams of notes tied with rubber bands, first one pocket, then the other. Puts them back. They laugh again. Now he has found what he wants. Sugar packets.

"Have some sugar," he says in his broadcaster's voice.

"No thanks," one man replies. "I'm watching my sugar." I don't want to laugh because I don't want them to know I am listening.

He is leaving. The other two stay, saying back and forth (I can't tell their voices apart, they speak as one, in perfect mockery), "Oh no, there's that hat of his. What did he do, pick it out of a garbage can? A lady's hat. He's got that ridiculous hat on." I am angry. They have no right to make fun of that neglected old man with his gift of sugar. What have the poor to give but what they take? It's almost time for my interview. Better get ready.

4:07 P.M. — In a dark corner of the Periodicals Reading Room. Worst interview ever. I was on time but Mrs. Faustid kept me waiting. Her office was too brightly lit. She was slovenly. Coffee stains on her blouse, tobacco leaves in her teeth. "Yes?" she said when I came in. No smile. Her glasses magnified her eyes' imperfections — warts and mucus, the surrounding membrane red.

I introduced myself and explained that I wanted to work in the library, asked what kinds of jobs were available.

"What can you do?" She stared like a bug.

"Well, anything, if I'm trained. That is, I'm willing to do anything . . . except windows." I thought a little joke might break the ice. She was encased in a rigid no-smile.

Finally I said, "Shelving books?"

"Oh, that."

"Not necessarily. I just mean I'm willing to do anything."

"Hmm." The telephone rang. She told someone "the key codes are you know where . . . I can't talk. Someone here, nobody that knows Anthroparion I'm sure where at the union yes I will Azazel sure I see bye." She gave me a funny look. I pretended not to have heard anything. So then she stared me down again. "Those jobs are for disadvantaged teenagers. You're no teenager, are you?"

I laughed, thinking she was kidding. No response. "I'm not

disadvantaged either," I said. "Just unemployed. I have a B.A. I'd love to go for a degree in library science, but I can't afford it. Maybe if I were working in the library I—"

"Hmph. Right away they think we should send them to school. Everybody loves learning at someone else's expense. Don't you know the — oh, never mind. I assume you can dictodigitabulate." I shook my head. "You do know the library keys?" Again I shook my head. "The decimal system, don't you know the Dewey? Union Catalogue? Library of Congress? Prestidestidigitation? Legerdemain? Concinnity? Oneiromancy? Magic code boxes, at least?"

"Couldn't someone show me how—"

"We have oodles of time to train people who don't know the rudiments of stichomancy. Keys and codes. Personnel with nothing better to do than—" A gold ankh slipped out of her blouse. She pushed it back and buttoned her blouse all the way, looking to see if I'd seen. I acted blind.

"Well, I'm sorry I bothered you then," I said. "You obviously have nothing for me." I started to leave.

"Sit down," she said. "Maybe you could be an information assistant, faute de mieux. Would that interest you, my little kraken? Infundibular with all the lamia, so to speak."

"Um — well, I guess. I don't know what that is exactly."

"Have you ever called the library for information because you couldn't come in person?" Suddenly she seemed nice. I smiled back.

"Well, yes, I have. I was a copy editor for 17 years and used to call the library often to verify information."

"I see, so you made use of the services but probably never gave us a dime. Who did you edit for?"

I told her it was a schlockhouse, no magazine she'd ever have heard of, and that I wanted to move on to something else. "I'd love to be an information assistant," I said. "I'd learn a lot."

"Hmmm," she said. "Let's say someone wanted to know what day of the week January 3, 2006, falls out, what would you do?"

"Uh . . . uh, well, I would look it up someplace. A calendar?"

"A calender? Where would you find a Sufi wandering dervish, and what makes you think he'd know? Oh, a calendar, I didn't understand your pronunciation. From Brooklyn, aren't you? Well, go on, where, how? Come on. I haven't got all day."

"Couldn't someone tell me, till I got the hang of things?"

She laughed, then shook her head. "How about if someone wanted to know the hypotenuse of an illegitimate quadrangle found in Southeast Humbungoland?"

"I, uh . . . I, uh . . . well, I'd look it up someplace."

"I'd look it up someplace," she mimicked my voice. "Where? What do you think I'm asking? Didn't they teach obeah where you went to school? I know it wasn't Yale, but still. What number Dewey? Don't you even know the Dewey?"

"Not by heart. I could memorize it, I just haven't needed to till now. So I'd look in the catalogue under whatever it is, Hum—"

"Good luck to you. You have to look up 'illegitimate' and the number 13. No, I don't think you're information assistant material. Even an assistant has to know basic onamastics."

"I'm not good at math or geography. My field is art, actually, and literature — that is, I read a lot. So maybe if—"

"OK, let's say someone called who happened to ask a question right in your field, by a strange coincidence. Where would you look up the ascendant and moon of Vincent Van Gogh?"

"Van Gogh?"

"You've heard of him, haven't you? Isn't he in your field?"

"Well, of course I've heard of him, but his moon? As far as I know his moon was in his pants."

"Look, I don't have the time or energy to quibble quodlibet with you." She opened a book and riffled the pages. After being ignored for quite some time, I started to get up, figuring the interview was over. I was shaking with anger. "Yes?" she said.

"I-I—"

"I'm just consulting the job description paginanotator, looking for something you can do. Felo-de-se, perhaps. Have you ever thought of becoming a special investigator?"

184

"A spec — you mean a spy?"

She didn't look away till I did. "The library conducts investigations of people who don't return books. After archimages study an omnium gatherum of objets trouvés, of course."

"Of course."

"Have you ever not returned a book?" she suddenly shot at me.

I shook my head, feeling gummy with guilt.

"No, of course not." She smirked. "But you'd be surprised at the kind of theft that goes on in the library. Some people take out books and never return them. It is not they but the professional thieves we want to track down, crooks commissioned to steal particular volumes. Let's say you were missing a volume of your sortilege encyclopedia, for instance. As I'm sure you know, you can't get one volume of a good sortilege encyclopedia these days, not without going to Egypt. So you might hire a professional to steal, let's say, volume 13, on scapulamancy, mightn't you?"

I nodded and her eyes opened wide. "You would?"

"No, I wouldn't, but I might. You asked if I might, meaning that it was possible. I would never do it. I'm no thief. I—" The more I defended myself, the guiltier I sounded.

Suddenly her tone changed. "You just go to people's houses, check their bookshelves, arrest them for not returning library material. Nothing demanding. You don't have to be a shamantvo to do it. No transmogrification. Does that appeal to you?"

I didn't want to turn down any library job, but it had never dawned on me that I'd be offered this sort of work. I had trouble responding, couldn't find the words. I stared, mouth open.

"What's the matter? Cat got your lepsy?" she asked, then grew very serious. "You're not subject to fits, are you? Nympholapy's been going around. My aunt came down with ruah raah and had to go to a thaumaturge recidivus, you know. A top specialist, no less."

"I, uh . . . well, I don't think I really see myself doing that," I said. "I mean about the job. I-I—"

"Well then, I don't know what I can say. Nothing seems to be right for you. Here, come with me. We'll see the chthonian librarian." She took me down a back stairwell to an elevator. We came out in a basement room. She set me up at a table with 15 thick reference volumes about library science and graduate programs.

"Maybe these volumes will give you some ideas. Make another appointment if there is any way I can be of further aid." Suddenly she was as sweet as sugar in an old man's pocket.

"Good afternoon, Mrs. Faustid," the young chthonian librarian said. "How's your granddaughter's doppelgänger?"

"Daedaling, daedaling." The two librarians talked for ten minutes as if they were on a street corner, making no attempt to whisper. When I coughed, they both turned. "Shhh," said the chthonian. "This is a library," said Mrs. Faustid.

After she left, I brought the books to the librarian's desk.

"Just leave them there, with the other books on Docetism," she said, waving her hand at the table I'd been sitting at.

"Can you tell me how to get out of here?"

"The way you came." She seemed surprised, as if I'd asked an extraordinary question. I started to go to the back elevator and she called out, "Where do you think you're going?"

"That's the way I came."

"Oh, ensorcellment, envoûtement," and she convulsed into laughter, pointing me in the other direction. "Through the nummular opening skull." Just then the phone rang. I heard her say, "Yes, hello, Mrs. Faus — uh, yes, she's still, no finfinella she's . . . the famulus told me something funny at the union I think . . ."

I walked out, my ears burning.

April 15 — Important to get out every day. The pizza man talks about me in Italian as I walk by. People humor me, speaking as you would to a woman on a ledge. "Yes, dear. That's right. Absolutely. Now step here, that's it. Grab her, Harry."

*

Fri. — Uncle's seizures: first he'd fall asleep. We couldn't wake him. Then he'd be awake. Wouldn't know us or see us. Take everything out of his pockets, rip paper into tiny pieces, pace back and forth. After a while he'd begin to sew. Put the needle in, pull it through. Over and over, a tiny man sewing. Bunching the tablecloth, oblivious to the dishes. It eased him to sit sewing emperor's clothes. He'd look up suddenly. The fog would clear, you could see it rise behind his eyes and dissipate. "So?" he'd say, a smile burning through like sunshine. "What are you doing here?"

One time in college I got up too fast. The blood drained from my head, everything turned black, crispening around the edges, like a picture burning, constricting till reality was squeezed out. I could feel myself falling but I couldn't stop. I was going down in jerks, unable to catch my balance forward or back, crying for help, but the words were garbled. I heard twisted sounds as I called for help. Time stretched so that falling and crying took forever, like jumping off a movie cliff or falling into movie love. I heard voices. Laughter. "What is she doing?" a friend said over and over. Then I couldn't understand her voice. I was alone.

When I came to, my boyfriend was staring down at me on the floor. "What are you doing?" he asked.

I was furious. "Why didn't you help me? Didn't you see I was falling, crying for help?"

"You were making such silly faces," he said. "We thought you were kidding around."

Sat. — In park, watching an old man shadowbox. He throws his chin back with imaginary punches, laughing. Nearby a shopping-bag man talks to an invisible friend: "See that lunatic over there? Yeah, what he doing, man? I don't know. Look stupid, don't he? Yeah, know what you mean."

And the one who is jotting this down? Feel like I've caught sight of myself in a mirror, dancing naked on a table.

*

April 18? — Everywhere I look I see uncles. Keep thinking of how they tied him down. His arm, attached to tubes, was bent like a broken wing. It twitched violently, without pause. I begged the nurse to unhook him, let him go. It was like the shiver of a frog's tendon in an experiment. In the home, he told me, they forced medicine down his throat. He cried, begging me to free him from demons. I didn't believe him — I, who have always identified with the girl who discovers aliens are invading the earth, the one no one believes. He cried, "My watch they stole. They beat me." His watch was missing, he had cuts on his head. The staff said he fell.

I swear it wasn't a terrible place. He adjusted, learned his way around: how to find the library — its volumes left by generations of the dead — how to find the peanut machine. They let him walk up and down the halls muttering to himself. The social worker would take him to parties in the basement. I once saw him dancing with a nurse. He was laughing, shuffling in place as she twirled. Another time he stood before all the old people, performing on a makeshift stage. He sang in his crow's voice, raspy, stuttering, a big smile. He made funny sucking noises with his tongue and teeth, to signify percussion, the tapping of a coin.

I visited the day he discovered the peanut machine. The peanuts were salted. He was on a low-sodium diet. I knew he shouldn't have them, but he was so excited. He asked me for change. I gave him all I had, like a grandmother giving candy to a child. He sat munching peanuts, the dreadful mash spraying out of his mouth as he told me a long story: he and the others went to a park. They threw a big ball to one another — it must have been a beach ball. Maybe he dreamt it. The picture stays in my mind. Fragile bird-people throw a ball against the sky. You can hear the sea.

He also told me they took him bowling. He and another old man got on the wrong bus and hid, eating all the sandwiches. Maybe. He said he'd been dancing on the boardwalk under the moon. He said the nurses came to him at night to smoke. They kept him up with their whispers. They tickled his feet.

Should I have believed him? Them? They were strangers in uniforms and he was my uncle. People who work with the elderly grow crazy too — from sickness and death and obstinacy. How can I know who told the truth, what happened when no one else was around?

One time as I was leaving the home I heard a voice crying, "Help me, nursey, help me, nursey. I'm stuck on the toilet and I can't get up, nursey, nursey." It was a little voice, one of those old voices that can be male or female, the secondary sexual characteristics retracting into an undistinguished blob of flesh like a baby's. I said to the nurse, "Someone is crying for help. Someone is stuck on the toilet."

The nurse gave me a fed-up look. "I can hear. That person has to go and doesn't know it, doesn't have the patience to sit. They cry to be put on, then cry to be taken off. They don't know what they need." She gave me a big smile. "I know it's upsetting to hear, but believe me, we know what's best. We're with them all the time and you're only here a few hours a week."

There was a monster in the basement once but no one believed me. Then I found myself on the other side of belief. What was I to do? Take Uncle to live with me? Let him die on the street? I had to be deaf to his stories. I chose not to believe.

Mon.? — Saw the unbaked child alone in the elevator. She had two black eyes, as if she were wearing the Lone Ranger's mask. "What happened?" I asked.

"The baby ate a pin."

"Yes, but what happened to you? How did—"

She said, "The baby swallowed the pin and I was diapering him and ran to Mother. I was supposed to be watching him, and she hit me 'cause I let her down. I didn't watch careful and—"

"Ethel!" Mrs. Unbaked screamed from her doorway. "Get over here *now!*" The girl ran out. She's all of seven.

There's no doubt. The whimpering in my walls must be her — I heard crying again last night. I must call the police.

Evening — Called the child welfare agency. They're sending an investigator tomorrow. Told me to be home.

Saw a nude woman in the park. A black giant as huge as a statue come to life, naked but for a piece of torn sheet draped across her back. I asked if she needed help. She gave a beatific smile, answering sweetly. "No, thank you, darlin'. I'm Sophie."

Tuesday — Investigators came to the unbaked family. (Their real name is Hansel — I asked Aldo.) They called me in to repeat what the little girl had said. I did and she denied it. "She didn't understand," the liar said. "A boy in the schoolyard hit me. That's all."

The Hansels gave me the evil eye. No one believed me. The social worker thinks I'm some sort of crank. The child was playing a joke on me. I can't bear not to be believed.

Thursday? — Watching a man poke through garbage, I was disconcerted when he sat beside me. "Give me something and I'll bless you," he said, reaching into his bag for a bell. He was not the Philosopher, although I recognized his shtick.

"I'm sorry," I replied, "but the unpleasant financial straits I find myself in necessitate I cut back on almsgiving."

He sat quietly, then said, "OK, I'll do it for nothing." He proceeded to ring bell, blow horn, and chant. I tried to hide my discomfort. Afterward I thanked him, hoping he'd leave. "Lost your job?" he asked.

I nodded; my eyes turned red. I thought how absurd it was to cry to a shopping-bag man. "What line of work were you in?" He had a white beard, a great hoary head, and looked, with all his layers of red rags, like Santa Claus after New Year's.

"Editing," I said.

"Me too!"

"Oh."

He looked down. "What sort of editing did you do?"

"Um . . . magazine," I said. "I'm free-lancing now."

Again that delighted face. "What a coincidence. Free-lancing. Magazine editing. Same here." He sidled closer to me on the bench. "I used to edit *Mansions in the Sky,* do you know it?" I shook my head. "Didn't figure you would. Trade publication. Funeral business." He laughed. He had a pleasant laugh. I could see that maybe he had been someone important once. He had the deep masculine laugh of a man in a tweed jacket.

"What was that like?" I asked.

"Kind of fun, if you like morbid jokes. When I got laid off, I decided to free-lance. The freedom, you know. What about you?"

"Similar sort of thing, in a schlockhouse, which was an odd place to work. I decided to risk free-lancing. Hard to get a foot in the door, don't you find?"

He nodded. "Yes, indeed. I met with a fortuitous coincidence, actually. I sent my curriculum vitae to *Modern Mansions.* They assumed *Mansions in the Sky* was also a home-furnishings publication. I never corrected the mistake. They supply me with a number of articles on a monthly basis to edit. I also get book work. I live simply. I make enough to get by."

I smiled, but in the back of my mind this conversation made me uneasy. I kept wondering if he could help me. This caused a feeling of duplicity, as if I were trying to charm him for aid. Naturally, I couldn't ask for a recommendation then.

He rummaged through a bag while I tried to think of something to say. "I'm working on a magazine article," I blurted. "What do you think? Something like 'What the Ten Most Visible Homeless People Advise You to Take with You'?"

He tasted it, rolling it on his tongue like a suspect wine. "Title's a little long." I nodded, knowing this to be true. "What magazine do you see it in?"

"*New York,*" I said.

"I like the concept," he said. "Title needs punch. How about 'Advice from a Shopping Bag'? Subtitle: 'What New York's Ten Most Visible Homeless Can Tell You about Life on the Streets'?"

"That's much better," I said. "Um . . . would you, do you think — that is, may I interview you, if you have time?"

He had lovely teeth when he smiled. You could tell he once had had good dental care. "I would be honored," he said.

"Well, uh, how can I find you?"

He looked uncomfortable, then gave me another terrific smile. "I'm often at this bench. The East Side has very good garbage."

This was an interesting bit of news for my article.

"Zoroaster's the name," he said.

I shook his hand. "Unusual."

"My parents were Gnostics."

"Mmm-hmm."

"Zoroastrians, actually."

"I see. I, uh, didn't realize Zoroastrianism was still practiced." Suddenly everything seemed askew. I imagined James walking by. What would he think?

"Oh yes," he said. "You'd be surprised at the number of us. A minority but, well, aren't we all?" He laughed and I laughed. "I didn't catch your name."

"Louise," I told him. I don't know why.

"Louise," he whispered. "Funny, you don't look like a Louise."

Dressed in a lie, I felt naked, as if he saw through me. I quickly asked about his religion. "Zoroastrianism is like . . . there's Good versus Evil, end-of-the-world stuff. You know Jews for Jesus?"

I nodded, thinking, "Uh-oh."

"Well, Zoroastrianism is like Christianity without Christ."

That was it. He didn't proselytize. Instead we talked about other stuff. At one point a woman with hair dyed lavender to match her poodle stooped over to clean her dog's poop. Zoroaster said, "Look what she does now." We both watched as she threw it loose into the can. "That's a liability in my line," he said. "You have to be careful."

"Thanks." I smiled. "Can I quote you in my article?"

"By all means."

"I'm surprised, aren't you, that a woman like that, obviously rich and all, wouldn't hire someone to walk her dog."

"You kidding? The rich are the biggest cheapskates. Don't bother approaching anyone well-dressed for a handout."

I changed the topic. "I once saw Cerberus in the park," I said, "but on closer examination it turned out to be a dog-walker with five pooches leashed together. Reminded me of a Futurist painting. By Giacomo Balla, I think — 'Dynamism of a Dog on a Leash,' something like that. Do you know it?"

"Very well," he said. "But wasn't it by Duchamp?"

"No, you're thinking of 'Nude Descending a Staircase.' "

He nodded and said, "Yes, I believe you're right." We sat a bit longer. Somehow we got to talking about my uncle. I said, "He was a dreamer," and Zoroaster said, "Which makes you a dream."

Then he got up. "Have to be going now. Port Authority." We shook hands, wished each other luck.

So now I'm basking in the warmth of his understanding, writing this, trying to figure out what's bothering me. I feel scared. Why? Zoroaster wouldn't hurt me. It's not that. About him being an editor: I doubt it. If it's true, where does he pick up and drop off assignments? Do production editors send messengers to garbage cans in the park? Does he go to their offices dressed like a discarded Santa Claus? His story makes no sense. I am alternately astonished at my naiveté and ashamed of my suspicion.

Sat. — Someone is watching me. A spy gazes at my window, follows where I walk. When I turn, he hides. A shy man stands in the street and looks as I undress in the moonlight. Eyes tug invisible scarves around my hands. I know he is staring but I don't know who he is. The man who has found my notebook, has he fallen in love?   .

Liz White: I was terrified when I learned of Gabby's disappearance. You know the posters of missing people that families put up? I always look at them, particularly the faces of children — ever since my sister's boy was kidnapped, a long time ago. He'd be all grown up now. I like to think he's okay, that he was adopted illegally, but — you know what you think. So I saw the poster with Gabby's picture. I don't know who put it up. I didn't think she had any family, but I didn't know her well. No one knew Gabby. She was quiet, a loner, but she had a sweet way. After reading the notice I thought how I should have made the effort to befriend her. When the articles began to appear about her artwork, somehow it all fell into place. I used to see her drawing in the park on her lunch hour. I never asked her about it. I didn't want to pry. It's horrible to think her body may never be found. Twenty years is a long time.

Sun. — I. K. called. Wants me to come over tomorrow, Apr. 26, to pick up Uncle's book. I have sold my father's watch. Overheard conversation between 13-year-old boys on train. One said, "We're doing the Seven Deadly Sins and my sin is pride." I don't want I. K. to know anything's wrong, but he'll probably be able to tell. Mrs. K. will surely pick it up. I have to be prepared to accept their offer if they want to lend me money.

Mon. — Told I. K. I lost my job. Know what he said? "With the dreck you publish, I'm not surprised."
Turns out I gave him Uncle's last diary, written in the nursing home. The Roman numeral two was really an 11. That means his second book is missing, lost or stolen, as my notebook was. Parallel between us — frightening, exciting. What does it mean?

What is this place? Prison? Living meat can't walk, they cry, "Help me. Get it off me." Think, Moisha. Where am I?
The last thing I remember I was in the library. Decided to go to the boardwalk. After that, nothing. They must have kidnapped me. Caught me alone on the boardwalk, hit me on the head with a rock, stole my body (my watch too is missing, my wallet it goes without saying, but my clothes?). They brought me to this place.
They say for three days I didn't know my own name. Lies! I'm Moisha Segul, who do they think they tell such cockamamie stories to? My own brother, the fool, believes them. They want to keep me here, that's clear. Why else have they hidden my coat? When I get up to go, they come running.
They tried to steal my blood. I fought them. I read of a great

shortage in the blood banks. Can it be they steal my blood and sell it? They keep us like cows, instead of milk it is our blood they suck — so this is some sort of blood barn? Okay, but why does my brother go along? Maybe they hold his family ransom? I'll ask him in code next time. But he's so stupid when it comes to a secret tongue, I have to repeat myself a thousand times and still he acts like I'm crazy or he's deaf. What if the demons know? Maybe they don't want me to study in the library.

Aha, here they come. I must be invisible. Hard to do under stress, everyone looking just write anything maybe they won't want to disturb a man from writing if I

Oh woe! They held me down. They stole my blood. I'd bang my head like a piece of wood, but they've tied my arms to the chair, leaving me only enough slack to write. Maybe I should be grateful they didn't take this book, my record for the woman who has no eyes. Or are they planning to read it? Do demons know Yiddish? When I speak Yiddish, their faces grow blank as grocery bags. I have to get out of here before it is too late.

Tues., Apr. 27 — Signed for my last unemployment check. Saw Zoroaster. Described how my uncle built a museum in the mind. "When my parents moved him from East New York," I said, "they threw out all his paintings."

Zoroaster said, "Maybe they didn't actually throw them out. Maybe they just left them."

I knew what he was thinking. Aunt Sadie left all the family photos in her building's basement when she moved. "Shmutz collectors," she called them. Grandparents, great-grandparents, gone. Someday I may recognize my ancestors in a thrift shop being sold for a dollar without frames. A painting may draw me to make out its signature — in this way Uncle could come home. Zoroaster said I might even find them in the old man's basement.

Wed., Apr. 28 — Went to a thrift shop, browsed through old photos. Came across one of Miss Tweety's home in Nova Scotia.

It had to have been stolen from her room. The bottom even had her elegant penmanship: "Biggest snowstorm in March."

I went to the woman who ran the place, asked where the photo came from. She didn't want to be bothered, but I wouldn't let her get away. I said, "I knew the woman whose house this was."

"Impossible. That's a daguerreotype. Any woman who had lived in that house, even as an infant, would be well over 100."

"She was old — 93. But maybe she lied about her age."

The woman looked away. "The snowstorm mentioned on the bottom was in 1888." Before I could stop her, she shuffled off.

I looked again at the picture. I know it was Miss Tweety's. What could I do? I put it on the bottom of the box so no one else will find it. When things get better, I'll come back. I'm suspicious of this "antique" dealer — is she in cahoots with the two graverobbers who broke into Miss Tweety's room?

Friday — Writing letters to the dead, burying them in Aunt Sadie's soil. I imagine my mother leaning her weight on one hip, dishtowel in hand, sour look on her mouth. She reads my note, annoyed that not even in Sheol can she rest in peace. I imagine my uncle, the paper pushed up to his nose. He peers with eyes magnified behind lenses.

Is there love after death? I feel myself on the point of a pinnacle, as if there really were a tip to a mountain like children draw. I stand on one toe atop this tiny tip, dangling above a terrible collapse.

I sit in the dark with the curtain closed. I write in the moonlight. Everyone snores like the ocean.

When he was a boy, the peasants when he was looking for birds' nests in the woods took him to a cave, made him eat of the tree of knowledge, a snake's filthy wisdom. How did he survive? He learned to leave. I don't remember. I am afraid. Dangerous. Sometimes you can't get back. Someone takes over unless you set the precautions just so. I don't remember what Golda taught.

When he was in the cave, they tied him to two planks of wood, hanging him on his head. It didn't hurt him. Not one bit.

When he was in the cave, he put a spell on the guard so that he took him down, to do him dirty. The boy got a rock.

When he got home, the rejoicing! They had given me up for dead. Everyone came, clapping their hands, singing, "A miracle, a miracle." The prayers they gave, my mother, my sister and brother. Everyone wanted to touch me, like I was a mezuzah. Everyone wanted to kiss me, hold me, rub me for good luck. I told them I fell out of the tree of knowledge and slept in the woods. Why should I tell them? It would break their hearts. They are not strong like me.

Sat.? — Sitting near Fifth Avenue when someone called, "Hey, Louise, how's it going?"

"Hi, Zoroaster," I said. "Sit down."

"You can call me Zoro."

"You mean like the Masked Avenger of Evil?"

No reply, just a smile. It was funny, though. Zoro is fat, not at all the dark, romantic type. "How's free-lancing?" I asked.

"Comme ci, comme ça. Turning in an assignment now, as a matter of fact, but I'm early." I glanced in his shopping bag, and sure enough, there was a manuscript-size Jiffy envelope.

Looking at his beard and grimy clothes, I had an idea. "Let me run this by you," I said. "What would you think if someone were to take an old Persian lamb coat — what if this person, a woman on the streets, let's say, cut a beard out of it, and a mustache, glued it on? I mean, do you think that would protect her? You got to figure she'd be wearing filthy clothes. Women have it harder than men, don't you think?"

He was quiet, then made a funny motion with his finger, like he was drawing a Z across my face. "It can't hurt," he said, "to look like a man. Or a nut. Here, let me show you." After browsing through his bags for a time, he pulled out his bell and horn. "This is my 'beard,' if you will. You know the Philosopher? He taught me. You see, no one wants a raving nut around, not even another raving nut. If I think I'm in for a hassle, I take out my bell, my horn, begin chanting loudly." He laughed. "You're welcome to use it."

"In my article, you mean," I said. "The beard is—"

"Hang in there, Louise. Got to drop off this manuscript."

"Yes," I said. "And thanks . . . about the bell. And the other ideas. For my piece in *New York*. I'll quote you, OK?"

He made the Z sign and left.

Joe comes, brings socks. The girl gives chocolate kisses. I tell them to get me out of here. What good is socks when the world is in danger of being blown up? Who cares about candy when they are locking up my water? Devils bring food, I won't eat. I caught them putting poison in the juice. They want to cripple me like the others so I can't escape. What is the purpose? Do they know about my studies?

They want to kill me. What do they do with all the bodies? They can sell the eyes, the intestines, but a body makes new blood. If they sell off the organs, they make a fast buck, that's all. Demons are smarter than that. Capitalists wouldn't sell off the machinery. The time with the sewing machines, Finkle laughed at us, that we wanted to own our machines and pay him a rental.

The girl comes, brings a newspaper, pencils. She tells me to draw. I think only of escape.

DREAM: My old relatives were coasting down the street on roller skates. Uncle was leading the pack, gliding fastest. I was running after them but couldn't catch up. I had no wheels. They didn't hear my cries of "Wait!" They rolled away from me so fast that I was soon left far behind.

May 3? — Should I try to get "The Jew in the Thorn Bush" published? I could send it to a few magazines. Cover letter would explain that the writer, my uncle, is dead and was unrecognized in his lifetime, that he was a great artist whose works were thrown out. Isn't that, after all, the way it happens? The dead are geniuses, the living merely mad. Van Gogh died unknown and would have been forgotten. His work didn't sell. Contemporaries thought him insane. Afterward, they saw what he was about. It was V.G.'s sister-in-law who saved his letters and drawings. She believed in him, saw he got the recognition that was his due.

I could try to get "Jew in the Thorn Bush" published. Maybe even publish Uncle's diary. The super of his building might have saved the drawings. I must look into that. Stranger things have happened. The effect on Kolokoy would be terrible.

I want to comfort Uncle, as if I can beyond death . . . as if we can correspond now through a diary when we never did in life.

Weekend — Hungry for spectacle, my eyeballs eat everything in sight. I explored the city. It struck me anew how it is a museum in the round. On the weekend, when there isn't an ocean of workers sloshing back and forth, you can appreciate the gigantic sculptures in midtown, entering art to walk through lobbies, tunnels, alleys. The Chrysler building pokes up from behind Grand Central like King Kong peeking through a window at Fay Wray. From Vanderbilt Avenue, Grand Central is belted by a road that sits on stilts. When you see cabbies zipping around as if the road were solid, when you imagine the weight that rests on those toothpicks, then you realize people have no idea how slight the foundations are on which they've built their lives.

"All I ask in painting is a way of escaping from life." — Vincent Van Gogh

I dream of escape. Joe and I were racing down the street on wheels, flying like we were young. A crowd was with us. People from Uzlan, people from when I first came here. We were rolling on wheels. I was laughing, shouting so hard I woke up. I looked around and saw the cold room of my cell, my drawings gone, my mandolin stolen, nothing but a few pieces of clothing hanging in a closet, who needs them? No one here but me. No sun, no skates. Just an old man who can't fly.

Tues.? — What does it mean, that Uncle and I had the same dream? Can't think about it. There's this sound I've been hearing. In the museum I close my eyes, I try to draw it in. I sense him. Someone is watching me. He found my notebook. He saw my name. He remembered. He never forgot, never stopped thinking about me (else why have I thought of him all this time?). James is reading my diary. He can't stop thinking of me.

Wed.? — James once said he knew me from a past life. An odd smile played about his mouth. Amused, disturbing — as if he knew a secret. "You respond like a magic dream," he said.

DREAM: James was teaching an art class. All his famous paintings were before us. A pupil asked how he came to do the one of the woman bursting through a wall into art. He said, "I send dreams like letters. She can't not respond to correspondence."
Isn't it clear? He sent this dream because he thinks of me— that's why I can't stop thinking of him. Our astral bodies are lovers. My nipples are hard all the time from his pulling, there is a tingle in my groin. I am iron, his presence is a magnet. He is shy and sends his spirit like Cyrano de Bergerac to pitch his woo.

May 13? — All the people I saw today were subjects of famous paintings. The woman standing in the beauty parlor was Manet's maid in the "Bar at the Folies-Bergère." Sitting on the train was a peasant from Daumier's "Third-Class Carriage." The doorman on Fifth Avenue was about to be shot in Goya's "The Third of May." Even the little girl in the park was one of the "Maids of Honor" by Velázquez. I still don't know what it means, but today was like walking through Janson's *History of Art*.

*

Friday — It happened. I wasn't surprised. I'd felt him for days. And yet . . .

I was in the museum, staring at a Kokoschka, when his shadow cooled me. I knew at once, before looking up. Sure enough, James stared intently at the painting to my left. Lanky and fair, dressed in silly cowboy clothes — I took him in at a glance and knew him as well as I know this is my hand. All day I'd felt the chimes closing in, the crystal vibration in my groin.

Perhaps I was a fool to play the coquette, but I wanted to be found, to be discovered among paintings like a deer in the woods. I wanted to feign surprise, as if I hadn't waited years for this chance encounter. My heart set to shuddering like a steeple bell. I thought I might faint, so I closed my eyes for a moment, to regain my composure. When I opened them, he was gone. I just had time to catch sight of him leaving the room, the heel of his boot in the door. I ran after him.

He didn't walk fast but his steps were long; each one seemed equivalent to ten of mine. He glided down halls as if on skates. I pursued, running without ever gaining on him — ashamed that he might turn around and see me, afraid I might otherwise lose him. Each room I entered just in time to see him leave —the fringe of his cowboy jacket swaying past, the brim of his hat galloping away. Always at the vanishing point like a Cheshire cat, and it never occurred to me that this was his game.

At last he entered the room of De Chiricos. I knew I had him. It was a dead end. My prey trapped, I took my time, preparing like a huntress. Ran my hands through my hair, smoothed my eyebrows with spit, moistened my lips. Then entered, eyes down. And was alone!

I know well that place of perspective. Have often wondered down De Chirico streets for hours. There are no hiding spots. There are no other doors. I had seen James enter it, not his foot, not his back. I had seen him, the man, the length and breadth of him walk through the door.

So I paced the four walls, touching them, as if I thought an optical illusion hid him from me, a ray of peculiar light. I searched for the unseen hole.

All along I felt him watching. A woman knows when she is being looked at. His eyeballs rolled my flesh. I smelled his desire, the steam of his sweat. Then I heard his laughter. It rang clear and shook me as if I hung on the tongue of a bell swinging across the countryside. He was mocking me. Wanting me, yes; to shame me more.

I believe in the foresight of peripheral vision. It often detects what cannot be seen directly. And so, from the corner of my eye, I caught his gaze in a sunlit plaza. He didn't have the time to elude me completely; perhaps he didn't want to, part of his game. In any case, his is the shadow of the unseen man in the painting "The Nostalgia of the Infinite."

No sooner did I go to confront him than his laughter rang from "The Seer" across the room. Then he stood behind a wall in "The Melancholy and Mystery of a Street." Wherever I looked, he vanished down the point of perspective, hiding himself in art.

Why does he play this game with me? Such mockery isn't good. It's entered my soul like a sorcerer's arrow. Why does he sport with my heart? Does he think it's a ball? I am a woman, not a toy.

Dear James,

Your eyes drank me. They sucked away my soul. Why did you eat me up in the dark, that night you drew the phantasm from my eyes and swallowed me whole like an oyster? The bar light greened you garish as you charmed me. Why, if you meant to turn away, did you woo me? Even now you haunt my thoughts like a spirit in a closet. You won't stop thinking about me, so I can't stop thinking of you.

I know what you're up to. I'm wise to your game. I saw your picture in a mirror once. The hollows under your eyes. The grin flopped to snarl. You were death. Your eyes seethed cold.

Stop hardening my tongue, pulling me taut pulling you. You must stop wanting me. Or else you must come.

People often fall in love by accident, drinking potions meant for others. Lancelot and Guinevere, Tristam and Iseult. It happens all the time. I may have been hit with a spell meant for someone else. There were many arrows flying about the art department then. I know of at least one witch with voodoo pins for you. I am stuck with a tip meant for another. I try but can't stop probing the infection. My fingers thrum the sore till pain vibrates your name.

Dear Uncle Moisha,

Forgive me. Can the dead forgive? You must know I'd do it again. I couldn't leave you to die on the street. And where would you have slept if I took you here — in my bed?

Imprisoned in a home, what can you tell me about my state? I haven't paid the rent. There have been phone calls, then the phone was shut off. Still it rings. The dead are calling me. Who else would call and breathe, not answer when I cry, "What do you want?"

Uncle, enough of this act. Leave off your death and tell me the secret of life. Teach me to be an artist without faith . . . or show me where faith resides. How am I to live?

What is it in me that so loves an absence? Must I always crave Judas because I have betrayed you, Uncle, and would do it again, weeping and betraying, because there is no other way? Now I find that I too stare into blankness, willing possession. Trance, whether madness or god or sex, something is taking me away from me and I let it. No, I *encourage* it . . . because it feels like art.

When you sank into your final repose and I spoke to you though you lay with shut eyes just as you do today (only more so), what I told you is true. I know you. I see past your disguise — even the one the corpse wears. I call upon you to visit me. I am lonely and need you to teach me. How am I to deflect evil? Teach me to charm. Protection — I need that and a promise of meaning. Where am I to turn if not to my mentor?

Dear Momma,

How are you and Daddy getting along? Have you adjusted to the change? Do you keep in touch, do you know what's been going on?

I'm sorry to bother you this way, just when you're probably getting used to the peace and quiet, but I've been upset since you left without saying goodbye. My stomach hurts. I bring up bitter bubbles of missing, belch an anger soured from being kept in so long. Nothing stays down. I'm sick and I'm tired.

And my back, Ma, is killing me from schlepping that heavy sack you filled with guilt. It turns out no one will take those coins. I can't pay the rent with them. So I'd like to ask you, would you mind so terribly, would it hurt so much (you being dead and all), if I lay this bag of blame at your feet?

I guess you can see this won't be a pleasant letter, but don't turn your head and act like a corpse. Can't we make peace even now? It's not that I don't love you. I love you too much. I miss you with the longing reserved for what we never had.

You left so abruptly. We've played hide and seek before, so I know this is your way of teaching me a lesson — not to take you for granted. You won't make peace because you fear I may let you rest in it.

The strongest bonds are produced with threads so thin they don't exist. You've tied me with invisible twine. Knowing how "absence makes the heart grow fonder," you removed your love, stood behind empty dresses to see me miss you. Do you remember telling me this, how you hid from me in a department store? It would have been to your benefit to have me forget how you stood behind the dresses, but you could not resist reminding me of your prank.

How old was I — four? — when I wandered in childish curiosity suddenly to find myself alone? "Ma!" I bleated. Strangers stared. None wore your eyes. The dresses, invisible women hanging on empty necks, shamed me in their sway. Every place I looked was devoid of meaning, for it did not have your face. "Ma," I wept, an orphan among racks. Then you appeared, your arms open to gather me in. "I didn't mean it, mommalah, I wanted to teach you a lesson. You can get lost, kidnapped." How I wept to think I had ever mistrusted you.

I didn't mean to tie you down, Ma, so I know you didn't mean to tie me either, but tied I am — to the past. I have no future. A childless spinster is tied to the dead. And if that weren't enough, you tug me with longing. Do you really miss me so?

Ours was an unusual love, even in the land of mother and daughter. Blind to stereotype, you conformed to cliché. Innocent of travesty, you invented Portnoy's mother to play the role Rothless. "Rothless?" you ask, throwing your hands up in exasperation. I hear your voice all the time. The phone rings with the urgency of your neglect. I pick it up. *Forgotten, she has forgotten me.*

Ma, it isn't true. How can I forget you? You won't let me. I'm dying to talk to you, but you won't let me do that either. You talk through me as if I were deaf. *She's having a good time. Can't be bothered to light a candle, remember my Yahrzeit with a prayer.*

I hear your complaints. When I try to answer them, you play dead. Oh, what's the use? You refuse to hear me make amends. You're bored, you're tired, but you won't let me go. So act this way. I know you're glad to hear from me. *Look how she mourns us,* you nudge the rock by your side. *It's a pity on her. Mommalah, go about your life. Have a good time. Don't worry about us, in dreard arein, just you go have fun. We're getting along.*

This bag of guilt must weigh a ton. How many stones did you put in there? Or is it that the mud won't hold? I am sinking into your arms. Let's be honest now. I never made you happy. The closest you came to being pleased with me was when I was incompetent. If I clung to you, afraid, you'd sigh, "My big baby," only to me revealing your secret smile. When I had nightmares, you groaned in annoyance but made room in your bed. When I was sick, you stroked my brow.

The day came when I betrayed you. "You don't love me," you cried with red eyes. As a child, crying this to you, I heard you say, "That's right, not when you act like a meshuggina." But I was no longer a child, and my crime was wanting my own apartment. "What, I don't cook for you? I don't clean for you?" you asked. You didn't sound like a woman about to be relieved of a burden.

That first night in my apartment, I was afraid to be alone. You and Daddy knew. After all, to whose bed had I crawled with my sack of nightmares? "Come back," you said, hurrying to my door. "There's always tomorrow. And if you can't do it, so? You have a home." Is this where you are pulling me now? I've read that when you're sinking in quicksand, the thing is not to struggle. I was younger then, stronger than I am now. I refused to cry. "I am not afraid," I said. I waited for you to leave.

You stood your ground, you would not go. In the hall the bulb had blown. Lit only by a rectangle of light from my foyer, you stared at me in the passage. You and Daddy, framed in the door, refused to move, like a painting, a mysterious translation into Yiddish Gothic. You would not go from that frame but forced me to close the lid on you. I had to nail you down in darkness like vampires to shut myself off from your love, and my own, with locks and bolts. I was sick, trembling and crying long afterward from killing you. I knew you would never so easily let me go.

Why did you give me such impossible choices? I'd complain about being too tall. You'd say, "Would you rather be a midget?" Would you rather have two heads or no arms? Why did you make me choose between the impossible and the absurd? Whenever the longing to be an artist came up, I thought, *It is the most important thing to me in the world,* and a voice would ask, *Would you rather be a successful artist or have your parents alive?* Who is it that held you hostage, demanding my failure as ransom?

Surely you didn't mean to hurt me when you said, "She's so tall she'll have to marry a basketball player." How could you suspect that warning a 13-year-old not to take the last piece of bread "or you'll wind up a spinster" could fuel my worry till it came true?

Perhaps it was my fault. I didn't want you to know you hurt me. I learned to act as if nothing you did could wound. *She didn't mean it,* I remember thinking when you said you were prettier than me at my age. *She doesn't realize what she's saying,* I told myself when you said you were embarrassed to be pregnant in your forties so you kept jumping off a chair. But when you said I would never have children, I was too old, no man would want me, I should lie about my age, I shook my head. "I have no intention of getting married." Your arrow hit its mark. I didn't want you to know my terror, that I'd die unloved.

This game we played — you hurting me as if unintentionally, me pretending not to notice — how can I forget these things? How can I forget you? I'm crying, from missing you. How is it that I love you so much? What is the secret of forgetting the dead? Do you know, and if you did, would you tell me?

I saw a documentary about chimpanzees once. A mother chimp had a baby when she was old and couldn't nurse him properly. As a result he stayed in infancy, clinging to arms too tired to hold him. At an age when other chimpanzees were experimenting with independence, he would not leave her side. She was preoccupied, sick, but there was no pleasure in that little chimp's life unless it was in his mother's gaze. It was terrible to see; children are so vulnerable, and the chimp was like a child's child. When she died, he wouldn't leave her body or let anyone take it. He stayed grieving, he couldn't eat, and at last died longing for what he had never had.

You prefer me dead than happy without you. Even now I see

206

distaste on your face. "Chimpanzees she's talking. I'm dead and she's comparing me to a monkey."

I have to tell you now. You have to know. The further I get from my childhood, the happier I am. Even now, as I dangle over despair and only a hair keeps me from falling in, I am still happier than the time I spent dependent on you.

I tell you these things only because you are dead and can't hear. I'm asking for your help because I know you have nothing to give and never did. I send you this letter because you aren't alive to read it. Kafka was a courageous coward, to write thus to a living father. I hear you, Ma, you don't have to shout. "Who's this Kafka and who cares? Talk about something real for a change. Like, what did you have for dinner? Have you moved your bowels yet? Do it every day. Make it your business." I suppose this is the business you'd have me succeed in.

Dear Gabby,
So, you miss me? Sorry to hear you not feel well. Me too. It takes some getting used to this place. Finally I am sitting under the drier by the beauty parlor and thinking. I hope you go see Uncle Moisha. If not, O.K. We were at Uncle Shloimie's, a nice house but a lot of land to clean. He feels O.K. I got along with Esther. She had work and I was busy cleaning up the leaves enough for 10 people. We went out for dinner. I didn't have to cook, didn't see each other much. Daddy is fine. Here is a leaf from their yard.

Dear Gabby,
We busy getting settled here in Florida, now we can enjoy the weather. It's too hot. We having Shloimie Esther over, then they have us and you can see that I am quite busy. Everything here is the same as last year. I got my card games back in the club house. I play Tuesday Thursday. Wend. we play bingo. Sat. night we have our polka game with the family and that's how we keep busy. Daddy has games too. He feels good. We will talk to you Sunday as usual. I am learning to bake cakes and cookies. Aunt Sadie shows me.

My daling Gabbalah,
Thank you for your byootifull letter it was byutifull the picture was so pretty it was byutifl. I saw by me yourn Mama and yourn

Papa. They both vell and look as always beyutifull so stay vell and stay mine beayutil neese so byutil like no one.

With Love and Kisses from your
Tanta Rose

milk
oranj jus
creme chese
toilette paper

Dear Gabby,
Hi! It was some trip. The most important thing we bought a new car we should be well to enjoy it. We didn't get it yet it take 10 days. I can't believe we only here a week it seems forever.

Dear Gabby,
We went with Cousin Selma to Disneyworld. When we get to the gate the car decides not to go. We push it on the lot. She calls the AA we went in. Selma sat a whole day in the garage. By the time it fixed was time go home. The poor thing was a whole day in the garage and it cost her $75. Besides everything something it is to see very beautiful with the fish jumping. Jed's girl likes to help out in the kitchen, she should only be Jewish. The reception was nice the food was not what we like. It is real hot here. I am cooking a cabage soup it is 7 AM everybody aslep.

Dear Gabby,
We bought a new TV. The other stoped playing and you know how Daddy loves TV. Driving in the new car he has troubly finding the bottons that takes time he will get used to it.

Dear Gabby,
We fine. It is beeter this way for Uncle Moisha though we feel bad it is good. He in the home gets his meals. They clean him around. When we come home maybe we take him out if he so unhappy. But really we can't let him walk around fall down go to hospitol be busy our whole lives with him. God willing better he should ajust.
We settling down after Daddy came back. He exhausted from the whole bizness and says it freezing to death in New York. I forget already winter. I got started cleaning while he was away so I could do a good job with him not under my feet a whole day.

Now my shoulder kills me I am looking for a doctor I have numbers to call.

Daddy is pleased with the new hearing aid. The weather is great. Too hot for me. We are going on a boat trip toomoro and you know how I love that. I hope I don't get too nauseus from it but Daddy wants to go and I don't want to sit a whole day by myself in the house getting blue while he having fun.

If you can't you can't you do what can that's all you can do but go visit Uncle Moisha, it shouldn't kill you the whole day. I know in the home he is lonely for a family face. It's a pity on him.

The woman who has no eyes was here, weeping. Why doesn't she help me? The red rims around the holes in her face are horrible as she cries, "We had to do it, Uncle. We couldn't let you freeze."

"Help me," I whisper, "escape." She moans. I am in horror of the pools in her face. Can I tell her my secrets, this woman with her bag of chocolate kisses? I have to get out of here, to continue my work in the Jewish Room of the 42nd Street Library. Why doesn't she help me? At night the demons tickle my feet. The woman with no eyes, can't she see?

May 25? — I read Uncle's diary. It's almost as if he's telling me where to find him. What sort of work was he doing in the library? Perhaps I can continue his research.

The girl was here. I told about the dead man we found frozen in the snow. He had a hole in his head like someone took a stick and poked it through his skull. People began talking of vampires. There was an old man, a water-carrier. No one knew where he came from. We said he was a fool. He shook so bad, water spilled out his buckets. This water-carrier said, "He was killed by an icicle." We knew it to be true. The next day I went to his hut. He was gone. We never saw him again. People said Elijah had come to Uzlan. He likes to come to a town, see what's going on, do a few miracles, then go.

The girl put on her look of mud, staring with clay eyes like one who doesn't believe. Have I made a mistake? I thought she was the one. Later her heart reached out to me like a hand. I think she is the one. When you are in a bright room and you look out the window to see who is looking in, your own face often gets in the way. I almost see you, or is it only me?

May 26? — Periodicals Reading Room, a room filled with uncles. Look at them all, with their crooked glasses and nubby pencils. Last time I was here six old men peered at yellowed newspapers with magnifying glasses, scribbling notes. The time before, nine! This time three. A tiny man jots words from a magazine. He has a small smile, like a baby who's just belched. Another looks up numbers in a pamphlet, compares them to a list copied from a tabloid. Checks a set of numbers against this with a Sherlock Holmes glass. Numbers are keyed somehow to dates. I hear him mumble: "Six million people times 1776 equals mutter mutter." Working out a correlation between history and numerology?

The room is like a Dutch Masters cigar box. Dark panels. Oval murals. The brush of Frans Hals tickles my nose. I feel like the subject of someone else's art. Surely Uncle spent much time reading papers in this room. I sense him hovering over my shoulder. OK, Uncle, don't shove. I'm going down to the Jewish Room now.

Jewish Room: surprisingly bright. Musty as a Cairo synagogue of fragments. Dust motes fly about like spirits. Where to begin?

A demon took me to a room, she gave me cookies. There was music. She made me dance. She pushed me before the crowd and said, "Ladies and gentlemen, Moisha Segul is going to sing for you a song." It got quiet. She gave me a coin. I clicked it. They swayed.

June? — When I first enter the library, I practice a form of self-prophecy. I float to a book, flip its pages till a line catches my eye. I make the dead speak. The advice of the dead must be taken seriously.

"In art we break bread with the dead." — W. H. Auden

When the demons stole me I was reading about Bruno the magician. They burned him at the stake. A long time ago, they don't do that anymore. Now they lock you in a crazy house. Everyone's got a wand to make you sleep. They jab needles full of dreams into your tochis. I pretend to sleep. Demons are easy to fool. I stay by the window. The moon shines. I hear the ocean.

June 3? — Found an article on Giordano Bruno, the magician of memory. He must be the one Uncle writes about. His theory of erotic magic describes love as theurgical bondage. The emotion of love produces phantasms of lust that are then used to bind one to a magus's will. The magus is susceptible to self-sorcery. If he succumbs to the passion he invokes, his phantoms can bind him with his own rope. Is this what happened to Bruno — tied to a pole and set afire? In order not to have this happen, a sorcerer must learn to burn with cold indifference. Who does this remind you of?!

DREAM — I was admiring James's self-portrait. Something in his painted eye disturbed me. I peered more closely at it, till I saw a naked woman screaming for release. In startled recognition I awoke.

"Once upon a time, I, Chuang Tzu, dreamt I was a butterfly, fluttering hither and thither, to all intents and purposes a butterfly. I was conscious only of following my fancies as a butterfly, and was unconscious of my individuality as a man. Suddenly I awakened and there I lay, myself again. Now I do not know whether I was then a man dreaming I was a butterfly, or whether I am now a butterfly dreaming I am a man." — Chuang Tzu

*

Wed.? — James's magic uncle was Rasputin. It came back to me today as I read about sexual phantoms bloated with passion. Is Uncle trying to warn me? The wizard arouses heat in the woman he would possess. Her enamoured response brings into existence phantasms of lust. He uses these to bind her soul to his.

What are the tricks of the demon lover? He shoots her with pangs of yearning, burning arrows that give the impression he has fallen under her spell. Flames ping out of his eyes like hidden, unwilling revelations of desire, but they are really erotic spirits that, once inside her, inflate till she is gorged on phantoms, swollen with lust, and falls heavy as a passion fruit to rot.

The magus must be in control at all times. In sorcery one gains what others give up. The sorcerer pretends uncontrollable lust; all the while, detached, he observes precious fluids spill, laps them. If he but once succumbs to his own desire, his imps have him to torture eternally, tickle tickle, with his own scorchery.

What must it be to burn and not be consumed, to reach always for a climax never come, in the heat of passion to detach and observe one's victim writhe? Even as he burns he remains cold. The higher his indifference leaps, the more excruciating his victim's raging . . . and the tighter the ropes that tie her to his will like a witch to a stake.

Do you know how eagles fuck? They soar above clouds and swoop in ecstasy, join, falling almost to the ground. But something stops them short; one eagle must take his eye off phantasy or eagles would be as extinct as phoenixes. In such a way does a magus love, hot and hard and never there. He injects invisible unejaculated seed to work from inside like maggots, infatuating and infesting, till she makes him a nest, a home for wandering phantasms in her breast.

JAMES KOLOKOL: Gabby was always intense. Her problem was, she had no sense of humor. She acted like I was a holy man, like I could give her the secret to life. I'm not a magician, but it's hard not to play the part around a woman who thinks so. There was a sex thing too, though she wasn't my type. I liked looking at her. She had a way of changing. She'd appear as an old woman, then a child. There'd be the whore in Gabby, and the virgin, it would swirl and I'd be fascinated by the changes, trying to think how she did it, how I could capture it. There was often a dark woman in my paintings at that time. I'd try to get some of Gabby into her. I'd look at her, she'd catch me. It felt odd, like I was stealing her image. Of course, I was. And you know what? She wanted me to.

Another thing was how responsive she was. I only had to think of her to make her appear. Even now I dream she's walking in the park, talking to me, but I'm invisible. So when I'm in the park I look for her. One time after I left PP, I saw her. It was in a gallery, right before she vanished. She didn't see me. She was like someone sleeping with her eyes open. Staring into art, her face so naked, like a dreamer. I realized what it was. She didn't have her glasses on. It scared me, you know, to see her lost in a dream. I watched over her, like you do when someone is sleeping next to you. A woman came over. She was dressed in leather and fur and had sharp teeth like a rodent. She said, "Can I help you?" It was clear she was telling Gabby to move on. Gabby shook her head and ran away. I followed her for a few blocks, but then I stopped. She wanted something from me I couldn't give. The time was wrong. I thought it best to let her go.

You know, I was so busy answering her questions back then that I never got around to asking my own.

June 15? — Saw the unbaked girl in the elevator. She was alone. I made up my mind to ignore her. I don't like being the butt of a joke. She gave me a big smile. Her front tooth was missing. "What happened this time?" I said. "Get mugged by the tooth fairy?"

She was nervous. "Listen, I couldn't say anything in front of the cops. No one would have believed me anyway."

"I believed you," I said, "and you made a fool of me." Her

shirt slipped off her shoulder. I saw welts. Before I could ask her about them, her mother yelled, "Ethel, I told you not to talk to that crazy lady!"

I must get to the library. I leave my body. It is dangerous but what choice is there? They think I'm asleep. I set the Recording Angel. It makes notes on what goes on. Lilith pods try to steal my seed. I'm not mad. I'm only pretending. Today in the library, I read scientists say 92 elements were made half an hour after Creation. Cabalists say that 32 paths of wisdom were created from 10 sephiroth. Secret scientists all over the world prove the truth of Cabala. Music is the soul of math; magic is its will. Science and Cabala match like if two people should dream the same dream and each would understand it in his or her own way. Am I making myself clear?

Weekend — I was dreamwalking in the shine of a wet street when I became afraid. The sun was in my eyes, black in its brightness, and I was blind, provoking something to take me away. Suddenly I knew I was willing the Uncle Moisha state.

The walking trance is both heightened and scary, as if one skipped on the brink of fit. I had been walking in fantasy, on the verge. Trancing is a holy state of union that merges one into another. I want to lose myself in it, whatever it is — art, madness, sex, God. The surrender of identity pulls; the pleasure of terror is like dangling over a precipice, enjoying the view. Perhaps it's a function of the dream itself, this titillation of dreamwalking. They've attached electrodes to the genitals, eyes, brains of sleepers, measuring the rate of excitation during REM. They say you are aroused when you dream. Perhaps that's all it is— chemicals, nerve endings, an overstimulation of the pleasure nodes. Today it occurred to me like a voice outside myself: *I am on the verge of seizure. I shall be seized.* I suffered Uncle's terror, all those years of shame in a restaurant, dreaming, and the next thing you know you're writhing on the floor, strangers saying, "That girl sure can dance."

214

The height before dropping into fit, the accompanying state of freakishness — I can't give it up, the genius state. Like being on the edge of orgasm, just this side of screaming. In between panics were sessions of revelation, image upon image. I can't resist.

Saturday — Saw Zoro. He made the sign of the Z and came over. Asked about my article, suggested I send a query letter before doing any more work. Somehow we got on the subject of childhood. I sang, "We will rise and proudly claim you, dear old 203." Zoro sang, "Strong as an eagle, swift as a vulture, we are the kids from Ethical Culture."

I told him some of the strange experiences I've been having. "Sounds like someone's put a spell on you," he said. He looked through his bag. "When you're dreaming someone else's dream," he mumbled, "the best thing is to deflect it." He found a small object, handed it to me. It was a bit of broken mirror. " 'I'm ink, you're glue. Whatever spell you've cast on me sticks on you.' That's the anti-spell," he told me. "Say it while you reflect this mirror shield at the reflection of your face."

I thanked him, pocketing the bit of cracked glass. Then he said, "Why don't you meet me in the park tonight?"

I was frightened and backed off, I don't know why. Zoro began to laugh, pointing finger darts from his eyes to mine. "You might meet your dream man some night, little dreamer."

They think I'm crazy. I want them to think that. I chase a demon into the elevator. The doors close. I watch the numbers. It stops on one. I take the next elevator. I see her white skirt. She walks into a room at the end of the hall. I race, a young man's heart in an old man's breast. The room is a library. Just one wall of books. On the other side, a TV set. All the demons are sitting there, making smoke curl out their noses. The demon I was following is by the books.

I run to her. She puts up her hand. Fire shoots from her nails. I am frightened. She grows to be a black giant, dressed in a sheet like the Statue of Liberty. I can't look at her, she is so beautiful. She says, "I am Sophia. Do you love me?"

I nod. She starts pulling out books, setting them on the table. "Sit," she says. "Here, read this. And that. Where is that book of Greek myths? This magic text will be very useful—"

"Wait a minute," I say. "I'm an old man. How will I understand such things?" Better they should think me a fool.

"If you really love me," she says, "you'll understand." It's then I know she sees through my disguise. I'm about to say, "Okay, so you know," when she vanishes. I look around. The others don't notice. I begin to read.

June 20? — Glancing in Aunt Sadie's flowerpot just now, I noticed three ciphers. I figured the soil must have sunk as it does in a grave, that my own letters to the dead were poking up. One began to beckon.

I walked to the soil. Two bones stood as blank witnesses to my terror; the third crooked to hook me. I stood above it. It straightened itself into a treasure map. I plucked and unrolled it, reading:

> Oh, my name is James Ilyich Kolokol.
> I hunger for your heart and your soul.
> If you fly to the moon,
> I'll catch you with my spoon,
> and eat you lying naked in a bowl.

I looked down. The second finger was motioning for my attention. It stiffened, waiting like news in a dog's mouth.

> Oh, my name is James Ilyich Kolokol.
> I hunger for your meat and your hole.
> I'll put me above you,
> and moan that I love you,
> while I burrow in your sorrow like a mole.

Previously I had found limericks amusing. Now they held me in their drum, giving me the final finger. The last parchment danced in that obscene way of dead notes. I exhumed it.

> Yes, my name is James Ilyich Kolokol.
> I've ice and indifference for a soul.
> My eyes, full of fire,
> seem to burn with desire,
> but it's mainly that I plainly want to roll.

"You are a lousy poet," I said to the three bones writhing with laughter. "Stick to art." Then I realized magic is also an art. My double-entendre caused me to curse myself. What a sneaky sorcerer. In dreams he plumbs my soul, monkeys with my pipes. He becomes me. I used to think he read my mind, but it isn't that. He has placed his thoughts inside me. Night after night he stares into my eyes, sips at my soul through twin straws.

"The poet . . . is a failed magician . . . who has substituted metaphor for metamorphosis." — Andrei Sinyavsky (Abram Tertz)

Sophia runs into a room. There is a peanut machine by the window. I turn the knob. Nothing. I hit it. Nothing.

A hand reaches out, gives me money. I put the coin in the machine. Nuts drop down. I shove them in my mouth, chewing, a pleasure. I turn and see Sophia the giant librarian. She shrinks herself to normal size but doesn't stop. She continues to shrink, crinkle, whiten, changing till I recognize the little old woman from someone I knew long ago. I can't believe my eyes.

"Sophie Herring!" I cry.

"Sophie the Nut," she says in English. I laugh, thinking she is making a joke. She doesn't. "Time soon to crack the shell."

I think maybe this is one of Meshuggina Sophie Herring's tricks. I figure the demons caught her too, she's also an old lady. In this country old people are handed over to demons to manufacture urine and blood. I look away, look back. What do you think? Sophie Herring has become Golda the Wise from Uzlan. The shock on my face must have been funny. Golda starts to laugh. Mashed nuts spray out of her mouth. I'm afraid she shouldn't choke. Instead she disappears.

Sat.? — I fuel my dreams by walking. My steps drum up fantasies of genius and beauty. I am hypnotized by the beat of myself. Madness pounds on the other side like a landlord demanding rent. Every fantasy requires payment. For fantasies of grandeur there are fantasies of debasement. First you act the mad genius; then it's clear you're no genius, you're no longer acting. Walking down a long passage, I am struck by inevitability like a grain shooting down a funnel.

Mysterious Uncle, teach me the ways of wizards. I am preparing to take a magus on. Teach me spells and exorcisms, rituals of secret design. Help me beat the sorcerer at his own game, Uncle.

> Death, beloved of my heart,
> do not separate me from your protection;
> do not leave him a quiet moment;
> bother him every instant;
> frighten him, worry him,
> so that he will always think of me.
> — Mexican love spell

June? — Magus, I tire of the same old trick, how you vanish down a point of perspective. Don't you realize that in vanishing you reveal yourself? I see you in your robe, your arm slivers in sleeves empty but for stars. Why do you hide behind spell anymore? I see through you. Come out. A duel. I challenge you. Your wand and my hat. We'll see who makes whose bunny hop.

June? — The fakir is on his bed of nails. His wife snores gently beside him. He stares up, his cold eyes gleam. He imagines a woman's parts, how she tastes, how she moves, until she begins to move, miles away, in rhythm to his demands. A puppet dancing on the strings of his lust, she performs for his ghost in the dark.

Rubbing to make a genie come, I have learned also to work such spells. I fantasize a sorcerer so hard and pull myself in so tight I feel his ghost throb between my legs. A ghost must depart before the cock crows, but this cock will crow ere I depart. I ride his phantasm and groan beneath the moon. Magic by masturbation is an ancient art.

"We are all, without conscience, magicians in the dark."
— R. P. Blackmur

The way to catch a dream: to be an artist you must throw away your eyes. Shhh, listen. They think I'm crazy. They don't know. All my life I pretended to be a meshugginer. Now I am one.

"If a fool would persist in his folly he would become wise."
—William Blake

June? — I walk around the city blind. I've thrown away my glasses. At first it was disconcerting. Now fantasy sits atop reality. A man sleeping in a field is watched over by a brown pheasant. Its long neck stretches, its tiny head turns to look at me. I draw close and it changes into the twisted top of a brown paper bag. A woman has a great cockatoo on her shoulder. It reveals itself to be a big white bow.

When I wear my glasses, I am pushed left and right by cyclists, runners, anyone coming toward me. But blind in uninterrupted dream, I can't be jostled by the jab of stare nor cut by the calculations of men, the assessments of women. Instead I am free to imagine the materialization of a certain sorcerer.

June? — It is very sunny. I am in the park. I walk directly into the sun. Blinded by the light, I head sightless into the arms of a willed destiny. Someone calls: "Gabby?" I look but cannot see.

I peer across the road, where the voice seems to originate, and see a silhouette against the bright light. "Who is it?" I ask, shielding my eyes with my hand. "I can't see."

"James," says the center of the blind spot. "James Kolokol."

The edges of my blindness flare like a god's aura. Should I cross the street, should I wait? As many times as this has happened, I still can't make it perfect all at once.

He crosses the street to my side. "Gabby? Is it you? You look . . . beautiful." He tells me his wife left him, she took the child. He is so glad to see me. We fall to walking together, our steps in perfect match, like horses that have been hitched for years.

"Gabby?"

"Yes, James."

"Do you know I look everywhere for you?"

"Then why did you hide from me in the museum?" Oh damn, damn, why did I say that? Accuse him practically the first moment I see him. Though I am the god of my universe, I still must create myself several times before coming up with answers to questions never asked at meetings never met. Whatever isn't perfect I take out, polishing my dreams till they shine. I walk in the sunlight.

"Gabby?"

"Who is it?" I call into the dark center of the sun.

"James. James Kolokol, remember? The artist."

"James. James Kolokol, the painter."

"James. Gabriella, stop playing this game, stop torturing me."

He joins me. "My wife left me," he says. "She took the child. I look everywhere for you."

"You've gained weight. Why did you run away in the museum?"

"Run away? I never run from you, Gabriella."

We fall silent, walk on, into the sun. The light sparkles my hair, my eyes and lips. I shimmer like a reflecting pool when the wind passes. It whispers at my side, accompanying me like a shadow.

"Gabby?" I stare into the sun but cannot see. Who can be

calling me from the sun? Apollo? He's not my type. Hermes? "Who is it? I cannot see."

"James. Ilyich Kolokol. I hunger . . . your heart, your soul."

"Who?"

"James Kolokol, remember me?" He crosses the street to my side. "Isn't this funny," he says, "that I bump into you destiny-walking? I was just thinking about you. Of course I think about you all the time."

"Oh pooh, you say that to all the artists." We fall into rhythm, walking like twins. My stride matches his. We seem to fly. And then we are flying along the bridal path, as if Pegasus had two heads, one heart. Walking into the sun, I cannot see. I am as powerful as art, as sex, a blind goddess of come, a seer without eyes, I am my dream. I am I am

"Gabby?"

✦ ✦ ✦

Lara reread James's reminiscence of Gabby. She lit a cigarette, disturbed, not knowing why. Could she be jealous of a dead woman? She bit her lip. After all, no one knew for a fact that Gabby was dead.

The clock in the living room chimed ten times. She was meeting James for a drink, as she had almost every night since she had first written to him of her project. He was an oddly attractive man — not handsome, not witty, certainly too old for her, but he had a power. Lara understood Gabby's fascination. James was an homme fatal.

She left for Lucy's Bar, knowing she was late, and felt a tinge of glee when she saw him waiting. "I'm sorry," she said. "Have you been here long? I got caught up in writing."

James smiled. A glass of Scotch was ready for her, the ice still hard. "Tell me about the great artist," he said.

She sipped her drink. "I liked your reminiscence," she replied, "though it certainly took you long enough." James neither smiled nor frowned, but Lara got the feeling he was mocking her. "I feel funny saying this," she went on, though she'd had no intention of doing so. "Just, Gabby thought strange stuff about you."

"Like?" He stared through her.

Lara shivered, then shook back her hair. "She thought you bewitched her." She paused, then laughed unconvincingly. "Did you?"

"Interesting," he said. "Flattering. What else did she say?"

She wanted to change the subject but found herself unable. James's smile changed subtly. There was a funny reflection in his eye, a tiny triangle of bright light. It seemed to grow bigger, then explode into space. She blinked her eyes hard. "She said your uncle was Rasputin."

James laughed so long people turned to look. He seemed unable to control himself. Finally he chuckled to a halt. "Such nonsense. And me a sorcerer? She was mad. Always looking for holy men . . . and not so holy." He took out his key chain, swung it absentmindedly back and forth. "She wanted answers," he continued. "When there was no one to ask, she talked to herself. What do you think a diary is? Look at me, Lara. I'm a man, can't you tell? Can't you see I'm not a wizard? Your eyes are red. Are you getting sleepy?"

Lara closed her eyes, just for a moment. She heard James say, "You've been reading too much. I could help you with the diary. Your eyes are bleary. Aren't you tired . . . of working alone?"

She shook her head. It moved slowly, as if through syrup. She pried it loose of his voice. Pulled herself out of thick liquid, forced her eyes open, coming back as though from a great distance. "No," she said, her voice suddenly too loud. People turned to look at her. Like a woman caught talking to herself, she was startled, embarrassed. She must have dozed off. Her glass was empty. Her cigarette was out. She was alone.

✦ ✦ ✦

Listen, there's not much time. In China a painter entered the scene he created and disappeared. Get the picture? In New Guinea they call leaving one's body *lulu*. Ring a bell? I'm not mad. I'm only pretending. You are what you pretend to be.

Sunday? — Listening to Stravinsky on my headphones. A pigeon marches in perfect synch to the second movement of the *Rite of Spring*. Wouldn't you know — just as I dotted the period of my last sentence, I lost the station. Music replaced by voices. Fooling with the wires. Can't get it back.

Odd. Turning dial doesn't change murmur. Also, battery light is out. Must be people talking nearby.

But without headphones, nothing. Put them on, voices. Strange. Removing batteries doesn't matter. As long as headphones are on, I hear whispering.

Birds' movements still synchronized to headphone sounds, only instead of Stravinsky, whispers link to wings. Can it be? Is it possible — I am almost afraid to write this, it's so crazy, but the headphones seem to allow me to understand the language of birds. They are saying, "Look at her—"

But no, it isn't that. A little boy just ran into the grazing pigeons. He flapped his arms and frightened them off. Still there is whisper whisper:

". . . look at her she thinks she's a genius look at her writing in her notebook she wants everyone in the park to see she is writing drawing she's an artist a prophet she is everything she thinks she's crazy love magic wisdom Hermes holy moly what's he waiting for death oh pooh he was at the dropoff on time look at her hubris if there's one thing I can't bear what fools these beings so soon wases thinking willbes. Gray-eyed Athena, hail and how's it going?"

"Haven't heard that in a while. What're you two up to?"

"Philosophizing, watching our story. Aphrodite had some ideas for plot development . . . naturally. Remember the time she got mad at Eos, Aurora, Dawn Whatshername — I forget if we're doing Roman or Greek — so she made her be in love all the time?"

"Just one of my plots. Not much, really. But that bitch of a Dawn had a lot of nerve sidling up to my war god. Ares and I go way back. How he used to tie me up. And then my stupid husband comes in, burning with rage. Calls the other gods. About rosy-nippled Dawn, though, it was Zeus who really made her bed."

"Yeah, what happened again? She fell in love with a mortal and begged for immortality for him, right? Oh, wait, I remember. She forgot to ask for eternal youth, so he became a doddering old fart jabbering incoherently. Senile altah cockah she had to lock up in a nursing home. He kept wandering off, getting lost, falling down."

"Hmm, yeah. Anyway, listen, Athena, Aphrodite's got a wicked angle — love and violence. Can you hack it?"

"Hey, Uncle Hymie was my idea."

"Who?"

"Uncle Hermes. Can't get much clearer than that, can I, with her listening? Quest is best, but remember, we're not supposed to interfere. Like Daddy says, look but don't touch."

"Jumping Jupiter, just 'cause you hatched out of your father's head doesn't make you a bright idea, Athena."

"Let's get down to business. Do you have the station? Where is Hermes' caduceus? Where's all the doctors on *General Hospital*?"

"We're not watching *General Hospital*. For a goddess of wisdom, you can be rather thick."

"Hey, you two. Quit jabbering and watch, otherwise I'm going back down. If you'd pay attention and quit yapping, you'd catch on. See how everyone is looking at her, how the sun shines like a spotlight she chose the sun she was cold and didn't want a secluded place in case you know as if she can spoil our plot she sits in light complains a lot that everyone looks why didn't she stay home if she wants to be alone we'll lull her with goddess chatter fall in stupor soporific she goes to sleep hypnotized by the lullabies of goddess milk ingested lies and warmth and soothe and sooth and truth and health and wealth and a happy marriage and a happy prince in a baby carriage tickle up tickle down tickle all around a pinch and a squeeze and a cool summer breeze whewwwwww—"

What's going on? I can't stand this! Feel like I've hooked into Mount Olympus, been translated bodily into an epic poem. The gods are plotting something and I can't bear to listen.

"Something wonderful has happened to me. I was caught up into the seventh heaven. There sat all the gods in assembly. By special grace I was granted the privilege of making a wish. 'Wilt thou,' said Mercury, 'have youth or beauty or power or a long life or the most beautiful maiden or any of the other glories we have in the chest? Choose, but only one thing.' For a moment I was at a loss. Then I addressed myself to the gods as follows: 'Most honorable contemporaries. I choose this one thing, that I may always have the laugh on my side.' Not one of the gods said a word; on the contrary, they all began to laugh. From this I concluded that my wish was granted, and found that the gods knew how to express themselves with taste; for it would hardly have been suitable for them to have answered gravely: 'Thy wish is granted.'" — Sören Kierkegaard

July? — Uncle, after his operation, pushed an IV-covered scepter like a caduceus hung with tubes. I remember his trembling hoary head, but Hermes was a young god with winged sandals. He flew away. Uncle, poor Uncle, they tied him to his insignia and made him walk the halls before he sank into death. Hermes traveled between celestial and earthly realms, taking the dead to Hecateland, acting as intermediary. (Interme*diary?*) What does it mean that Hermes is the hand, eye, and cock of the goddesses gabbing in my ear?

July? — I put the headphones on at night and stand transfixed as the gods plot my fate. I am like a soap star without a contract sitting in on a story conference.

Escape. Help me escape. People lie, they boast. They waste your time. You could die from their stupidity. The thing is to listen when they don't know you hear. If you have a question, think about it and take a walk. Strangers on the street don't know what they talk.

I often used to hear someone say something, then ask, "Why did I say that?" I know why. Ignorant people will call you crazy. They speak from the hole in their pants.

Long ago I asked, "Should I try again to convince Molly to come back?" I took a walk. A fat woman says to her friend, "I wouldn't go back there if you paid me a million dollars. The food was lousy and too expensive."

That's it, my answer. The food was lousy and too expensive. She took everything I had and gave me a soup from shoelaces and bellybuttons. I got a better soup in the cafeteria, and cheaper.

July 8? — Uncle's diary is an *I Ching* without sticks. I am nearing the end. What will I do? I don't

A man just walked by and said to his friend, "I'm going to the library. Meet me later?" And so, to the library.

I'm a meshugginer, I never knew why. If I tell you a story, maybe you'll see. There was once a princess who couldn't laugh. When she was with a crowd of people who were all laughing, she'd smile and jerk her head, they should think she was laughing. Her father watched her carefully. He knew she was faking.

He felt it was important for her to learn to laugh or she'd get cancer. He put an ad in the paper for a comedian. People came and told jokes, did routines. She'd pretend to laugh till everyone left but the comic. Alone with her he'd ask, "Why did the chicken cross the road?" She'd shrug. He'd say, "To get to the other side." He'd slap his knee and she'd say, "That's funny?"

Comics complained to her father — she was killing them. Things get worse before they get better, so one day the princess didn't laugh at the joke of an evil magician. He put her behind a wall of dreams. The father pleaded with the wizard to remove the spell, but it did no good. The magician moved somewhere in Chicago, who knows, he left no forwarding address.

Now the father had a real problem. Not only a daughter without a funny bone but one altogether unreachable. Since things also get better before they get worse, a nobody from nowhere showed

226

up. He claimed he could get past the wall of dreams. The father said, "Try. I've nothing to lose. You, maybe your head. We'll see."

Everyone watched as the nobody from nowhere did nothing. At first people were patient. The nobody took off his shoes and socks and cleaned between his toes. He put his socks back on, his shoes. He picked his ear. He read the paper and made notes, all this with his back to the wall of dreams.

Behind the swirling colors and stretching phantasms you could see the princess staring out. Her mouth moved as if she were trying to scream. She looked like a fish in a bowl with her mouth opening and closing as she wavered behind the wall of glass.

The nobody took out a mandolin. Everyone's ears perked up. Now they'd hear something. But no, he tinked a tune shakily, humming to himself. Maybe he dreamt of people dancing. The girl behind the wall started to cry. The colors of her dreams ran and smeared.

The little nobody put down his mandolin and sat back in his chair, resting his hands on his knees. He stared out the window at the ocean. He sighed. The crowd was getting restless, a few started to leave. Many checked their watches, stifled yawns. The girl behind the wall of dreams cleared a window and stared out.

The little nobody took off his glasses and rubbed the sand from the corners of his lids. He hummed a song, then began to sew.

The girl's eyes behind the wall formed black rays that narrowed to meet at the nobody. Her stare was so strong, it started to pull her through the wall. Nobody noticed. Everyone was looking at the little man.

He had gotten up, complaining the light was bad for sewing. He was looking for an outlet to plug in a lamp. In English he kept saying, "Where is the testicle? I know there's a testicle to plug in here. The king must have a testicle. He wouldn't be king and live in a place without a testicle." He kept speaking like this as he walked around his chair. The wire from the lamp twisted about his leg. The lamp toppled, and he, caught in the wire, fell too.

The girl, whose head and shoulders were jutting out of the wall of dreams like she was a figurehead on a ship, tried to look blank. She didn't want to laugh at the little nobody from nowhere.

"A testicle!" the lunatic shrieked, throwing up his arms. "Where is the king's testicle? Did you ever hear of a palace without a testicle?"

The girl hid her smile behind her hand, which she'd just managed to pull out of the wall. To keep from laughing, she worked on wriggling her hips free of dreams like someone taking off a girdle.

All of a sudden the nitwit stood still. "Testicle?" he said. "What is a testicle?" The girl by this time had planted her second foot on the ground of the nobody from nowhere. He glowered. "I mean a receptacle," he told her.

"I know," she said. The girl turned her head to the wall of dreams to chuckle as she put the plug in the outlet. He stopped her. "Then do you also know you are dreaming my dream?" The lamp came on.

July — Private eyeless, agent provocateur, as powerful as a naked woman, I dreamwalk James into existence: "Gabby?" he is about to call. Each footstep taps on his consciousness. I'm rapping my toes on the door of his mind. He is going to answer. I can almost hear him. He wants me to cast back his spell. Soon he will call, and I will hear, "Gabby?"

"Gabby?"

Someone calls but I can't see. The voice comes from the sunlight. I am blinded, looking into the sun. I try not to squint.

"It's Lee, Gabby, don't you remember? Yeah, how are you?"

And so it is. Lee's nipples stare out of her tight white shirt, like another set of eyes. I am wearing invisibility clothes — brown cords and an old beige blouse to drab me out of existence. I fade from the view of most people, but Lee sees through my clothes as I see through hers.

"Hi there. So what are you up to?" I ask.

"Oh, I'm doing great. Got a job on *Cosmo.* I love it."

I ask fast questions so she won't have a chance. "Hear from anyone?"

"I haven't kept in touch . . . but I did see Happy not too long ago. She got a contract to write a diet book, so she's busy. Oh and Frankenstein, this is horrible, but he was found gagged and tied in his studio. Murdered. They think it was sex that went too far. I mean, someone got him without his leather pants, you know."

I started to laugh, then realized that was inappropriate. Frank was a character but now he was a dead character. "What else?"

Lee looked up for a minute, as if reading the sky. "Oh yeah," she said. "Tessa got a big promotion after we all left. She's the marketing V.P. for Goddess Comics, isn't that a surprise?"

"Really," I said. "And she was just an editorial assistant when PP folded."

"You know about Liz and Suzy?"

"No, what?"

"About their fortunetelling business, didn't you get a notice?" I shook my head. "Oh, it's great. They both tell fortunes. Liz reads palms, Suzy does auras. Suzy is the real psychic of course. Liz mostly handles the business end. Happy was so funny. She said Liz reads palms to see if there's any money in them. Oh, here, I have one of their cards in my wallet. Take it. Maybe you'll want to stop by and say hi. They'd love it."

I took the business card. "Probably not," I said. "I'm so busy. As a matter of fact, I have to get going. I'm on my way to an interview." As soon as I said this I was sorry. Who goes on a job interview in washed-out pants and shirt, torn sneakers? But I wanted to get away before Lee asked me questions. "It was great seeing you," I said, trying to make amends.

"OK, Gabby, you take care of yourself, OK?" Lee smiled and her eyes looked as concerned as a Labrador retriever's.

Suzy McGill: I was so sad to learn about Gabby's disappearance. I used my powers to try to find her, but every time I was closing in, a mirror would go up and deflect me. I didn't understand at first. Now I do. Gabby doesn't want to be found. She's all right. She's out there, disguised. If she were dead or being held against her will, I'd be able to find her. I'm really very good at that sort of stuff. My friend's nephew was missing for years, and the family kept hoping. It was a sickness for them. So I set my mind to finding his body and did. It's in the Hudson River. If they want to send scuba divers to bring it up, I can tell them exactly where. It's stuck under an old car someone drove off the pier.

DREAM: Uncle was sleeping on a park bench. I was so glad to see him. I cried, "Uncle, wake up." Nothing. I shook him. He still wouldn't awaken. I realized I could see into his dream. There was an old woman in it. I knew that this was Golda the Wise. Uncle was dreaming that Golda was dreaming of him dreaming of her. But actually Golda was dreaming of someone else dreaming of her. Now I had to wake Uncle. I needed him to explain.

I shook him, crying, "Uncle, wake up, you're dreaming."

He opened his eyes and gave a half-smile, saying, "And you?"

I wouldn't let him off. I said. "Whose dream is this?"

Again that half-smile. "Don't you remember?" he said. "We heard the madness was coming. Rabbi Nachman told us that the whole world would catch it from poison grain. Not us, because we stored uncontaminated food. We have cut ourselves off from madness. Look."

He parted the draperies of life and showed me a movie-screen image. In it an audience was watching us. People were coming in, going out, changing seats. "That is reality," he said. "Dream their dreams. Or dream your own." Then I awoke.

I can't figure it out. It is like an Escher picture, where the repetition of one thing in a pattern metamorphoses into something else in its negative space. Actually it is more like that one of a hand drawing a hand drawing the hand drawing it.

Have I made my uncle a fiction . . . or has he dreamed me into being?

Escape. Sophie Herring acted the nut to fool people. All my life I pretended to be a meshugginer. Now I am one. You are what you pretend to be. In 50 years if the angel of death should say,

230

"You never had talent, you were insane," so? It's not like you get a prize at the end of your life for having guessed right. There's no satisfaction when you're dead to say, "At least I always knew."

Who is the meshugginer? They hang him by his foot, make him wiggle. It didn't hurt me. Why? When you hang upside down the blood rushes to your head, your thoughts grow wings, you fly away. What's the use of a meshugginer if not to have the laugh shook out of him? They think it's coins that fall from your pocket. I had the last laugh. The laugh was on my side.

I know, I know. For a long time I dreamed other people's dreams. My father, my mother, Molly, even you. Everyone dreams about the meshugginer, comes up with a reason why. Do you see the joke? A homeless man imprisoned in a home, sewn back into his body just when he was about to fly free. All I had to do was refuse.

Look at her, scribbling away, past me. I give her the wisdom of the ages, she gives my secrets to an imbecile. Think you had trouble finding a translator? You shouldn't know from it. People say I'm mad? Good, I want them to think that. I am not mad. I am only pretending. I was afraid to die. I saw my mother at the sink scrubbing a pot. She turned. Her eyes met mine. "I dreamt of you, Moishalah," she said. "I dreamt you woke my granddaughter from a dream." That's when I died. The secret is

Listen, I used to sit in the park and watch people walk their dogs. Look at a dog. A dog doesn't wash. A dog doesn't wear pajamas. He finds what to eat in the garbage. He walks around, he is happy, he is free. One time in the winter, I was sitting. A woman walked by with a plate of steaming meat. I got hungry. Then all of a sudden I realized she was carrying dogshit to the garbage. Don't you see, it's all shit. The secret is

I used to watch these people with their dogs. The men's dogs would stretch like penises in the direction of females. It amazed me how people could bear to watch their animals piss and sniff. I laughed at them, thinking, "If only they could see themselves." Then one day I realized that they were watching their animals, but I was watching them. I had a good laugh then. The audience is the show. The draperies are opening. They are coming. The picture is coming on, it takes a while to warm up the tube. I see an old man leave his body. The stars are dreaming. The curtain opens. People come in, go out, take their seats. The picture is about to begin. It's of an old man asleep on a bench. He is pretending. Inside, he laughs like a madman. You are what you pretend to be. A laugh was the beginning of creation. It ends with a joke. Laughter is creation. It's in the *Zohar*. The secret is we are dreams dreaming. The secret is you are lost in someone's dream. The secret is laughter. The kibitzer hanging from his feet is laughing. Turn me over, set me free.

A man asked a turkey what he should do with his wife. And the turkey said, "Holdherholdherholdher." Did you hear the one about the book who thought it was the universe till someone got to the end and shut it up? Draperies are parting. Demons are coming. All I had to do was wake up you're dreaming. Do you hear me, Gabby? Wake up you're dreaming escape help me escape snap out of it wake up Gabby you're dreaming

July — I was reading the translation of my uncle's diary. All of a sudden he began talking to me! I was so startled, I dropped the manuscript. When I picked it up, the pages ran together. I couldn't find my place. English was like a foreign language. Nothing made sense. The page on which Uncle began talking to me was missing. I was scared.

"Be calm," I told myself. "This doesn't mean you're nuts. You address Uncle sometimes, not only in your mind but right here in this book. Perhaps it was in such a way that he addressed you." I was trying to fool myself and knew it. It's true that we talk to the dead in our minds, in our diaries, and that's not madness but a function of grief. But when the dead start talking back . . .

I ran to the shelf with Uncle's original notebooks. I took one down. They say a little knowledge is a dangerous thing. It must be true. All this time, knowing that Yiddish and Hebrew are read right to left, I'd held the book backward when looking at it. Being distraught today, I held it upside down, opening it as you would an American book. The letters started dancing, turning into English before my eyes, telling me to help Uncle escape, burn his books, let go of his dreams.

July — I went to the building in East New York where Uncle used to live. In the basement, covered with dust, I found his paintings and his mandolin. I took everything home. "See, Uncle," I said. I opened his diary at random and found the page where he asks to be set free. I remembered a place where bums dance around a burning can. I went there, threw his books on the flames. Zoro gave me wine. I clicked my coins. The bums began to dance like Cossacks. I recognized this as a fragment of someone else's dream. I stopped and went home. I stood before a mirror, willed the image of a great artist. The telephone rang. It was a girl from the Painting Place. They have been trying to reach me for months but couldn't because my phone was disconnected. "I'm so glad to talk to you," she said. "Tom really wants your stuff in his next group show." An old woman was sitting on my heart. She cried, "That garbage, like a baby makes with a crayon?" I lulled her to sleep. "Lie back, mommalah," I said. "You are tired. You are dreaming. You are getting sleepy. You can't keep your eyes open. Sleep, sleep."

I resumed my conversation. "I was really hoping for a one-woman show," I said. "When can Tom and I meet to discuss that?" We made plans to have lunch.

When I got back upstairs, I noticed life had restarted in Aunt Sadie's soil: a vegetal phoenix was being born from shriveled knots of wandering Jew. Two shoots snaked up Miss Tweety's cane. I stood staring through déjà vu eyes. Mundane became miracle and miracle grew mundane, the world glittered with insight and blindness till I recognized the caduceus had been handed down. It is time to go.

✦ ✦ ✦

Lara Jacob closed Gabby's diary. She felt her aunt watching her. The telephone rang. She did not answer.